Conquistador's Lady

A Novel by

Anita McAndrews

Fithian Press ❖ Santa Barbara, California ❖ 1990

LIBRARY OF CONGRESS CATALOGING-IN-PUBLICATION DATA
McAndrews, Anita G.
  Conquistador's lady / Anita McAndrews
      p.   cm
  ISBN 0-931832-48-9 : $10.95
  1. Cueva, Beatriz de la—Fiction. 2. Alvarado, Pedro de,
  1485?-1541—Fiction. 3. Mexico—History—Conquest,
  1519-1540—Fiction. 4. Guatemala—History—To 1821—Fiction. I. Title
  PS3563.C29C66 1990
  813'.54—dc20   90-30127 CIP

Published by Fithian Press
Post Office Box 1525
Santa Barbara, California, 93102

CONQUISTADOR'S LADY

In Guatemala, in Santiago, Beatriz's lost capital and known today as *La Ciudad Vieja* (The Old City), only the tower of her castle rears above the earth mounds. The shattered walls of her chapel are overgrown with weeds. On the ruins is a stone marker engraved with the following words:

Pause here, traveler,
This is the Palace of the Conqueror of Guatemala,
And here perished The Hapless One,
Beatriz de la Cueva
and her eleven ladies
in the Catastrophe, September 8, 1541

CHAPTER 1

"MY LADY, BEWARE the dark waters!"

It was the shaman warned me. I think of him now. They named him Witch, and he suffered that fate designed for witches. But I knew better. It was life the shaman practiced.

"There are no goodbyes." He said that too. I understood, and I have held those words close, more comforting than prayer.

Now, at this moment, I have need of comfort. Not even Belial, that gypsy fiend, could have brewed such a storm as this. It shakes the foundations of my castle. Belial—poor wretch, she was jealous of me.

Yes, many have envied the lady Beatriz. I am twenty-two, and Spain's appointed queen of a territory so vast its boundaries are not all explored. One hundred Indian slaves attend me and I have gold, silver, and jewels beyond counting. My husband wore the crown of Guatemala and Honduras, and the Cross of St. James. Charles V, Sovereign of the Spanish Empire, appointed my husband, Pedro Alvarado, Don and Conquistador, Captain General of those lands south of Mexico to the Isthmus of Panama. My city is Santiago de los Caballeros; our castle and cathedral are the finest in New Spain.

I am nobly born: the purest blood runs in my veins. I am cousin to the Dukes of Albuquerque, and the favorite niece of Don Francisco de los Cobos who is Secretary to the Council of the Indies and trusted advisor to our sovereign.

But they are far away now, these aristocratic relatives of mine. They cannot help me. I am alone in my castle, mistress of an edifice that crumbles under the assault of a storm the like of which I have not seen before. Indeed, I believe myself and my ladies, my town, will vanish, swept away as if we had never been at all.

I protest! Life is unfair! I have come a great distance, at such cost, from the child I was. And always in a hurry. I wanted forever now, promised at once. Did I sense these black waters then, racing at my heels?

That little Beatriz. I carry her within me—her fears, her shyness, her desperate loves. My young self. She felt confined, oppressed. She shrank corner to corner of that great castle called Bedmar, in Valladolid, Spain. She saw ghosts in the hallways. No one to run to, so Beatriz believed, except Ana, her duenna.

Ana, her eyes milky with age, her fingers clenched to her palms as if she clutched the last shreds of her life—hers was the lap small Beatriz sought. Because Ana was love, and Ana knew magic. Ana could read the future, she said, and she would brush my hair slowly, then spit on my mirror and tell me of that princess she saw reflected there. "'Tis you, little one," she would croon. And sometimes I believed her magic, and I could smile then, held close and comforted.

There was little love in that formal court. All paraded like puppets, I thought, hating their spiked ruffs and stacatto heels. Only the king was kind. He is a melancholy man, and I believe my pranks made him smile. He never chided me as others did.

I escaped whenever I could. There was an apple tree I liked to climb. From the nest I had made at the top of it I could see beyond the castle walls. I watched the sheep boys on the hills and I longed to be one of them. I counted the caravans coming and going on the road that lost itself behind a tall hill. I felt imprisoned. There was a world out there and why was I forbidden to explore it?

"Nobility is responsibility," my mother preached.

"Boys may seek their fortunes, girls remain at home," my father intoned.

I thought mine a cruel fate. I sulked. I wept. I considered running away. But where to go?

"Does no one want me?" I cried. "Who will understand?"

"You are incorrigible," Mother scolded. And she would lock me away in my room where I would kick and scream—that someone hear me.

Wicked Beatriz! Even the Church considered my

escapades sins, and my skinny knees were blistered raw from my penance prayed morning and night.

I would not practice humility or reverence. There were three of us: my older sister Francesca, myself, and my brother Francisco, nicknamed Paco. Francesca was all a girl should be: a sugar lump, her two black braids polished smooth and her pretty hands overfull, so it seemed to me, of comfits or lengths of lace, white and neat as that soul of hers she so endlessly boasted. A preening dove, she and all the other girls, toys of the Court, fondled and petted.

I sucked my thumb, brooded in corners, envying my brother Paco's freedom from restraints. When he rebelled, he was dubbed "brave"; my mother adored him.

I was ashamed of my freckles, my lank and pinkish hair, my clumsy fingers which could not knit one inch of lace without it looking as if the moths had got at it. To this day I have not mastered that woman's pastime called embroidery. Perhaps I never wished to?

I was a moody child. *"Intolerable!"* my mother said. Because nobody seemed to want me near, I pretended I preferred to be alone. It was a habit hard to shed—this surety that not a soul loved me. Truly, I have held love bright, like a pearl in the hand, and not recognized it or refused to see it clearly. Folk wiser than myself have told me that. Yes—richly gowned, envied, admired, I have played a beggar woman, begging treasures I already possess. Of course people laughed at me, and eventually ignored me.

The Spanish Court was austere. It was one long dull parade of processions, candles, and tolling bells. I believed the courtiers and their ladies wore masks; their faces were chalk, unsmiling. My petticoats scratched and my boots were too tight. I envied the flight of the lark high above the cathedral spires.

After supper, abruptly dismissed, I would run, panic-stricken, through the long hallways, dodging ghosts—truly I saw them there. The servants tittered when I told them of my frights; Paco pulled my hair, pounced at me from dark corners. Francesca smiled, chided me for weeping. "Mouse," she called me, because of my pink eyes; she said that tears and tempers pleased neither God or man.

But the world and God had set me apart, so I believed. I pretended I did not care, but I would have given my life to sing an Ave as Francesca did, her dark head bowed, her hands folded plump and neat as a pigeon's wings.

My father: I saw him tall enough to step on me. He was entitled to wear purple, but he preferred black, and a great many rubies. He stank of wine and, if he acknowledged any of us, his children, it was his son Francisco. Paco is with me now, a great comfort; then he was a bully, tormenting my pets just to see me cry.

It is Mother I should pray to today. Dear, perfect soul who never knew how much I yearned to be exactly like her. Thinking of her face, it becomes one with that of the Virgin. My mother glittered, sharp as the diamonds she loved. She tried—God rest her soul!—to ease the bonds I fought against. She advised obedience, humility, acceptance of the woman's role I must play. I craved loving, her arms about me. Did she deliberately withhold that which I most needed? Did she hope I would forget love, knowing I was unlikely to find it? She did not succeed. Always I have clutched at hands, wanting but not daring to believe another's offering.

I refused to heed Mother's firm instruction to give my fate to God. When I prayed, which was seldom, I asked for freedom from all restraints. When I could escape, I shed shoes and petticoats and climbed to the top of my apple tree.

I had one accomplice: my page, Négri. He had been given me when both of us were seven. Négri taught me somersaults, and stole cakes for me from the kitchen. When I was frightened of the dark, Négri consoled me with an African story of how the dead are planted in the ground and their souls bloom as flowers. Négri is a hunchback; I mind it terribly when people laugh at him because his soul is beautiful as any flower. Négri and I—we grew up together and I have never questioned his devotion to me.

One afternoon, I remember it well, Négri and I, treetop high, feasted on the small green apples there. We were greedy, and that evening I was in bed with a bellyache. Sleepless, I woke late the next morning and felt the world a dull and bitter place. I would not get up, I decided. Tio Francisco rescued me. He brought me some message from my mother and, finding me listless, he rebuked my laziness. He lent me a book which contained engravings of legendary beasts. Turning the pages, I touched centaurs, and unicorns. "Someday," I told my uncle, "I will ride a white unicorn!"

He looked sharply at me. "You have an imagination. Is there a brain there too, somewhere?"

"Girls do have brains!" I flared.

I believe he began the lessons out of kindness. Uncle looks stern as a hawk; few people know he has a heart like butter. He is interested in all the world, and because I was interested too—well, I had the key, and he opened to me and gave me what he knew. Dearest Uncle! There have been times I cursed him, believed him to have forgotten me. Not at all. He has been my touchstone. Would that I could tell him so now!

Eagerly I devoured the Greek legends. I mastered the rudiments of French and Latin. I memorized the names of principalities and seas, and my small finger endlessly rehearsed the seaborne trade routes from Spain to the Western Indies.

My enthusiasm delighted Uncle, and I responded and knew real affection for the first time in my life. By the time I was twelve, books had become my passion. I would never be lonely again, or so I earnestly believed.

Had I been born a boy naught would have stopped me. By now, at twenty-two, I would be sitting at the king's right hand, as Viceroy to the Indies perhaps. If I had been born a boy....

But I am a girl. I think it is cruel to give books and learning to a girl. And wasteful too, because women are denied position and leadership. Tio Francisco told me to keep my learning secret. "Mask your knowledge with frivolity," he warned me. "Learn to smile, Beatriz. Fold your hands, stay quiet." Often he said, "What a wife I will make of you!" He was moulding me to his own designs, I didn't know that then—all that mattered was his loving me.

And I would not marry. I had decided that. Tio Francisco had opened books for me; soon he would open still another path. So I learned to smile, to fold my hands and listen; I obeyed my uncle in all things, and put my questions to him alone.

His interest in me quickened my spirit; my world was a brighter place. Late at night, I remember, Tio Francisco would send for me and we would sit by his fire, he in his great chair and I on my pillow at his feet. Poetry, he read me then, or brave tales from the Conquest of the Moors. He taught me the lyre, and many times I sang him to sleep.

But it was the Conquest of the Indies that obsessed Tio Francisco. It was not long until I knew the names and deeds of captains and bishops, admirals and Indian kings. Their treacheries, their greed and ambition appalled me. "Who can I trust?" I asked.

"I trust no one," he replied. "Beatriz, remember, all men fear power. My power, and yours, child, lie in our wealth and our nobility. There is not a man we cannot bribe or buy. Hold a gold mirror to a man's face and give him time to study what he might become. Remind him it is you who can place him wheresoever he desires."

"General Cortes is dazzled by his own reflection," I said, "but that one the Indians call Tonatiuh, Child of the Sun, Captain Pedro Alvarado—I doubt he can be so beguiled."

"But he can…he can be…" my uncle chuckled.

I was excited because the young Captain Alvarado, fresh from his exploits in Mexico, was coming to Valladolid to request the governorship of Guatemala, a territory in New Spain Alvarado himself professed to have conquered. My uncle told me the captain was accused by fellow officers of deserting his post and withholding monies from the King's fifth.

"He is a fool to present himself here," Uncle said. "I can

order him imprisoned—before he reaches the King."

"But you will not," and I smiled. "You respect courage, Uncle. Tell me, will the captain seek a wife among the ladies here?"

He cocked an eyebrow at my eagerness. "You would wed him, Beatriz?"

Oh! I remember my heart leaped. I knew Captain Alvarado was not yet thirty; he was fair-haired and brave. Even the Indians stood in awe of him. I clapped my hands. "Yes, I will wed the captain!" I cried. My sworn spinsterhood forgotten, I glimpsed escape and romance.

I see myself then: a stalk of a girl, flat-chested, my legs straight as a boy's from riding hard. My green eyes brooded and my red hair hung straight to below my waist, unbound. I was clumsy, just past thirteen, between woman and girl with no knowledge of men but ready to worship the first available hero.

"Promise me to Captain Alvarado," I begged. "Command him to request my hand."

Tio Francisco was gentle, but firm. "It is too soon, little one. I will not give you to the first adventurer who comes begging favors. This Alvarado is a nobody, Beatriz. He was born in the Province of Estremadura, the son of a minor *hidalgo* and a woman named Léonor. We know little of him except that he sports a blood-soaked sword."

"But he is a hero," I protested. "Uncle, you yourself have praised the captain's extraordinary concern for the safety of his men. You have said he is a true soldier, that he should be knighted. And now you belittle him because he is not wellborn!"

My uncle shrugged, made a gesture of dismissal. I persisted: "Would you have me wed a fop?" I demanded. "Should I choose some scented creature from this Court, a pretender to knighthood?"

Uncle hushed me, and promised me a royal husband, one worthy of me, all in good time. "You are too young yet," he said, and that my sister Francesca was to wed Captain Alvarado—it was all arranged.

"Francesca! That mealy mouth!" My temper bolted. With

both hands I beat upon Uncle's chest and, failing to move him, I turned and struck the globe. It was his pride and joy and, horror struck, I watched it whirl, fall then and crack—a chasm sundering Guatemala, a veritable earthquake!

I stood aghast, ashamed. Globes are rare, this was Uncle's treasure. "Oh..." I faltered, "and Guatemala, too...."

His lips white, Uncle stared at me. His silence infuriated me. "I don't care!" I shouted. "Cursed be that part of New Spain called Guatemala! May its volcanoes swallow it! And Francesca too—she will never be queen!

"Alvarado..." I hesitated, not wishing my hero harm. "May his horse bolt from under him, may his men see him fall!"

"Careful, child, words are like arrows, someday they reach their marks."

A silence then, and Uncle made the Sign of the Cross between us. He righted the globe, touched Guatemala gently, as if he would heal it.

"Go to your room, child," he said, regarding me with such icy distaste I might have been a gypsy beggar ranting some evil prophecy.

CHAPTER 2

PEDRO ALVARADO NEVER loved my sister. He accepted her as one more of the honors bestowed upon him by our king. I know that now, but then I suffered, body and soul, standing beside Francesca at her wedding Mass. So serene was she that no one there could have guessed her days previous, days of weeping and prayers.

Francesca did not want to marry the captain. He was a commoner, she cried, a murderer, a beast. "And where on earth is Guatemala?" she asked. "Have mercy on me!" She pleaded and wept: she would die, taken so from family and friends, all that was familiar.

To no avail, Francesca's tears. She went to the altar, to her husband, mournful as a sheep to the shearing, but looking so lovely in her *manta* of white silk and her girdle of pearls that I longed to unveil her for the sniveling fool she was. Because he must love her, I was certain of that—what man could resist such docile beauty?

Pedro did not look at me. He has told me since he does not recall my presence though I stood as near to him as was allowed. My eyes never left his face. Tonatiuh, Child of the Sun...yes, I thought him a god come among us, and I yearned to touch his crisp yellow curls. He had the most extraordinary blue eyes, fringed with lashes thick as gilt.

That morning, his wedding day, Pedro wore crimson, even to his belled boots. A gold medal on a golden chain was about his neck; he was never without that talisman, they said. The Cross of James sparkled above his heart.

The captain's allegiance to Spain had been secured with many honors, but I do not believe he thought of himself as bribed. Pedro stood tall and proud, knowing himself victor. Here is a man, I guessed, who sees his reflection clear in the mirror of his mind. It would take more woman than Francesca to ruffle this soldier's self-esteem. I could, I thought fiercely.

When Pedro turned to kiss Francesca, to receive her plain metal band and place a jewel on her finger, my heart almost burst. Because the little fool dared not look at him! But the tears on her cheeks were like the Virgin's own, and Pedro's smile, I imagined, was one of pleasure.

Later, at the feasting, I fled the women's table. I slipped out into the night, into the garden where I gathered marigolds and rosebuds. I bound the flowers with a lock of my hair and returned to the dining hall where the gentlemen sat at ease. All were so tipsy-merry they did not notice me, and Pedro himself does not recall my pulling at his sleeve, my curtsy, and my gift of flowers that drooped already in the heat of the room. He may not remember now, but he was pleased then and he chucked me under the chin, pulled me close and kissed me on both cheeks. *"Hermanita,"* he murmured, and he set my bouquet in the clasp that held his Cross of St. James. "God keep you sir," I whispered, and fled.

I found the flowers the next morning, under his window. They were crumpled and brown and I imagined how he had held Francesca close. In that night of love, my flowers perished.

Francesca...I might have pitied her. She was given against her will, packed off like baggage to a land she knew not except that is was embattled and heathen. She was just fifteen, and soft clear through, content as any kitten in a furry litter.

"Francesca will never be queen!" My angry words came true. She died of fever in Mexico. She never reached her kingdom and her grave lies we know not where. Did Pedro mourn? Every night, imagining their crossing of the great ocean, I prayed Pedro would discover the empty-head he had married. When word of my sister's death reached us, I felt no sadness, only relief for him. I wore the yellow mourning clothes, but I could not mourn.

CHAPTER 3

IT WOULD BE eleven years before Pedro returned again to Spain. I had sworn before the Blessed Virgin to love the captain through eternity, but I was young and, in the ensuing months, he faded to dim memory.

I returned to my books and studies. As I have said, New Spain obssessed my uncle. He swore he would have it all, this mysterious land of uncountable riches, for the Empire. He made me privy to his ambitions, and to many of the documents pertaining to the territories. Soon, I was half in love with another captain, a certain Don Bernal del Castillo who faithfuly chronicled Cortes's victories. Bernal's pen was an artist's brush, painting the lush detail of gold and pearls, dark Indians and their valiant conquerors.

Castillo's accounts of the land across the sea made the seeming endless rituals of my own court life unendurable. I fretted and chafed. Nothing pleased me. I could not rhyme my verses or complete a melody. Once, discoursing on Indian rituals, Uncle caught me sketching unicorns. "Bah! Girls are dreamers!"

"I am not girls," I retorted. "I am Beatriz de la Cueva, and I learn what I want, when I want to. Not dreams, Uncle, I am bored."

"Woman's vagaries..." and he turned his back on me.

"I am not like that," I protested. "Look at me, dear Uncle, I am troubled, feeling neither here nor there." It was true, I wanted everything, and nothing.

He smiled then, and drew me to my feet. "The king has a gift for you," he said. "He is fond of you, Beatriz. He has remembered your fifteenth brithday."

We went down, and out into the courtyard. I saw my page, Négri, his face glistening in one wide smile. He stood beside a dappled mare and she so finely made I could only stare, speechless. Her neat black hooves, her mane like rippled cream. She sported a crimson leather saddle and a bridle hung with silver bells. "Oh, how splendid!" I whispered. "She is yours," said my uncle.

I called her *Señorita*. The king could not have given me a more perfect gift. But our sovereign is like that. Some call him arrogant and moody, but I think he broods on unfulfilled desires very like my own. King Charles is but a few years older than myself, and if he is melancholy it is because few dare approach him. He is lonely; he thinks too much about his wretched mother, Queen Juana, who, it is said, went mad loving Phillip the Handsome. King Charles is afraid he has inherited his mother's melancholia. But I have made him smile—with a new game, or a kiss, when he least expected one.

Señorita was made for me, and her saddle too—I could ride astride, which I preferred, or side-saddle when I must. Mounted on *Señorita*, I wore full soft skirts and boots that reached above my knees. I rode her like a boy and she was out ahead at every hunt; we left all the gentlemen behind. But what I loved most was riding out alone, only Négri to accompany me, and leaving him too. Across the hill and past the willows beside the river I rode alone, singing to *Señorita*.

I was up at dawn; gone for hours. Mother protested, Ana scolded, but I went my headstrong way. Tio Francisco shrugged off my parents' complaints. "Give the girl her head," he advised. "Beatriz must run her own course."

My fifteenth birthday was celebrated with a fete and fireworks. It was noted, with some relief, that I had grown passably pretty. There was talk of a husband for me, but I managed to prevail upon Uncle to wait a year at least. He agreed, I think, because he had grown fond of me. It was my mother who wished me off her hands, properly married. "Naught but ill befalls a girl who passes her fifteenth birthday without a husband," Mother warned me.

"When I am ready, then I will choose," I said, tossing my hair which I refused to braid and twist high as the other girls did. They spent hours slicking their tresses with oil, pricking their scalps with pins and combs. I refused stays and stockings; I pretended I did not care how I looked. Ah, but I lied! Hours, all alone, I would stare at my reflection,

18

tipping the mirror this way and that, and liking what I saw. A crown set with emeralds, I dreamed, they would match my green eyes.

It was then Alonso came. A Venetian, wellborn, the son of a wealthy merchant, Alonso arrived at Court with a caravan of treasurers. I believed he stepped from the love legends of my favorite books. He was black-haired, black-eyed, a poet, and an artist with a gift for mimicry, a wit to match my own. He came to Court on Saturday; we fell in love at Matins, before the sun was full up, on Sunday. Quick as magic working—yes, it was that....

Leaving the chapel, I stumbled on the steps and Alonso caught me. He did not release me immediately, as a gentleman should, but held my two hands and gazed deeply at me until I blushed, and dropped both fan and rosary. In that confusion my *manta* fell back and my fresh-washed hair tumbled loose, and the king came up beside me and I forgot to curtsy. Tio Francisco wished me good morning, but I swear I never heard him. Alonso filled my eyes.

And so it was—through springtime into summer, I was loved and loving. We became inseparable. For the first time, without a backward look, I gave myself into another's keeping. My books gathered dust, my scribblings faded; Tio Francisco was kept waiting. Alonso possessed my days and nights. He lingered at Court and made himself most welcome. We lived, as I have said, half-stifled in tradition and formalities but Alonso, like myself, could make the king laugh. Alonso designed new fetes; he played the clown; he rehearsed the court in a new theater from the streets that kept all ribald past midnight.

From his own coffers, Alonso presented me with a gown so thin I pulled the length of it through a golden ring. He gave me a leather book, and the story in it, brush-painted in royal colors, told of the first unicorn, my most beloved beast. I clasped the book to me. "Have you seen the unicorn?" I asked. Alonso answered, telling me we would see the animal together. "All mysteries are ours, Beatriz," he promised me.

"We will be wed before the year is out," Alonso said.

19

"Soon, Beatriz, I will ask your parents for your hand."

"Not yet, *querido*." I was uneasy. There was no reason why I should not wed Alonso, but I felt Tio Francisco's disapproval. I resolved to talk to him. There was a hunt planned for that next day and I told Alonso I would approach my uncle when he was weary, content from hard riding and the inevitable kill.

"Uncle will not deny me my heart's desire," I assured Alonso, and myself.

That dawn was splendid. I was betrothed and my secret caused me to smile on everyone. Négri held my stirrup and wished me fine hunting. Merrily I told him I need hunt no more. Tio Francisco, mounted near me, overheard my remark and he scowled. I gave him a brilliant smile and said, lightly, that I wished to speak to him later. "I will send for you, Beatriz," he replied, and struck his horse so cruely the animal reared; *Señorita* shied and almost threw me. I lost my reins and Uncle mocked my momentary imbalance.

Alonso rode out beside me. We raced ahead of the others, then pulled in our horses. "I have no taste for killing on a day like this, Beatriz," Alonso said. He reached across the space between us, taking my hand. "Shall we hunt the unicorn?" he whispered.

"Where?" My thoughts swam dizzily in the summer sun.

"You know the legend," Alonso pressed.

"Only a virgin can see the unicorn," I said, and blushed, and would have spurred *Señorita* forward but Alonso held me back.

"Go to the river," he said. "Ride over that hill and behind the willows. You know the place, Beatriz. Close your eyes and wait for me." Alonso smiled. "Whistle for the unicorn," he said.

Across the hill, behind the willows. The river sang in the shallows. I dismounted; *Señorita* would graze contently, never far from me, and I loosened her reins. I remember how the grass felt, soft under my heels when I removed my boots. I sat down, near to the river as I could, then I lay back, my arms beneath my head, and gazed at the bright sky until my eyes blurred. Full of sunlight, warm, I smiled, and dared to whistle, softly.

Alonso was beside me. I did not want to open my eyes. "The unicorn will eat from my hands," I murmured. "He is white, he has black hooves, and he is very near, I feel him, Alonso—I am frightened...."

My body trembled, I remember, and I bit my lips to stop their silly quivering.

"You have nothing to fear," Alonso said. Gently he removed my gloves. His kisses were warm in the palms of my hands.

Grass tickled the nape of my neck. I smelled wildflowers, and I heard, far away, the music of the river. The horn of the unicorn, I wondered—is it hurtful?

It is strange and wonderful to me now, as it was then, the first time—how a man loves a woman. There is nothing more marvelous—to be held so, and caressed. Alonso's gift to me. Ever after I would treasure that moment's knowing—a body different from my own, but fitting perfectly.

I had heard it whispered that the love act is pain and blood, that women submit because they must, without pleasure. I have never felt so. In fact, Alonso awakened a new hunger in me, a curious craving that I have had to discipline.

That first time—it is important to a girl. I felt soft, rounded, flowers growing from me. I told Alonso, and he laughed and said he felt the same himself. We lay there, sated, in the sunlight; careless, my head on his chest and his arms tight about me.

No, it was not a sin. Over and over again, Alonso told, me we were promised to each other. *"Te amo*—I love you!" I am certain the echo of our vows then blends with the river music now. And the white unicorn bends his head to drink....

CHAPTER 4

TIO FRANCISCO FOUND US. He came on horseback, smashing like a thunderbolt. I saw his dagger drawn and I believed he would strike Alonso dead. "No!" I screamed.

Uncle reached and swung me up in front of him, across his saddle. He struck *Señorita's* rump and she whinnied in pain, was gone before I could call her name.

"Beatriz!" Alonso shouted. I never heard his voice again.

My father swore; my mother wept. Uncle ordered me confined to my rooms. Even Ana's kindness was denied me. It was Négri who scratched on my door—nights, days later—and whispered that the Venetian lord was gone.

"Gone?" I beat upon my door, begging Négri to open it.

"Hush, my lady," Negri's voice was low. "Don Alonso was ordered from Court. Rumor has it that he was beset by thieves on the road south and murdered. God rest his poor soul!"

"Murdered?" I leaned against the door. "Négri, tell me Alonso is not dead!"

I struck that door until my hands were bruised. I wept, crying for Ana, for my mother, and at last, demanding my uncle. He came; I heard the key turn in the lock and, when he entered, I flung myself at him. "Murderer!" I hissed.

"Not I, child," he said, catching my flailing hands. "It is the Venice peacock who has killed—killed you, Beatriz! If word of this is told about, you will not be wed. Used goods!" My uncle thrust me from him with such force I fell to my knees. "Who will want you now, Beatriz?" he demanded.

I managed to stand. "Praise be to God if no man wants me now," I said. "Alonso and I were betrothed, Uncle. We planned to ask your blessing."

"I would not have given it," he told me bluntly. "Beatriz, small one...." his voice broke. I felt no pity. He would have touched me, but I retreated. "Beatriz, I planned a crown for you, an Empire...."

"I have lost a kingdom greater than all others," I replied. "Love was all I desired, Uncle. You are both thief and murderer."

He pleaded then, like a father confronted with a disobedient but still beloved child. "Your books, Beatriz, once they meant everything to you. Do you forget so quickly all I have taught you?"

"Your teachings but filled an emptiness until Alonso came," and I turned my back. "Leave me," I begged, struggling to control my tears.

"Plan no more for me," I cried, "I want solitude now. Take that from me and you will have my soul."

We stood, looking at each other—we who had been more than friends. I believed I would loathe this man to my dying day; so it is when one is young and filled with grief.

Uncle cleared his throat. "The scandal," he said, "perhaps we can bury it. Your mother has taken to her bed. Your father would have you sent immediately from Court. The king—he does not yet believe the gossip prated already from stable boy to house servant. Ana must hold her tongue. Beatriz—" Uncle seized my shoulders, "you will never speak his name again. I order it."

I tore loose from his hands. "Whose name?" I mocked, "Alonso's? It is Alonso dead, murdered in a ditch—his name I must not speak? But he is my husband in the sight of God! Day and night, I swear, I will pray aloud for him."

"And lurch about, careless as any kitchen maid, his child in your belly," Uncle sneered, his face pale.

"Alonso's child?" I was stunned, past understanding. Then it came to me—Uncle, and all the others, they believed I had lain with Alonso more than once! I stood convicted by those who were old enough to believe the worst. Dazed, I shook my head. "It was only once, Uncle. I was a virgin, it was only once...."

"Enough—" he interrupted harshly. "I will send your confessor, child. You have sinned, but..." he shrugged, then straightened his shoulders, "perhaps things can be arranged...ah, Beatriz, the plans I've made for you, and now..." his voice faltered, and he spread his arms to me as he had done in the past. I had run to that comfort then. Now I fled to the other side of the room.

"Ogre!" I cried. "Do not touch me, Uncle. I believed you were wisest and kindest of all, and knowing me best—" my voice broke on a sob. "Now even you believe the worst of me. Love is a vile word in your mouth too. By our Holy Mother, I cannot bear the sight of you!"

Grief struck me hard then, as a winter wind. I stood in a blight of loneliness and disillusionment.

Tio Francisco spoke, his voice strange in its harshness. "You will remain alone, Beatriz, until you can control yourself."

CHAPTER 5

ALONSO'S BODY WAS returned to Venice in a sealed casket. Négri told me and, true to Uncle's word, Alonso's name was never spoken again. I thought this callous, and I insisted on wearing mourning for a year. The sour yellow of grief is unbecoming to me but I persisted, forsaking scents and powder too. Only when the king ordered it did I appear in public. I knew the gossips marked me demented, wanton.

My mother was heard to call me "changeling." My father played so royal and aloof I thought he had forgot my name. Paco was surprisingly kind; I felt his sympathy and reached out to him and it was then we became friends.

Ana coddled me: "My fallen angel," she said, wringing her hands. Négri tagged my footsteps, trying to make me laugh. I could not...would not; all I desired was solitude. But the Court—ladies and gentlemen both, they worried at me as a pack of dogs pick at kitchen leavings. The ladies sucked sweets and prayed aloud for my lost soul. My alleged sin spiced their gossip, and I knew they gloated over my "fall."

The gentlemen—hypocrites, all of them! Straight- laced and laced, there was not one among them who did not believe himself capable of taking Alonso's place. If I had had one lover, then of course I must have more —or so these gentlemen would lead me to believe.

But no suitors for my hand. Indeed, I was told repeatedly, it might be impossible to give me away! I smiled when they said that because I knew myself promised to one man only, and that man dead. If I had had my way, I would have joined a convent then and there. A convent in New Spain, I brooded, naively believing a nunnery meant freedom.

My mourning became my prison. There were nights when I thought I had lost my mind. Mad Queen Juana—losing Phillip, she had been half-crazed; they had shut her away. I asked Ana to tell me the truth of that story, but she laid her finger across my lips. "Speak not of that poor lady." she admonished me, "Rather, pray for her soul."

We knelt together, Ana and I, and I was ashamed then, I remember, because I had forgotten formal prayer. "I cannot pray for any soul," I told Ana. "Not Queen Juana's or my own. Especially mine—it is with Alonso and I do not know where he has gone."

The seasons' changing stirred me not at all. *Señorita* grew fat from idleness. Valladolid, Burgos, Madrid...I moved like a sleepwalker in the Court's processions. I did not mark the passing of the years. My mirror lay face-down; I knew I had aged. I was nineteen, but dry inside as yesterday's apple core.

"Beatriz, wake up! You've a life to live," Tio Francisco urged me. That angel-devil man! He had the patience of a saint with me. I returned to my books because they helped me to forget the hours and hours of time to be passed.

"I am not living," I told my uncle. "I am nineteen now, I see no future."

"Pah!" It was his turn to set his globe spinning, and the world turned twice under his fingers. "What can I give you, Beatriz, to make you smile again?"

I saw Guatemala under his thumb, and the crack I had made in it. "A convent in New Spain," I said eagerly. "I would teach girls as you have taught me. Panama is a well-established colony. Send me there, Uncle."

"It has a foul climate, Beatriz."

"I am not frail, as Francesca was," I replied.

"God rest her soul," Uncle said. Then he looked searchingly at me. "No, you are not Francesca...but you are a de la Cueva. It is a name can be used."

He was silent for a time, his fingers stroking the emerald he wore on his thumb. "Beatriz de la Cueva, and not yet uncomely...." He grinned then, and winked at me. "Thank God you have not spread to fat, though a bit more above the waist would help."

I sprang to my feet. "Do not make fun of me, sir! If you

will not give me my convent, I will ask the king." I walked rapidly toward the door, calling for Négri.

"Stay—" Uncle's voice was sharp, and I obeyed as I was used to do when much younger. "Hear me out," he said. "Captain Alvarado returns again to Court, Beatriz. He comes once more to plead his own cause. There are serious charges against him. He deserted his assigned post in Guatemala and, with the king's monies, he attempted a disastrous expedition to Peru. He faces prison, and a fine of 15,000 ducats."

I smiled, remembering that tall and errant hero from my past. "Alvarado is as restless as myself," I said absently. "Does he still mourn Francesca?" As I grieve for Alonso? But I did not say that: I needed my uncle's good will. Carefully I had planned my convent across the sea, a voluntary isolation, my freedom.

"Alvarado mourns no one and nothing but his own misfortunes," Uncle said. "But I admire the man's courage. I need his sworn loyalty to Spain." He paused, his eyes were like a hawk's—keen, marking his prey. I felt a tingle of unease slide up my spine.

He spoke slowly then. "This Alvarado—gold buys him for a month or two...but there is something else will anchor him. He is lowborn and ashamed of it. A noble name, and...." Uncle snapped his fingers, loud as a sprung trap.

"But this captain, lowly born or not, is a knight, a don," I remembered. "What more can you give him?"

"Much more," Uncle murmured. He leaned closer to me. "Pedro Alvarado will accept you as wife. He has said as much."

My mouth went dry. "But I have sworn never to marry," I whispered. "I do not love this man. I refuse."

"You dare not, girl!" Tio Francisco stood squarely above me. "I offer you a kingdom. Consider yourself fortunate, Beatriz. In your position..."

"Yes, my position!" I cried, and stood, confronting him. "I will beseech the king. He will understand."

"The king is pleased, Beatriz. He needs men like

Alvarado. Do not be obstinate. I offer you a brilliant future. A moment ago you had none." Uncle sat down again, and gestured me to do the same.

I clutched at the back of my chair, my mind reeling. "The Pope..." I said, "he will not permit such a marriage. I believe it is forbidden that a girl wed her sister's widower. Yes—I will appeal to the Pope."

Uncle caught my hands; their grip bruised me. His voice was smooth. "The Church's dispensation for your marriage is easily purchased, Beatriz."

I saw his broad hands swallowing mine, the glitter of his emerald. "No!" I gasped, "no!"

"Why do you refuse? Think, child—once you begged to marry Alvarado."

"I was young then," I said, "and jealous of Francesca. She is dead now, but in the eyes of God she is still Alvarado's wife. And he mourns her, he must," I insisted, "he will not want me."

"Alvarado loves himself, Beatriz." Uncle was losing his patience. "Enough of these hysterics now. I need not tell you where your duty lies."

No. He need not tell me. I knew my fate—preordained, the fate of all young women like myself.

But I must try all escape routes. "The captain will want a virgin," I pleaded. "Uncle, you have said it yourself—I am used goods. And I am much too old. There are younger girls here, prettier than myself and untouched by scandal. Don Pedro is twice my age. I am sure his appetite is jaded. If he must wed to better his position—why he has a choice of...of...fresh morsels. Yes—from the king's own table!" I should have been ashamed of my blunt speech but I felt I was begging for my life.

Uncle shook his head. "Alvarado will wed a de la Cueva. My family, and my man then. He cannot ask more. Indeed, Beatriz, he will not guess your shame. Your mother—yes, the women will instruct you."

"Instruct me?" I wailed. But Uncle was sitting back in his chair, his fingertips together beneath his chin, and his eyes closed. It was his manner of dismissal. I knew my fate was sealed.

"But...I beg you...dearest Uncle!" And the room blurred then, the floor tilted, I was on my knees. Behind my uncle, his fire receded until its glow was shrunk small as the red tip of a unicorn's horn.

"Courage, child," I think Uncle said that.

"Alonso!" I cried, and I fainted.

CHAPTER 6

I AWOKE IN MY BED, rag-tag dreams clutching me and no sense of time passed or how I had got there. I opened my eyes and believed myself still dreaming because my mother sat beside me. I could not remember when she had last visited my chamber and her presence startled me. "Where is Ana?" I demanded.

"Resting, child," my mother said softly. "The old one has cared for you night and day. You have had fever, Beatriz."

I saw my casements shut, my altar with its Virgin pulled to the foot on my bed and candles lit. Citronella and other sharp scents burned my nose and throat. My head throbbed. "I want to die," I moaned, pulling my linens over my face.

"Die?" Mother was startled. "Beatriz, it is mortal sin to seek death." She plucked at my covers and dabbed my forehead with a wisp of cloth. "A sin, daughter," she whispered. "We must accept what is given us."

Always, she preached so! Bow the head and bend the knee. Sing hymns of thanksgiving to Him who deals the cruelest blows. "I will not," I said.

I sat up against my pillows. "Do you know what has made me ill, Mother? Can't you guess what sours my stomach?"

She knew, but she pretended not to. "Tell me," she urged.

"I am to be wed to a man who does not want me. He does not love me, but he needs my name. He is bought and I am given—and neither of us can refuse. It will be a cursed union, Madam!"

Hastily, Mother crossed herself, and then began to tell her beads. It was her way of shutting me out, and I called her back harshly. "Alvarado does not love me, Mother. Will you thank God to see me married to a bow-legged gramps, an upstart with a history of massacres to his name? Look what happened to Francesca. It was said she died of fever, but who can know the truth?"

My mother regarded me through the haze of her prayers. "The captain general was devoted to your sister," she said.

"Yes!" I shouted, and she covered my lips with her hand. I twisted free. "He still loves Francesca. He has taken no other to wife. Mother, do not let me go—unloved, unwanted, and unloving too."

She sighed, and I saw an immense pity in her eyes. But—"I cannot help you, Beatriz," she said. "The king commands this marriage and your father has agreed to it." I closed my eyes fiercely, but I could not stop my ears. "Such a small babe you were, Beatriz," Mother murmured. "You were all crimped shut, like a tight bud, from the start. Francesca, Paco—their little hands opened from birth while you, you were always starved, red-faced, your fists beating the air. Such a large hunger for such a small body...." My mother smiled absently.

I interrupted her. "I was a difficult child, wasn't I? A changeling—I have heard you say that, Mother, don't deny! Clumsy I was, you said, and wayward, and my nose always in some dusty book. I was never your own, was I, Madam?"

My words tumbled, like pebbles thrown at her still face. "Always hiding, wasn't I? Never at your beck and call like Francesca. I would not sit at your knee, pretend to pretty manners..."

It was Mother's turn to cover her ears. "Hush, Beatriz." But it spewed from me: "Naughty child. Bad girl. Sinner, and now spinster. Mother, I read my shame in your eyes. Nineteen years, and still you have not guessed what I need most? It is a life of my own, to do as I wish!"

She cut through my rantings. "Your life is not your own. Love God, Beatriz, and your heart's ease must follow." She sat very still, erect on her footstool.

I saw her hands folded, serene as white wings on her black crucifix. I wondered at her resignation. My father, haughty as a peacock, had she loved him once? Had the quick hooves of my unicorn ever wakened my mother? Or was her long sleep God's gift that left her undisturbed? I envied my mother.

"Help me," I whispered, with a longing I had never shown before. Did it startle her, my intensity? It must have, because she stood swiftly. She was walking away from me.

"Mother!" I cried. "Mother, listen—"

Her hand on the draperies at the window, she turned and gazed at me, her eyes vague, distracted. "God keep you, as bride and wife," she said, and pulled the musty brocades aside.

A flood of sunlight quickened the room, reddened my Virgin's painted lips, and turned the dust to dancing motes of gold. There was a knock on the door, and Ana's whisper: "My lady, Captain Alvarado waits below."

CHAPTER 7

I PRETENDED ILLNESS and would not receive the captain general. My parents must do the honors, I said, Alvarado's arrival was their doing, not mine.

But word was brought me day and night, of my lord's splendor, his extravagances. Négri appeared one morning in doublet and hose of purple cloth; his slippers turned up and around at the toes, and from the points dangled golden bells. How he strutted! And when I questioned the royal color he wore, Négri grinned and told me, "My lord Pedro insists this is the blue of his kingdom. He orders me to wear it as I am to be Master of the Bedchamber—in Guatemala, my lady. You will take me?" He knelt at my bedside.

"My lord Pedro prays your good health," Négri smiled. "He begs you will accept this small gift." It was a gold tray with a cup and plate of the same metal.

"And chocolate to drink?" I asked eagerly, greedy as a child and already addicted to the dark sweet Indian drink the captain had brought to Spain. Négri nodded. "He is a fine gentleman, my lady. Will you see him today?"

I shook my head. The captain had been at Court longer than a fortnight and, at first, I had been proud—let him come to me, I said, it was he who must insist. But after his first call and conversation with my uncle, he had not come again. He sent gifts intead. My apartments, drab and empty, were transformed by his generosity. Sweet-smelling mats took the chill from my floors, and painted cotton cloths made a fairyland of my walls. A silken swing—Négri called it a hammock—hung near my windows, and my new pillows were embroidered with birds and butterflies. I was given a leather casket full of paper-thin gold ornaments, and a basket finely woven and filled with pink pearls, round as pigeon eggs.

My suitor gave me a pair of parakeets, apple-green and wobbly on their feet, squabbling like two ancient lovers.

Inlaid dressing cases with silver clasps; copper-studded chests with fittings of sandalwood; coverlets stitched with jewels and feathers; a plumed headdress, and turquoises set in silver—did the captain general think he could buy me with gifts?

I wanted a word from him, his own tempestuous invasion of my apartments, a declaration of love from his own lips. It was not forthcoming, and I was hurt. Prideful, hurt, and stubborn.

If Don Pedro dazzled Négri, Ana was bewitched. She wore red silk and seed pearls, Alvarado's gift. "My lady," Ana begged, "he longs to see you!"

"Has he said as much?" I demanded, and Ana's downcast eyes told me, No.

"But such gifts, my lady," Ana fussed. "Your rudeness is a disgrace to us all. It is time you presented yourself."

"Perhaps, if I remain in my rooms, he will go away," I suggested. This was quite possible, I told myself; there must be fifty other girls throwing themselves at his head. "Is he well-liked at Court?" I asked Ana.

"Well-liked?" Ana clapped her hands. "My lady, he is springtime after winter. He makes the king laugh. Don Francisco, your uncle, he purrs like a tabby. Your mother, Lady Beatriz—I have seen her led out on the captain's arm to dance the pavane. Your father is full of smiles.

"Does the Captain General please the Court?" Ana pirouetted. "Ah, my lady, he has beguiled us all!"

But still I sulked. Pride held me solitary, then shame because I had soon waited past the time when I could meet the captain with grace. I grew more curious. "Does he appear old, Ana?"

"Ripe as summer, my lady!" The woman was besotted, and I was sharp with her. "Don Pedro is twice my age. He has turned your head, Ana."

"As he will turn your own, my lady," she replied impudently. Then she was serious. "You had best receive him, Beatriz. I hear the Captain General grows restless, wanting his own country."

It was my turn to applaud. "He leaves then? Oh God be

34

praised—Don Pedro will not wed me!"

"Oh, but he will." Tio Francisco had entered without knocking. "The banns are proclaimed, Beatriz. The Pope has sent his blessing. Don Pedro has been granted the Kingdom of Guatemala, the Writ in the king's own hand. The Council of the Indies approves. Your Betrothal Mass is arranged for this very evening. You will be present, Beatriz."

There was no escape. I remember the effort it took to hold my head high, to keep my voice steady. "Tell the Captain General I will meet him in church, at the appointed hour."

Tio Francisco nodded, gave me formal bow. I stayed him with a question. "What does this union cost you? How many ducats buy God's and the Pope's blessing on this unholy betrothal?"

"A third of Guatemala's revenue for the Holy Office, as long as you and Alvarado live," my uncle replied.

"He will go into debt—to marry me?" I could not believe that.

"He would pay more if asked, Beatriz. Think, girl, you are Alvarado's assurance of a fine inheritance for himself, and his heirs. Too, he needs the king's favor. He has many enemies."

"Yes," I said cooly, "you may count me among them."

My uncle ignored my remark. He ordered Ana to prepare me for the ceremony. Busy as cooks basting a lamb, my maids surrounded me. I was bathed, oiled, powdered, and perfumed. Wooden stays were pulled tight about me, squeezing my waist, wrenching my backbone to a posture similar to that of a Royal Guard on parade. Petticoat and petticoat, white on white on white. Then—suddenly, I sneezed, snapped laces, caused such a commotion I had to giggle. The tears ran down my cheeks. "Ana, have mercy," I begged, "you do not have to truss me so, I will not run away, I promise!"

"No, do not run—not from such a fine handsome lord," she crooned, holding me close. "Patience, child. Wait and see what comes to you."

What came then was one more petticoat; a scented sachet stuffed down between my breasts; the farthingale, and then the overskirt. My hair was stretched and combed over a wire headdress, and a framework of velvet and pearls clamped forehead and temples.

Stockings and silver-heeled shoes. The neck ruff which was ten layers, prickly and starched. Chalk powder, paint on my cheeks, and warm wax to hold my lips smiling. I wobbled on my high heels. The ruff pushed my chin high. I struggled for a breath of air and hiccuped, which sent my women scurrying for two new ribbons.

"Which of his jewels will you wear, sweet lady?" Ana asked, standing away from me and admiring me—her work of art, her painted virgin puppet.

"Not one of his," I said. "Give me the Venice filagree." It was Alonso's gift, soft and supple as cloth of gold. It clasped my throat, spilled to my waist.

Ana shook her head. "Look back, my lady, and you will turn to stone."

"I am stone," I told her. I did not lie. All feeling had left me, save a distaste for the duty I must perform, and an ugly contempt for myself and the man who thought to buy me.

Ana gave me the rolled parchment tied with ribbon that was my Betrothal Mass. I held it with my left hand and, with my right I wrapped my rosary beads about the scroll, and I said, slow and solemn as a prayer:

"All that transpires from now until my death is false. May God turn His face from me and mine."

Yes, before the vows were spoken, I had cursed my marriage. Ana made the Sign of the Cross above my head, but her love could not take the chill from me.

Later, walking behind my women through the halls, the last great door swung wide and we stepped outside into an autumn rain. The alley we must cross was flooded with a rushing oily stream; I was lifted into a chair but not before a drowned cat bobbed too near, its claws catching a moment in the mesh of my white stockings.

CHAPTER 8

I REMEMBER MY FIRST glimpse of him, waiting for me near the great altar. He stood taller than the others, his fair head bared, drawing all the gold and amber of the thousand tapers lit. I remember the bell chords, and the baritones of bishop and priests underscoring the high notes of the choir. I saw Don Pedro through a mist of incense and his splendor seemed a legend reborn.

It was nigh twelve years since I had seen the Captain General, and as I walked toward him now I saw myself as I had been, a small girl trailing her older sister. He had not looked at me then though I had done everything to catch his eye. Now, I swore I would not so much as glance at him. And I did not, not when we stood close, and not when he touched my hand at the end of the Mass. *"Doñita?"* he whispered, and would have raised my veils if I had not turned abruptly and descended the altar steps and kneeled for the King's blessing.

Then, in the rush and flurry of good wishes, it was easy to avoid my betrothed. I was redeemed for the moment, one of the flock, and each lady in turn clasped me to her jeweled bosom. Then it was time to dine, and I thanked God for the ruling that set the ladies apart, behind screens, for the feasting.

We sat, with little grace, on low cushions. I was put to my mother's right and I managed to smile prettily, to blush, to eat a sliver of venison and half a cold peach, the juice of which stained my gown. I could hear the men laughing, the clink of silver and crystal. My lord Pedro, it seemed, was a great story teller and Ana had told me true; my father's chuckles burbled like wine poured from a cask.

It was not long before I could gracefully plead weariness and excuse myself. I stepped between the cushioned ladies and I heard their whispers: "High and mighty, that filly—but he's the man to break her...." "Too good for the likes of us, but just wait...." "Lucky girl, " murmured another, "I thought her past giving away!"

I shuddered. It seemed there was not a soul to wish me good will. I followed Negri's torch through the chilly grave halls. Echoes and mold, portraits of dead kings and queens, tapestry scenes of vanished processions—I would not miss one particle of home. It was a sorry thought for a girl of nineteen on her betrothal night.

The feast blared hearty behind me and I heard Alvarado's deep laughter and—the ladies must have joined the gentlemen—the high voice and giggle of a girl. A flare of jealousy jumped my heart, startling me. Did I like him then? No! I could never like this man who lavished me with gifts but failed to ask even one question concerning my thoughts, my feelings.

I whispered my married name against the darkness. "Beatriz de Alvarado. Beatriz de la Cueva de Alvarado...." De Alvarado—of Alvarado! Meaning slave of, servant of, person of, woman of—belonging to. Dear God! I thought, at the very least a woman should be allowed to choose the man she must belong to.

I retired early that night, and every night following. I succeeded in avoiding my betrothed whenever he came near. Which was not often because he too became adept at evading any situation in which we might be brought together. Why? I began to wonder.

He had recognized my dislike of him and accepted it then, without protest?

Perhaps he could not endure the sight of me?

Once, we came face to face. I extended my hand. He bowed, his face inscrutable, and did not take my hand. I felt a fool, my fingers extended to the empty air.

Alvarado would not press his suit. I assumed he did not care to. It was humiliating.

I was intrigued, then perplexed and angry. The Court guessed our game, and I heard wagers placed as to when Don Alvarado and the Lady Beatriz would acknowledge their betrothal. I knew the Court was amused. King Charles fumbled an opportunity to bring Alvarado and myself together and I felt ashamed before the king's kindness, the captain's coldness.

The month dragged on; our wedding date was set for the end of October. On October 22, the year was 1538, King Charles, in a solemn ceremony, restored the government of Guatemala to Pedro Alvarado. The territory would belong to the Captain General for the next seven years. Alvarado would have the king's protection against any present or future sentence, or accusation, pressed against him by the Audencias of the Councils of the Indies and Mexico. The king awarded my lord Pedro the ceremonial sword, and a casket containing a gold arrow, a Castillian cross fashioned of rubies, and a lizard cleverly contrived of emeralds. [1]

Tio Francisco was standing beside me. I was puzzled by the King's decree. I asked my uncle, "Seven years, is that all? I thought Alvarado was to have Guatelama for his lifetime?"

"In seven years, your eldest son will be entitled to succeed his father," my uncle assured me. "Seven years is a long time, Beatriz. Alvarado is not a young man."

Ambition stirred me. "If Alvarado should die, the kingdom will be mine?"

He nodded. "Exactly. You will inherit the territory of Guatemala, Beatriz. You, and your children." My uncle's hand pressed my arm. "I promised you a kingdom. Have you forgotten?"

I had forgotten. Self-pity dulls the wits. Now, my future brighter, I looked long and hard at my betrothed as he knelt with bowed head before the king.

I wondered how long he might live. He was approaching fifty, but still virile, an adventurer.

Then I remembered how I had wished Francesca dead, and Alvarado fallen from his horse. With all my heart I had cursed Guatemala.

Some say there is power in an evil curse. And Francesca had died. I shivered: I must not wish Alvarado dead.

---

[1] At present, in a locked vault in Guatemala City.

Despite my fears, then, ambition gathered power. I might be queen, sovereign of a rich territory in New Spain. Was it possible?

My uncle read the question in my eyes. "Nothing is impossible," he whispered.

My lord Pedro had risen from his knees; I saw him surrounded by courtiers. Swiftly, Tio Francisco slid his emerald from his thumb and pressed the jewel into my hand. I had admired the stone many times in the past, and now I saw that he had had it engraved with the coat-of-arms of Guatemala: three volcanoes, with one erupting; a crown in the sky, and a knight on horseback above the crown.

"A kingdom for my lady Beatriz," Uncle murmured. "Keep this, my small one. Do not trade it foolishly for love or money."

"A talisman," I said, slipping the ring between the laces of my bodice. "Your promise, and my kingdom."

The Captain General turned to look straight at me. Our eyes met and held; his own so blue and full of teasing gentleness that my breath caught. Strange then, I felt a stab of fear (or pity, was it?) for this man so bedecked with and certain of the honors due him. Impetuously, I moved toward him.

My hands outstretched—he did not take my hands, but laid the casket in them. "Yours, my lady."

"No, my lord," I smiled. "Keep what you have won."

"But I am well-content," he protested warmly. "We are met at last, Beatriz."

I clutched the casket and blushed, and could not look at him again. Laughter and titters from the Court pressed all about the Captain General and myself.

He guessed my discomfort. "The air is oppressive," he said. "There is time for a walk in the garden. Will you join me, my lady?"

He was offering me protection, but, obstinate, I fled his kindness. I could not stroll careless, my hand on his arm when, moments before, I had considered his death and imagined his kingdom mine. Too, I was not completely won; I would not be paraded as one more of Don Pedro's royal decorations.

A moment's hesitation, then I cut him cruelly—with the sweetest of smiles, turning my back of him.

CHAPTER 9

THE LAST OCTOBER DAY in 1538—the autumn sun of that morning, my wedding day, was round and bright, red as an apple dropped in my lap.

A trumpet call awakened me—more visitors; Bedmar Castle was overflowing with uncles and aunts and cousins from distant provinces. Envoys from Flanders, from Rome, yes—even England and France sent emissaries with gifts for me. The world sought to please Spain. King Charles, de la Cueva, Albuquerque—these are noble names whose invitations are command, flattery and promise. The Council of the Indies sent Bishop Bartolomé de las Casas, self-appointed enemy of all the royal governors of New Spain and bitter critic of soldiers like Pedro Alvarado. De las Casas calls himself "Protector of the Indians"; he slinks about like the poorest of mendicant monks. I know he receives an annual salary of 100 gold pesos, and that he is overlord of an immense tract of land in Cuba, these hectares worked by his own slaves. De las Casas is a fraud, a watchdog mongrel, the tool of the Council whose members are always jealous of the king's soldier-governors.

This unholy bishop brought with him to my wedding another bishop, Marroquin, from Guatemala. He is one of the few true Christian gentlemen I have ever met. He is a Dominican, but with a faith generous to include all sects. He is elderly, seeming frail, but the strength of his hands gives healing. When we first met, I recognized a friend which is unusual for me. Bishop Marroquin has a mind much like that of Tio Francisco, and we enjoyed each other instantly, the good Bishop and I. I asked him to be my Confessor, and to officiate at my Wedding Mass.

"Yes—if you will keep your vows to the very letter, Lady Beatriz," he said, looking through my eyes to my soul, so that I must reply, "I do not love him, Father."

"You will, my child," the bishop replied. "He is a man

42

easy to love."

I might have answered honestly: I do not want to love
him. But that was but half a truth and, hours from being
wed, I was uneasy, frightened, wanting to trust but wary
of giving.

Yes, a majestic dawn, I remember it: trumpeted and
belled, the castle wreathed and bannered, music and
dancing all through the town. I could not help but wake
with a start, my spine tingling and my thoughts darting,
trembly as butterflies. Négri , respendent in still another
silk suit, brought me my chocolate and another gift from
my lord Pedro. It was a fan, its green plumes tall as myself
and streaked with iridescent blues.

"The tail of the Quetzal bird," Négri told me. "My lord
tells me the bird is the spirit of Guatemala and is
worshipped by the Indians. Only a highborn princess may
wear the plumes." Négri smiled. "Don Pedro asks you to
carry this fan because you are queen of Guatemala."

"I will be," I said, and it was the knowledge that
someday, perhaps, I would be queen that enabled me to
endure the prodding and pushing and plumping, the
annointing of me for my Nuptial Mass.

"Come true at last! She is my angel," Ana crooned,
stepping back at last to admire her masterpiece. My lips
were so waxed I could barely manage a smile. Ana spit on
and polished my mirror of quicksilver, and I looked at the
figure reflected there: white and ivory, pearls and silver,
her whole body armored as if she went to do battle. Poor
girl in there, I thought, she is changed to a statue; I doubt
she can walk—the creature must be carried everywhere!

But I would walk, I resolved. I did not want to be lifted in
a chair, placed here, then over there. I noticed Ana had
rouged my cheeks beyond reality and I rubbed them with
my mittened fists smearing paint and chalk until my face
must be done over again. Ana fussed, scolded, "You will be
late, my lady."

"No matter," I said, and I sat down on a broad cushion
and pulled Ana next to me. I spread my left hand on her
lap. "Tell me I will be queen!"

Ana gave me a sharp look. "If that be true, I will tell it so. If not..." she shrugged. "I will not please you with lies, little lady."

"Hurry!" I urged.

She studied my palm, traced its few lines with her gnarled forefinger. "Your way divides," she said. "I see two paths and you must choose. I see a pearl and a stone."

"Nonsense!" I exclaimed. "Ana, tell me what I want to know. Will I wear a crown?"

"Two paths," she insisted, her face so near my palm I felt her breath. "Look neither right nor left," she warned, "walk straight, though the way be hard." She raised her eyes and gazed at me. "It is you will choose," she said. "The pearl is peace, and the stone lies heavy."

"What does it mean?" I wondered.

"It will come clear," she promised. Again, she bent above my hand. "It is he who offers the pearl, Beatriz, and you who are blind."

I was uneasy and I pretended to a gaiety I did not feel. "I do not refuse pearls, Ana. Tell me, do you see me crowned queen?"

She shook her head and her eyes held mine. "You want no more than that, child?"

"What else is there for me?" I demanded angrily. Yes, what else, I wondered, love denied me and my freedom taken—what else but a crown would lighten my days? I offered my hand again. "I will be queen, Ana!"

"Even now, you refuse," Ana said softly.

I was disappointed and I spoke sharply. "We are late. You must paint my cheeks again—red as a harlot's," I taunted. "I am not a virgin—why pretend?"

Ana hushed me, too late. My mother had entered my room. She had heard my last words. We stared at her, Ana and I. She was all topaz, saffron, spiked ruff and a headdress pointed in two grotesque horns. "Hold your tongue in front of servants, Beatriz," she chided.

"Servants?" I clutched Ana close. "Ana is my own dear comfort, my heart's haven, my...my pearl, yes! Ana is more my mother than you have ever been! She knows all my secrets."

"Well?" Mother's lips were thin. "Shall I have your treasure taken from the room? Or will you send it?" She was hurt. I had never heard her so bitter. Ana fled, weeping.

My mother waited until the door closed and we were alone. Then she said, "I have come with one purpose only."

"Yes?" I was suddenly weary, and wondering if I could endure, with head held high, the seeming endless masquerade of the hours ahead. "If you have come to instruct me in the duties of marriage, there is no need, Mother. Your teachings weigh too heavy to forget."

I saw her stricken face, and I was sorry for my words. I stepped towards her. "I ask your blessing," I said gently. Yes, truly, I wanted my good mother's prayers; they would perhaps protect me against Ana's woeful predictions. "Mother, teach me to pray," I begged her.

But I had hurt her, or she was much preoccupied. She flicked my face with a bit of lace, complaining that my powder was too white. "Have you seen a ghost, Beatriz?"

She produced a silk scarf tied in knots and unrolled it carefully. She pressed a tiny crystal vial into my hand. "Careful," she warned, "it breaks easily. Keep it hidden. Later, tonight, when your husband sleeps, break it."

The bottle was warm in my hand. I held it to the light and saw it filled with a thick, scarlet fluid. I was puzzled. "What is it, Mother? A secret potion from the Moors, a love-water to fire an old man? Has my grizzled captain spent his vigor? Is he impotent, Mother?"

She had not the grace to blush. "It is your blood, Beatriz, kept from your first menstrual period. It is an old custom; the blood assures fertility." She smiled slightly. "Now it serves another purpose. The Captain knows nothing of your past, the scandal. He expects a virgin. The Court—there has been much gossip. When your sheets are examined in the morning, we...I mean, you will be exonerated."

I thought it a vile custom and I told my mother so—and threw that bottle to a corner of my room. "Madam, I have had enough," I said, and turned my back on her.

CHAPTER 10

M Y FATHER and Tio Francisco entered. They were imposing figures in black and purple silks, their long cloaks lined with sable. Uncle remarked the lateness of the hour, and my father, so pleased was he to be finally rid of me, said I was the prettiest bride he had ever seen. He spoke with such gallantry I wanted to believe him.

I took my father's arm, but when Tio Francisco offered me his support on my left, I refused. That blood—it was my uncle's scheme, I was sure of that. I would not be party to such revolting subterfuge and I said as much. "If Don Pedro wants a virgin, he will be disappointed, Uncle."

My ladies waited outside my door and, leading the procession, I walked slowly down the hall. Ana followed closely behind me, her arms piled with my heavy train and the gauze *manta* in which I would be wrapped before approaching the altar. I kept my voice low but my uncle felt the sting of my anger. "I will not be party to your trickery," I said.

Uncle shrugged. "Tell the Captain General whatever you like, Beatriz. He will not be pleased. You understand, of course, that if you do not satisfy him, he can leave you here. The marriage is brilliant enough. He need not take you to New Spain."

I teetered on my heels. "Not take me?" The thought had not occured to me. "But he must," I said, "I am to be queen. You have told me yourself, Uncle—New Spain has need of noble ladies. Alvarado too, he must be lonely. He is no fool—it would be beneath him to take an Indian wench...."

"He is a soldier first," my uncle said, and there was that in his voice gave me pause. Then he continued. "If you are difficult, he will leave you here at Court, Beatriz."

"You would permit that?" I stood still, staring at my uncle. Again that shrug, as if he no longer cared for me. "I will have little to say in the matter, Beatriz. You will be the Captain General's lady."

"I will not be anyone's lady!" I spoke so loudly that those just behind me heard, and they whispered, one to another, *"She will not...she will not..."* Négri, just ahead, turned in surprise. He was carrying my green fan and I saw the plumes waver. I stood, wondering what would happen if I refused to move at all? Tio Francisco would summon a chair, and I would be lifted into it, carried to my destiny. Writs and scrolls, stamps and seals —I was not, even now, my own lady.

"You will behave yourself," my uncle said, and he pulled my hand through the crook of his arm.

We proceeded. Doors opened before me, closed shut behind me. We crossed the alley, laved this time by a pale sun. I remembered that drowned cat, the day of my betrothal, and I shuddered and glanced up at the blue sky. I saw one bird adrift a wind I could not feel; a lark I think it was.

The bells startled me, their tone so rich it stopped my ears. I heard the choir. *Ave Maria...Ave...Ave....*

I climbed the steps and walked into a haze of gold, a light that dazzled and I blinked, remembering another sun, long ago, that had so filled my eyes.

The aisle was fenced with lilies, carpeted with rose petals. I felt Ana's hands, and my soft *manta* wrapping me, head to toes. *Ave Maria...*I did not know the prayer I needed now.

I was a cloud, a flower floated on a tide. Through my veils I saw the bright diamond tears on the Virgin's cheeks. I passed the chiseled faces of all the Apostles and, from habit, I breathed their litany of names. I stopped before the Cross, and genuflected. Then—on some impulse, I removed my *manta* and knelt to wrap His cold marble feet in the soft gauze. It was not His name I whispered, but Alonso's.

Strength, I begged, and felt pity then, for that figure crucified. He too was bound to His destiny.

I went up the steps, unveiled, to the high altar. The heat of the candles melted the wax on my lips. I felt strength flow through me, and a stillness. Unveiled, I could see clearly.

But I knew my act vulgar, unprecedented. Brides should hide their faces, stumble and seek support. My mother sobbed. My father's arm, beneath my hand, trembled. The face of the king's bishop was purple as his vestments. There was an unholy silence until Bishop Marroquin stepped forward. "Welcome, child," he said. "Such beauty should not be veiled."

I knelt. "Forgive me, sir, it was an impulse."

Bishop Marroquin raised me to my feet. "It was a gentle act," he said.

"Yes, my lady is kind." A deep voice near me. A strong hand sliding the length of my forearm, gripping my hand. He wore a quilted doublet of green brocade, a tunic of blue velvet with an ermine border, and a cap the color of his eyes and plumed with green feathers. He wore heeled Italian boots that day. I thought his height marvelous. "My lady has a brave heart," he said, and I knew his eyes approved my face. "She is pretty, too," he smiled. "The good bishop is correct. Such skin and hair should not be veiled."

I lifted my head proudly then, looked straight ahead. I remember little of the ceremony except that it was hours long, and my fingers cramped, crushed in Pedro's grip. I remember blisters burning both my heels, and I recall that one candle on the altar which guttered out, was lit again, and died again. It wilted, one black wick among a myriad of flames. There was such a fuss of altar boys over that small candle that Pedro cursed it and the boys—loudly, a soldier's rough curse. I smiled, guessing my lord had a temper very like my own.

To love, to honor, and obey...our vows were spoken. My lord's moustache scraped my cheek, and I stared past him at that vacant candle. What chill finger had snuffed it out? I wondered. The other tapers burned so bright and steady. Was it an omen? I pushed the thought away and turned to descend the steps and receive the king's blessing.

Standing near Don Pedro, my back to the spectators, I had forgot my unveiled face. Now, I encountered scowls and sneers. I had but wrapped Christ's feet against the cold, but the ladies and gentlemen present assumed I had brazenly renounced my virgin veils. How else would Beatriz behave? they whispered.

Even the king was displeased; he told me so, and he advised me to guard my manners in Guatemala. Twenty young noblewomen, he said, were to attend me there—twenty maidens, and I, their chaperone! I was nonplused, but managed not to show my feelings. I promised the king my Court would be magnificent. I wondered if my husband had been advised of the additional baggage. I supposed he had, and I knew myself foolish then, for remaining closeted in my rooms and allowing plans to be made without my consent.

I curtsied to Bishop de las Casas and he blessed me mournfully. "God keep you in that heathen land," he bleated. Don Pedro scowled. My mother, still shocked by my naked face, did not move to embrace me. Tio Francisco made me a formal bow; my father turned his back to me. Then my husband was swept from me by well-wishers, and I stood alone among all the people. Absently, I moved to recover my *manta*, but, His feet wrapped, Christ looked as if he slept. I knelt and prayed His resignation might touch my own spirit.

Paco lifted me to my feet. His brown eyes were merry. "You have set a new fashion, sister—the bride unveiled before the ceremony! The gentlemen will thank you." He laughed. "The unveiling, I have heard, can be shock enough to stun a man. Will you make a new ruling in Guatemala, Beatriz? All brides must reveal their faces prior to the ceremony."

Paco recovered my *manta* and wrapped it about my shoulders. "Smile, Madam," he ordered me. "Father has decided my fate too. I am to accompany you to Guatemala." He struck his forehead in mock dismay. "I am not certain where exactly Guatemala is, or how to travel there—by ship, I suppose? I have told them I belong astride a horse, not walking a deck or counting Indians!"

Paco hugged me close. "We are condemned together, my

sister. All insist they would be rid of Beatriz, and Paco, too."

I sensed his bitterness. Paco dearly loves court life; he is a born gallant. "I am pleased you will grace my Court in Guatemala," I said. And then I grasped his hands in mine. "Paco, we are not condemned, we are set free. I feel like a wild bird, loosed at last from its cage."

"You are wed, Beatriz, gone from one cage into another," he corrected me. I saw the pity in his eyes and it angered me.

"I am Lady Beatriz," I said. "Marriage will not clip my wings, Paco—it will not!" I turned away, but not before I heard my brother's light reply:

"Not marriage, no. 'Tis love will clip this lady's wings."

CHAPTER 11

THE DUKE OF ALBUQUERQUE presided over our wedding feast. The vaulted dining hall was divided in two by Moorish screens. The gentlemen sat at table, and how I envied them the comfort of their armchairs! We women crouched on our cushions, eating at low stools, and served last.

I saw the roasted peacocks carried past; whole splendid birds with tails still attached and spread like fans. Small *mantillas* of gold cloth circled the birds' necks and these *mantillas*, I saw were embroidered with the Cross of St. James.

We wore silk gloves to dine, and rose water stood nearby in which to dip a cloth and wipe our lips. Négri was my cup bearer, and that afternoon he kept my cup filled despite my mother's protests.

Peacock and goose; heron and white duck; eggs served whole on the tines of forks. I heard the crude laughter and jokes of the gentlemen when the testicles of roosters were presented. Fruit ices were followed by pomegranates and figs, and grapes both bitter and sweet. The Duke of Alburquerque sent me his own page, bearing a silver salver on which reposed a castle of spun sugar rimmed with chocolate mountains bursting yellow cream.

It was a feast intended to last past sunset, well into the night. I could not eat, nor could the other ladies because our stays were uncomfortably tight, and to sit gracefully on a pillow, legs tucked under, is always an ordeal. We pecked and nibbled. The air became oppressive; the scented air and perfumes, the stench of grease and aromatic oils combined to ache my head. I longed for fresh air, but the ladies were fearful of autumn drafts; they ordered more logs piled on the fire and soon the room was smoke-filled. My lord's deep voice and the sound of his comfortable laughter led me to suppose he would sit at the table most of the night. The musicians tuned their instruments. I did not want to dance.

I begged to be excused. I doubt any lady present remarked my departure except my mother.

She signaled me to remain seated, but I disobeyed her. Knowing her night would be worry-haunted, I wished her, "Pleasant dreams," as I passed her. Négri lighted me to my rooms where Ana awaited me.

I saw the shirred chemises, the cosmetic jars, the sponges and combs and tweezers. "Leave me, he will not come," I said. "My lord drinks heavily. He will not visit me tonight."

Ana chuckled. "He will come. He found you pretty, my lady."

Days previously, Ana told me, she had made a Neapolitan soap with fat of deer kidneys, hemp and ash. I wrinkled my nose at the sight of the steaming tub. "No!" I protested, but Ana and five waiting women did with me as they wished.

I was scrubbed until my skin was raw. I was patted dry and bathed again in a liquid made from the white of eggs, myrrh, camphor, and turpentine. And towelled dry again, and rinsed three times with rose water. Ana plucked every hair from my body with the sharp silver tweezers. "Smooth as a dove," she crooned, "sweet as an angel."

No less than three starched chemises were knotted and laced, my chin to my toes. My hair was brushed until it was free of the stiffening gum, and plaited then, with pearls. My feet were oiled, and bracelets with bells were clasped around my ankles. "Slave's bracelets," I muttered. "The music of love," Ana insisted.

"I will wear my uncle's gift," I said. I tied the emerald to the ribbon threaded nearest my heart. My courage waned and I needed this reminder of my kingdom.

"Your lady mother will be displeased," Ana fussed. "Not a drop of color for a bride. So it must be."

"My lady mother," I replied, "is up to her chin in peacocks and cream. I doubt she will trouble herself to bid me goodnight." My eyes probed the shadowed corners of my room, and I wondered where the vial of blood had fallen. "Ana," I begged, "leave me to sleep now."

"Little sleep for you tonight, my cherub," she cackled, and I saw the one tooth left her flash white and I pitied her. I wondered what it would be like to grow old and ugly. Dear Ana, what would happen to her without me? I was the last of her angels. What would I do without Ana? The thought smote me, and I clung to her then. "Stay," I whispered. "Sing me a lullaby, Ana, to keep me safe in the dark."

She dismissed my ladies and tucked me into the bed, all cambric cool, sharp laces, and broad as an island. I caught Ana's hands. "Sing of the green land where you were born." I knew the old one's story by heart, but I longed for it again, now. "How do you make a song of slavery?" I asked. And then I whispered, "Ana, have you known the love of a man?"

"Like a pearl in my hand, my lady," she said, and sat on the edge of my bed. I thought her frail as an autumn leaf. She sang softly in a language I did not understand, except that I knew it was happy.

I was lulled to sleep, and wakened hours later to find Ana gone and the weight of a man's hand on mine. In my sleep, I had rolled to lie curled against him.

My lord sat beside me, and because I could see the brilliant blue of his eyes, I knew it was near dawn.

I pulled loose from his grasp. "You come late to bed," I said accusingly.

"Do not pretend you have waited for me," he replied. Then, cool as you please, he stood and stretched lazily and began to disrobe. I heard the dull thud of his boots where he dropped them, the clink and clatter of sword belt and dagger. The small light through my casements etched his figure large. "If you lack a page," I said, "you may call Négri. I have closets for bathing, for changing clothes...." I peered at him, my covers drawn up to my nose. Must he undress completely before my eyes? A brute, I thought, well-mannered in public, but a mongrel born. Let him desire me to his dying day, I would fight, refuse! I tensed my muscles, waiting the assault.

But he paid me no mind. He went to my window, clad

only in tight britches, and flung the shutters wide. *"Por Dios!* This air breeds pestilence, my lungs ache!" He leaned far out, breathing deeply.

Then—turning on me quickly, he said, "My lady, I loathe a shrew. If I am late to bed, so be it. There will be times I will not come to bed at all. I am told you are difficult—" he shrugged. "Keep your whining for your ladies. Other than that, saving my honor—I will not play the cuckold—you are free to spend your hours as you wish."

He was standing beside my bed, across its white expanse from me. "I will make no demands on you," he said, and climbed between the covers making a small earthquake of my still island. The bed was wide enough to sleep six comfortably so my lord lay a great distance from me, on his side and his back turned.

There was no more spoken between us that night, or rather that dawn. I lay awake, staring at that lump of man beside me, counting the scars like white stars on his skin, and hearing the rise and fall of his deep breathing. He fell asleep instantly, like a hound home from the hunt, and sometimes his skin twitched, or a muscle. Once his whole body spasmed, then relaxed and he murmured from some aching dream, "Luisa...Luisa...." It was the way I knew I called Alonso, a love dream, and I reached to caress his heaving shoulder. In his sleep, my lord shrugged my hand away.

So long I lay there! Shame, pride, loathing, longing, tenderness, despair—all feelings battled in me. I wished to flee that bed. Or wake my husband with a kiss. Or slap him hard! He did not want me. He would make no demands on me, so he had stated, clearly and coldly.

Luisa? Who was this Luisa who haunted him even in sleep?

Perhaps he kept a harem of his own, across the sea? Indian women with black tresses, bronzed skins, and Luisa, the current favorite?

Who and what will I be? I wondered. No more than a pale princess, queen by title only, and captive far from home. Not even Tio Francisco could reach me, not there, and he cared little now that I was wed. Tears slid down my cheeks, puddled the pillow under my cheek.

The bells rang six. I heard the watchman cry his last round. All about me, outside my closed room, the castle was waking. I heard hushed laughter, the creak of wagon wheels, and the rustle of brooms sweeping away the debris of my wedding feast. Dogs barked—they would have the bones of last night's banquet. A bird sang and pigeons cooed—they would gorge too, on crumbs from that feast in my honor. Pig slop, corn and fruit for the horses, cream for the cats, wine dregs for the lowest servant—every creature would thrive this morning on the leavings from my wedding night. Only I lay alone, ignored.

The bells rang seven. My lord slept on, and on! I knew Négri was awake, waiting beyond my door. Ana would come soon, to light my fire. My waiting women; the lords and ladies; the wedding guests; my parents and Tio Francisco—I felt their prying thoughts seep through the very walls, slide beneath my covers.

I would be an object for pity, for laughter. "I told you so—" there were some who would say that. And, "Who would want her for wife?" others would sneer. "The sheets are clean, he never touched her!" So would gossip weave its net, holding me fast. I could hear the snickers of the ladies, the giggles of the fops. Poor Mother would not be able to hold up her head, my shame become her own. Which was worse, I wondered, to be called whore, or rejected bride? And then I thought: there must be a way to keep this secret.

Dare I use it - that vial of blood? "No!" I spoke aloud, and sat up in bed with such a jerk I woke my husband.

"What is it?" he exclaimed, and was out of bed and fumbling for his dagger before his eyes were half open.

"Wake me gently, my lady. I am a soldier and sleep with one eye open."

"No," I shook my head, "I have watched you. You sleep deeply, my lord. I might have killed you, between one snore and the next."

He looked like a schoolboy then, tugging at his britches.

"I do not snore," he said, and was back in bed, away from me again.

"You dream, my lord," I whispered, wanting to keep him awake. There was still time before we would be called. He must not be permitted to shame me. I touched the back of his head, the whisper of a touch where his yellow hair was thick and tangled. He made no response.

"Will we visit the Western Indies, my lord?" I asked, my voice ordinary as the new daylight on my ceiling. "Will we sail soon for Guatemala?"

He did not answer me.

"Tell me of the Quetzal bird. I like the fan," I said. Then I thanked him for his many gifts. I told him I was glad that Paco was going with us. I asked him about Santiago, his capitol in Guatemala. I praised his deeds in Mexico. I named his brothers and asked after each of them: Jorge, Gonzalez, Gomez, and Juan.

Still, no reply. I said that I could read Latin, that I could write in cipher, that I spoke French and Italian. Did he like the lyre? I asked, and I told him I could also sing. I knew he was a fine rider, I said, and that I, too, liked nothing better than to be astride a horse.

Desperate, I chattered at that silent back. "I can fence, my lord. I have the whole book containing the Conquest of the Moors, and I will read aloud you."

My throat grew dry, listing my accomplishments, inquiring of his pleasures and all those things I guessed he held most dear. He did not move. But he was not asleep, I knew that.

And I was angry then! "You will answer me!" I shouted, and I gave him a great push that sent him tumbling off the edge of the bed.

When he stood, I was frightened. The light behind him spiked him gold, tawny as a lion. I thought he would strike me. But he laughed. A great bellow of laughter, and I saw his white teeth under his yellow moustache. "Witch," I think he called me that....

"Sweet," he murmured, stretching himself beside me. "Is so much talent healthy?" he teased. "Will you steal my kingdom, Beatriz?"

Talking softly, he undid my buttons and ribbons. I felt his large hands on my breasts. He slipped my gown from my shoulders. I heard his sharp intake of breath. "Ah, yes...yes," he whispered, and I knew he found me beautiful. "You pushed the Captain General from his bed," he said, his lips near my ear. He laughed and held me tight against him. "Not a woman yet has so disturbed my sleep!" He ducked his head and I felt his mouth move over me, tickling, caressing.

He was so gentle, discovering parts of me, that I was not ashamed, and never frightened. "My small fox," he said, and he spanned my waist with his hands. "Are you strong, little one? Can you be a Conquistador's lady?"

"Your lady," I whispered. My hands moved, warm as his own, and curious too. I found him splendid and I told him so—again and again until he put his mouth on mine and we were so close we might have been one.

When he was spent, he slept. In repose, his face was young. I touched the fullness of his lips, the thickness of his eyelashes. And the wonder of it all, I remember well, was that I believed this man mine, all my very own. I saw my future green as spring before me. Nothing and no one could ever part my lord and I—so I resolved.

And when he moved in my arms; when he whispered again, "Luisa?" I pressed my lips on his. "Beatriz," I insisted.

CHAPTER 12

PEDRO HAPPENED TO ME like a thunder clap. The little I knew of love I had learned from Alonso. And he had been like myself: innocent, romantic, speaking the language of my small world.

Pedro was different. I had grown up surrounded by obsequious cavaliers, arrogant courtiers, tutors and savants with much knowledge but greater ambitions. I had yet to meet a man who did not wear a mask. My lord does not conceal his feelings; his face is his own. Pedro kneels first to God, and then to his King; his honesty is relentless. My lord is no pretender to his manhood.

We rose early, that first morning. I would have lingered longer in bed, but Pedro was up and fully dressed before Négri brought our chocolate. My lord said he had an appointment with the king, and later he would sup with Tio Francisco, alone in my uncle's chambers.

"You will tell my uncle you are pleased with me?" I asked.

"Of course," he replied. "But it is Guatemala that concerns me now, and my city, Santiago. Your uncle will help me."

"Which is why you married me," I said, half-teasing, more in earnest.

He gave me a mock bow. "I cannot deny that, my lady. You are a gift from Heaven, and the king of Spain. But—" he leaned and kissed me then, "a lovelier gift than I had hoped."

"I was sworn to hate you," I whispered, my arms about his neck.

He set me back against my pillows. "The few times you deigned to show your face, you scowled, Beatriz. At our betrothal—by God's grace! if we had been alone I would have spanked you. Négri your page, shows better manners than yourself. Why, Beatriz?"

"Because, my lord—you should have come and begged my hand. Pedro, listen and understand. I am the king's

59

bribe. Beatriz de la Cueva buys your loyalty to Spain."

He shook his head. "I will not be bribed. Spain cannot buy my loyalty, it has been hers since I first soldiered. I have earned the honors given me, you among them, Beatriz." Pedro looked at me sharply. "Why do you complain? You will be queen of Guatemala. It is a fair and wealthy kingdom."

"Offer me China," I cried, "naught would weigh if I did not love you. My lord, I will not be bought or given against my wishes. I will not be 'among your honors won'!"

I kicked myself free of the bed covers. "You and your kingdom be damned!" I said, and rushed on, ignoring his shocked face. "I am no man's prize. It is our unholy marriage that concerns me, sir. Francesca, my dead sister, your dead wife—the Holy Book forbids a union such as ours. Pedro, we are no more than pawns." I hid my face, ashamed of my ready tears.

"Beatriz...*querida*...." He stroked my hair, buttoned a button. "God would not have set you in my path if He had not wished us wed. I feel strong purpose in our union. Francesca?" He shrugged. "God rest her timid soul, she did not please me as you do."

"Ah?" I almost clapped my hands. "I knew she wouldn't ! I told them all so. I begged the king to give me leave to marry you myself."

"That," Pedro answered, "I would have refused. I loathe the royal market in child brides."

I held my lord close. "You never loved her? Swear it, sir!"

"Love?" He was genuinely surprised. "What has love to do with marriage? I am content, that is enough. And now, my Beatriz, I must leave you." His hands pressed firm around my waist as he set me back on my pillows.

"Wait," I begged, and scrambled from bed to hold him again. "I will not lie to you," I whispered, hiding my face beneath his ruff. "I am not a virgin. Does it matter? They told me to lie, to spill blood on the sheets. My uncle said you would not be pleased, that you would leave me behind. You won't, my lord? The scandal is years past. You are not angry, are you?"

Under my cheek, his chest rumbled with that easy

laughter I already loved. "Scandal is the gossip of jealous fools, Beatriz. This chatter of blood and virgins—it is garbage. Their talk is sour as their wine."

He cupped my face between his hands, looked deeply into my eyes. "Know that you please me, Beatriz. Let their tongues waggle. But promise me one thing..."

"Anything!" I breathed.

"Do not curse our kingdom, my lady. I have sought to put the Devil out of Guatemala. Will you bring him back again, Beatriz?"

"Never, my lord," I promised. "Never!"

He left me a kiss in each of my hands. I sat on the edge of my bed, memorizing his every word and gesture. I looked at my palms, their thinly etched lines. A pearl and a stone, Ana had seen—which hand held the pearl? I wondered. Was my jealousy the stone? If my lord loved me, I would hold a pearl beyond price....

"My lady?" Ana had entered my room.

I flung myself into her arms. "All is very well," I told her. "I please him, he said that, Ana. He did ask what love has to do with mariage, but..."

"He likes you," Ana finished triumphantly. "And why wouldn't he? Liking is good, child; it is a beginning."

A beginning, yes. But I wanted more.

Ana read my thought. "Greedy girl. You will go hungry to your grave."

She sat me on a low stool and flourished the hair brush. "Such tangles, Beatriz—and your mother will see you right away," she told me. "Your uncle waits too. I think the blue gown is suitable...."

"My riding habit," I said firmly. "I want to get away, not talk. I feel different, Ana. Tell Négri to have *Señorita* saddled."

Ana shook her head. "It would be unseemly to wander off this morning."

"Exactly," I laughed. "I like to make their tongues wag. Ana, I need a ride today, off by myself."

It was splendid. The sun stood directly overhead. *Señorita* carried me smoothly as a bird flies, low over the winter-brown fields. I gave her her head; she knew where

I wanted to go, to the willow grove and that river where I had imagined the unicorn.

The water lay sluggish, skinned with a brittle ice. The willows were not as tall as I remembered. I had not dared come here since that lost summer day. The bank, once stitched with daisies, was grey scrub, brambles.

"Alonso is dead." I said it loudly enough to startle a nest of quail. Their wings rattled.

Señorita whinnied, and I turned her head toward home. The turrets of Bedmar Castle were silver needles hard against the leaden sky. Always before, I had lingered, riding home. But now my heels pressed *Señorita's* sides. I wanted to move fast, into that land of spring and summer eternal, so Pedro promised, an ever-blue sky and singing birds. Tigers, Pedro told me, and monkeys with fur red as my hair. I could not wait for all of it to come true.

My mother awaited me. "Why did you choose to ride this morning, Beatriz? It is whispered you had run away."

"I am happy," I said simply. "It is a rare feeling for me, Mother, and I wanted to savor it, alone."

She stepped too close to me. "Is all well?" she asked. I thought her curiosity obscene.

Then I remembered—I am Don Pedro's lady! No need, not now, to fumble at confessions, to snatch at a love that forever eluded.

"Mother," I said, and it did not matter that she did not understand, "I have been given a pearl beyond price."

CHAPTER 13

I WORE MY RICHLY-EMBROIDERED Guatemala skirts and carried my green-plumed fan. Négri announced me: "La doña Beatriz de Alvarado!" I swept into my uncle's room and caught him trying to mend the globe. "Leave it," I said, merrily, "it will mend of itself." I curtsied low and kissed his hand. "I am content," I said.

"Of course. I knew it!" He set the globe spinning and when it lurched, we both smiled. "I will trust you to keep that part of the world steady, Beatriz," he said.

"I wear your emerald like a talisman," I said, showing him the emerald safe about my neck, strung on a golden chain. "I feel myself a queen," I said.

"You will be queen," he replied. "Beatriz, I must acquaint you with the problems in Guatemala. Your head is cooler than the Captain General's; I think domestic politics will appeal to you."

"Who is to govern the territory?" I asked with some sarcasm. "You, or Don Pedro, or myself?"

He did not smile. "You are to suggest, not govern, Beatriz. I am informed the Captain General is well-pleased with you. It is enough. He will listen to you. But be subtle; women do not sit at the Council table. The sky would fall, Beatriz, if it was even supposed I had appointed a *Señora Gobernadora.*"

"Would it?" I asked. "There have been great queens, Uncle. It is said that Isabella had a quicker mind than Ferdinand, that she exerted more influence. It was she who encouraged Colombo, the admiral. One might say the world opened wider when Isabella was queen. Perhaps, when I..."

"You are queen-consort, Beatriz," my uncle said quickly.

"If—in seven years, if something should befall don Pedro—"

"God forbid!" I exclaimed.

My uncle smiled. "You are too changeable, Beatriz. It

was not long ago that you cursed your marriage and your husband."

"I wish I had not," I said fervently. "But Don Pedro is sincerely Christian; I doubt a curse can hurt him. I will stand beside him, behind him—whatever you wish, Uncle. But I will never move against my lord, not even if the king desires it."

My uncle allowed his hands to pull his face into a weary grimace. "There are many prepared to move against your husband, Beatriz. The Governor Maldonado of Nicaragua has lately moved into your husband's territory. Another, Don Montejo of Honduras, plots to divide your kingdom."

My uncle's fist crashed to his writing table. "These are civilized gentlemen sent to control savages and they behave, among themselves, like beasts. Their personal greeds far outweigh their loyalties. Don Pedro turns his back, and they tear at his territory."

I asked, "If the king's laws are broken, cannot the Church intervene?"

My uncle shook his head. "The Church breeds jackals too, Beatriz. Dominicans and Franciscans are at each other's throats, and united together to destroy the soldier conquerors. Slavery is an issue," my uncle continued, "and the payment of taxes by the nobility."

"Are all the Spanish settlers noblemen?" I asked.

"No," my uncle said, "but I believe they have knighted themselves! Retired foot soldiers and opportunists—they demand land, then refuse to pay taxes. These self-appointed feudal lords are too grand to walk behind their own ploughs. I am against the enslavement of Indians, Beatriz!" My uncle's fist made his papers fly again. "An army of slaves predicts future bloody uprisings."

I could not imagine my brother working his own land, and I said as much. "And I will need servants," I said. "I cannot make a candle, or soap. But those who do this for me, I will call them servants, not slaves. That word sickens me, Uncle."

"You will get used to it," he said. He took my hands and chafed them between his own as if the room had grown cold, which it had not. "You go to a harsh country, Beatriz. It is alien to your upbringing. There are those who would have your head too, if they dared. You must take care, child."

I embraced my uncle. "Don Pedro will protect me," I assured him. He caught me close a moment, as he had used to do, and he told me not to trust all to love, to keep my wits about me, and to pray God for guidance.

"And yourself," I teased. "It is not God but you, Uncle, who has set my feet upon this path. You should praise all the saints that Beatriz goes gladly."

Indeed, I could not wait for our departure. "When do we leave?" I asked Pedro. Winter was upon us and I knew the road south would be closed soon, with snow and ice. I begged that we set out immediately.

But my lord was weary, he told me. He said he relished his soft bed, and that his limp, which is so pronounced and painful in New Spain, did not bother him so much when he had bed quilts and ready fires to warm his rooms.

Pedro had received an arrow through his thigh in a battle for Guatemala, and the resulting infection and cauterization of the wound caused his right leg to be shorter than his left. The heel of his right boot is made higher than the other but few remark my lord's imperfection. He does not complain, but I have seen him grimace from the pain. I learned to massage that wicked scar and there were times he blessed my hands.

I knew Pedro relished the Court's adulation. He had brought with him from Guatemala, for the king's pleasure, a company of Indians who could keep a stick aloft in the air with their feet. He had acrobats, eleven of them, tall bronzed men who could twist and swing like monkeys.

Pedro was served by four albino Indians, muscular men, grey-eyed, their hair like white silk. I tried to befriend these strangers, but they were arrogant and not a little frightening. It was Négri who managed to communicate with them. "My black skin and crooked back are as strange here as their pale hair," Négri told me. "As they pine for their homeland, so do I."

"Négri," I said, "you need not come to Guatemala. You

have earned your freedom. Let me send you home to Africa."

He grinned. "And what would you do without me, my lady? Who knows best when the dark mood is on you? Who makes you laugh? No, you cannot be rid of Négri. I am your shadow, *doña.*"

I wanted my Ana too, but Pedro said she would not survive the ocean voyage. She might as well have traveled because my leaving killed her. She sickened from idleness. My uncle wrote later that Ana had become worthless. My Ana worthless? If there is a God, she is His comfort in Heaven.

"We will have many sons," Pedro told me. It was a night after the Feast of the Kings and snow fell soft on Valladolid. We lay together under furs, and he had loved me generously.

"You are my Seven Golden Cities of Cibola," he said, touching my eyes and lips and breasts. Head to my toes, he counted seven cities, and I said I would make a song of that legend.

"It is no legend," he told me. "The Seven Cities are real, Beatriz. They are my heart's desire. The king has at last given me permission to search for this place where even the cooking pots are made of gold."

I had believed I was his heart's desire. "Gold cooking pots," I scoffed. "Pedro, you cannot believe such a tale!"

A shutter banged loose and a cold draft guttered our candle. "You never say you love me," I accused him.

"But I am here, Beatriz," he answered.

What does that mean? I wondered. He yawned and closed his eyes. I knew he would fall instantly asleep while I lay restless beside him. I felt forlorn. I could be any woman, I thought—just his being here does not mean he loves me.

I stared into the darkness. It was gold and power my lord craved, not even the Seven Cities would suffice, he must have more and more. Conquistador, conqueror—his kind were all alike, their greed was legendary. Plainsmen, most of them, crude, tough as bulls. Bull-headed? I smiled.

Yes, my lord was that. I might hold him a while, then he

would go. Unless...I clasped my hands tight in prayer...unless I gave him the sons he craved.

CHAPTER 14

PEDRO DECIDED that we would depart for the port of Seville at the end of February, when the first thaw set in. We would sail for New Spain in March. I could not sleep at night for my excitement. "You are not frightened, Beatriz?" my lord asked me. "Most women would be terrified."

"I am not most women," I replied. "All my life I have dreamed of escaping the Court. Nineteen years of cushions and gossip—ah, Pedro, you cannot imagine what it is like to be born a noble lady! I am impatient to see New Spain. Before you came, I begged my uncle for a convent in Panama."

Pedro chuckled. "You, a nun? Beatriz, you would turn the convent upside-down to have your way."

"Yes," I agreed, "I would give Christ's brides less of the Bible, and more of learning."

"Hold your tongue, my lady." Pedro's voice was sharp. He never liked it when I criticized things pertaining to the Church. Too, he feared the Office of the Inquisition, its spies who travel as far as New Spain, seeking the unbelievers.

"Beatriz," he warned, "you speak close to heresy. As my consort, you must guard your tongue. You are aware that you are to chaperone twenty young noblewomen to Guatemala?"

I tossed my head. "Where ten times twenty willing bridegrooms wait impatiently?" I snapped. "Pedro, there is not a one among these pouter pigeons who dare a flight from home. They do not look forward to your auction block in Santiago. Must we take them?"

"The king wishes my capital city to be settled by the true nobility," Pedro said. "My officers dine with their boots off. They don't know a French fork from a dagger. It is time we gentlemen rehearse our manners. I have promised fair wives to my Knights of Santiago.

"Command the ladies to prepare themselves for the voyage, Beatriz. Tell them that there a husband waits;

here is spinsterhood." Pedro laughed. "Not a one but will be begging passage to New Spain."

"Perhaps," I suggested, "there are those among them who do not want husbands."

"What else does a girl want—what else is there for her but marriage?" Pedro asked, truly surprised.

I knew he would never understand, but then I did not understand myself because, when I told Pedro angrily, "You men believe yourselves God's gifts to women!" and he answered, "What am I to you, my gentle lady?" I capitulated: "You are my gift from Heaven," with all truth and submission.

The twenty maidens did not want to go, and they blamed me, thinking I had asked for them as waiting women. I was impatient with them, not stopping to explain. It never entered my head then that I might need friends in Guatemala. I had little talent for making women friends, believing my own company and Pedro's love sufficient.

Pedro insisted that I choose a replacement for Ana. "Is there no one you are close to, that you trust, Beatriz?"

I shook my head, ashamed. Too, it was difficult to imagine a life without Ana. I thought hard. "There is one girl," I said slowly, "she is not highborn. She is named for a flower, which is not our custom—Rosita, little rose. She is said to have Turkish or Jewish blood. My father found her south of here, and saw some worth in her, and brought her home to be my companion. She is playful, but has no patience for reading and writing. We were never close, but Rosita has spirit, and as little reverence for solemnity as I.

"Yes," I continued, "perhaps Rosita will accompany me. But you will have to find her a husband quickly, my lord. I swear, from her chatter, she is half in love with you."

"Bring her with you," Pedro said.

Rosita was sixteen then, with a tongue as quick as my own, and an arrogant lift to her chin. Her sense of fun appealed to me, and I could not guess that, under her bright veneer, she was jealous, possessed by a miserable demon. My father had long forgot, or I was never told, that Rosita was a practicing Christian, adopting the faith only through necessity. She worships no god, save that of the flesh. Half in love with my husband? If she could have, she would have devoured his heart!

But she was sweet, sticky as honey then. When I asked her if she would accompany me to Guatemala, she kneeled and kissed the hem of my gown. "I would give my life to go with you," she said.

"Guatemala is a wild country," I warned.

"This Court is savage," Rosita said. "I am a slave-girl without protection; men pursue me without mercy."

I told her that Don Pedro would give her his protection at the Guatemalan Court. "You will attend me then?" I asked.

"With all pleasure, my lady!"

"Ana will instruct you in the duties of my bedchamber," I said. "Inquire as to the care of my gowns, my bath, and the scents I prefer."

I should have guessed the girl's conceit then, because she said she would not make soap, and she preferred not to roughen her hands with the scrubbing of linens. When I told Rosita that Négri did much of the heavy work, she sniffed disdainfully. "He is black and ignorant," she said. Her remark angered me; I should have been forewarned.

Ana knew Rosita well. She advised me against the girl. "Her hands will soil your laces, my lady. Your bed will not be smooth, and your stockings will go unmended. High and mighty, she pretends! It is her fault the gentlemen chase her."

I believed Ana jealous. "Hush, old one," I soothed. "No hands but yours make my perfection. But my lord has said you cannot go. The trip is too arduous. Ana, it is time you rest now."

"Bah! Rest is death, my lady. I will care for your rooms until you return. When you visit, a year or two from now, with your own babes, you will find your bed turned down and myself to welcome you home."

I felt a strange foreboding then. "Ana, I will not come home again. I will die in Guatemala!" I clung to her fiercely, feeling that first sharp terror of the unknown. I thought of Francesca and her lost grave.

"Ana, I will write. I will send you presents. I will never

forget you," I promised.

"I cannot read," she said simply. "But I will know the state of your soul."

"How, Ana?"

"Call a name seven times seven," she whispered, "Breathe on crystal and all is revealed."

"All, Ana?" I knew she had a crystal ball.

She nodded solemnly. "Hear me, my lady. I have looked upon Rosita's face in the glass, and found her evil. The living and the dead are revealed to me, their worth or malice."

I was curious. "Take your crystal and tell me of someone called Luisa," I said, because, more than once, Pedro, dreaming, called that name.

Ana shook her head. "I will not wake the dead."

"Luisa is dead? Oh, Ana, you invent! Luisa's name is strange to both of us. Enough of your ghost tales." I moved away from her, but she caught my hand.

"Listen, my lady—my crystal shows your future. The ghost of Luisa is tangled in your fate."

Ana spoke with such sincerity I felt afraid. "Enough—" I said sharply. "I do not believe in ghosts."

But the old one insisted. "Remember to pray as I have taught you, Beatriz. Look not to the right or to the left. Do not walk forbidden paths. Rosita will tempt you, Beatriz, and Luisa will make you weep."

I pulled free of Ana's hands. "What horrendous hauntings you predict," I cried. "A ghost, and a demon? Come—enough of this chatter, you must brush my hair. My lord will wonder what keeps me so long."

CHAPTER 15

THE FIRST WEEK IN FEBRUARY, 1539. I believe our departure was on a Monday because I remember the tedious Masses of the day before when even horseshoes and wheat grains were blessed.

The sun was a slice of lemon, the air crackly, and I remember the crust of snow breaking under my hands when I leaned from my window and saw the traveling city Pedro had contrived. A dragonsnake, multicolored, it wound six times around Valladolid.

There were wagons like barges; gilded sedan chairs, and curtained litters. Spaced between the conveyances were all the familiar animals of farm and ranch: horses, mules, donkeys; I saw a shepherd with his sheep, a swineherd with his pigs, and the shortcaped *vaqueros* driving milk cows, cattle, and squealing calves.

Our caravan was bright with banners. I recognized the flag of Santiago, the lion and castle of Castile and Aragon, the rainbowed penants of Pedro's captains, and King Charles' own doubleheaded eagle.

Drum thunder, and the cry of flutes. I thought the bells of Valladolid kept pace with my own heartbeats. There was a silver glitter over all, but I do not remember feeling cold though my breath was like smoke, and Ana's too, as she helped me dress.

My rooms had been emptied days before, all my chests and boxes packed. My gowns, jewels, shoes, cushions, books, candlesticks, wall hangings, Pedro's gifts—all were wrapped and packed aboard the wagons, even my parakeets. Their cage had been wound about with lamb fleece and set aboard the high-backed wagon like a boat on wheels, in which I was to ride.

It was twenty leagues south to the port of Seville. Mountains, plains, and rivers stood between us and our destination. Salamanca, Segovia, Toledo, and Pedro's own Estremadura—I could not wait to begin my journey.

Ana wrapped me warm. My mother wrapped me

warmer still, and she insisted on a woolen *tapado*, that heavy cloak which begins at the top of the head and hides all, even to a woman's toes. There is a way of arranging the *tapado* so one eye is left exposed, but Mother insisted I must cover my face. "It is only seemly," she said. "A good wife does not show herself to strangers, child; you go into a world far from familiar faces."

"Thank God!" I exclaimed, then wished I had bit my tongue instead, her eyes showed such pain. "Mother," I grasped her hands, "know that I will miss you. I will try to behave as you have taught me."

"You will behave as you see fit; you always do," she said quietly. "Do you have your Bible, Beatriz?"

"My Bible, and my new boots," I said, and lifted my skirts to show off Pedro's latest gift—emerald green boots of dyed chamois, supple as my skin. "Aren't they fine, Mother?"

She clucked her tongue. "Unsuitable for traveling. You must wear your clogs over them."

My clogs! Those heavy clumsy wooden things which lifted me at least three inches from the ground, hobbled my walking. "No!" I argued.

Ana knelt. "Wear them, for her sake," she whispered.

I slid into my clogs and felt myself a swathed giantess. The room was not mine anymore, even my bed had been packed. I saw puffs of dust, and a spider weaving a web above the warm coals of my fire.

"Mother, will you miss me?" I asked it lightly; it was too late for any tenderness between us, but I hungered for one word, a hint of peace for both of us.

But—"Paco is going," she said absently. "You will be together. Yes, Paco is leaving." Her shoulders sagged, and she looked older, lonely. "Beatriz, your brother is impetuous, a trouble at times, you must..."

"I will love him as you do," I said, biting back my frustration.

I knelt to kiss the rusty edge of her skirt. "Mother, give me your blessing."

Hurriedly, she consigned me to the Virgin's care, and then she raised me to my feet. "Beatriz, when you reach

Veracruz search for Francesca's grave. Send me word of her."

I stared, blankly. I had felt some pity for her, but now I knew she thought only of Paco leaving her, and the dead Francesca. Angrily, I blinked away my tears. "I do not go to seek lost graves," I said, and would have spoken more and cruelly but my father knocked.

"They are waiting for you, Beatriz. Your husband begs you to make all speed."

"It is goodbye then." I looked at my father, his oiled beard and stiff ruff, the purple stuffs like armor that he wore. He did not hold me when he kissed me; his lips barely brushed my cheeks.

My mother turned her back. I like to think perhaps she hid her tears. I felt Ana's arms about me for the last time. "Look neither to right or to left, my angel," she whispered. I hugged her tight. "I hold the pearl," I told her. "I will not forget you."

Tio Francisco stood in my doorway. And Pedro behind him, splendid in scarlet. My lord wore breast armor, and a short sword. A bundle of fur stood next to him and I laughed when I saw it was Négri, wrapped head to toe in lynx and fox.

Farewell. *Adios*. Godspeed. Curtsies and bows, the falsely smiling faces—I passed through them all for the last time, and I looked neither to right or to left. They were more curious than kind.

King Charles waited in his sedan chair, near my wagon. I saw the latter gilded, its leather top oiled, and the silk curtains drawn back so that all might see my couch of pillows, the rugs on the wagon floor.

Rosita, already ensconced inside, beckoned gaily. "It is most comfortable, my lady!" I saw she had a brazier lit, and a kettle warming.

Despite my clogs and wrappings I would have knelt to the king, but he prevented me. "The ground is cold, Beatriz." He took my proffered hands and I felt the stiffness of his fingers through my gloves. "I will miss you," he said. His face looked stark as that winter day. He is sovereign of a mighty empire, but he is one of the saddest gentlemen I have ever known. If I am a slave, King Charles is a prisoner in solitary confinement.

"Remember me, and smile," I said. "Do not forget me, sir."

"Never, my lady," he said, so solemnly I knew both I and my kingdom would receive his favors.

"God keep you, sir," I prayed.

Then my uncle called me, and I turned to take his hand to mount the steps into my wagon.

"Uncle, I am really going," I said, and I put my arms tight about this tall man who had been father, teacher, and friend to me. "You will write often," I begged. "Oh, I am sorry for the times I angered you. I would take back my words, I am so happy now."

He pushed my hood back, and he cupped my face, holding me so I could look deep into his eyes. "Yes, you are content. A little love, and you are happy, Beatriz. God keep it so," he said, fervently.

"I will keep it so," I promised.

"Not too tight a rein," Tio Francisco warned. "If there is danger, Beatriz, send word to me."

"What danger?" I asked lightly, looking past my uncle at the color and pageantry of our imminent departure. Paco cantered by on his favorite horse, and he saluted me.

"Uncle," I said, " I cannot wait to begin! Perhaps I will sail past China!"

My uncle smiled. "You and Alvarado are two of a kind. But remember, he is older than you, Beatriz. He is hard, toughened by many battles. He coddles his ambition, feeds it first."

"He loves me!" I insisted. "See, Uncle, how he rides there." I pointed ahead to where Pedro reviewed his foot soldiers. "He will protect me, Uncle."

Pedro wheeled his horse, that splendid roan. He raced past my wagon, mud spitting from his horse's hooves. "Settle yourself, Beatriz," he shouted.

My uncle scowled, and I kissed the tip of his cold nose and scrubbed a splash of mud from his cheek. "My husband rides like the Devil himself!" I laughed, but looking after my lord, I saw him a true St. James on horseback, the image of his own coat-of arms.

"Uncle, I breathed, "you have given me a god!"

Tio Francisco embraced me. "Don't love the scoundrel overmuch," he whispered, handing me up the last steps into the wagon.

"Adios, querido Tio!" I cried, as the wagon lumbered forward, throwing me back against my pillows. We were moving at last, and the carnival tumult of our departure gave me no time to look back until all I knew was behind me.

A dot of a white kerchief or the wing of a pigeon fluttered at my window. Then Bedmar Castle vanished in a turn of the road, and a light snow began to fall. Négri raised the leather roof. I heard the caterwauling of my ladies in the two wagons behind my own. Cowards! I thought, and I prayed they would not wail all the way to Seville.

I leaned from the back window, catching snowflakes and watching their crisp perfection melt to nothing but a blotched stain on my gloves. I pushed back my hood and raised my face to feel the snow on my cheeks.

"You will fall, my lady," Rosita warned. I pretended not to hear her.

CHAPTER 16

SUCH HAPPINESS I KNEW then; at the start of my journey I was my own mistress at last. I, alone, gave the orders and this power was like strong wine. All of my mother's and Ana's admonitions and warnings were thrown out, like the slops left behind on the road.

Rosita had been ordered to sleep in the wagon with me. I soon changed that, dispatching her to one or another of the other wagons as soon as supper was disposed of and I was comfortable for the night. Pedro slept beside me, and I prevailed upon him, though he was not easy about it—robber bands beset all caravans, he said—but I enticed him to have our wagon set apart from the others at night. Sentries were posted, and we were able to sleep, when the weather was softer and we were farther south, with the wagon roof folded back. We lay together, my captain and I, beneath a canopy of stars.

I ate when Pedro was hungry, and Rosita did not complain because my husband dislikes rich food; he prefers bread and cheese, and bottled wine poured in crystal goblets. Pedro often tells me that our Spanish custom of storing wine in pigskins spoils the flavor of the grapes.

I rode *Señorita* whenever I could, and I was glad of the exercise. The wagon was confining, and monotonous. Reading was nigh impossible due to the bumps, the starting and stopping. My ladies complained constantly, conceived of every excuse to return to Valladolid. Two calves were born, and one lamb, the latter whose mother died and I took the creature into my wagon and dipped my finger in milk and fed him myself. Pedro told me I would make the best of mothers. Indeed, I had reason to believe I carried the seed of his child, and I told Pedro so and he was tender with me, and proud. Time proved me mistaken.

On those nights we slept within the walls of a city, we were royally entertained. It seems I have relatives everywhere. I have heard it said, often, that all the nobility of Spain are cousins and I believe it. Often Pedro was not recognized, and it was my name that opened doors. He was jealous, though I tried to bring him forward. Once he swore that when we reached Estremadura, he would search the plains for his small village; he was a hero there, he told me, but perhaps I had grown too vain to greet his parents kindly?

I protested I would like to know the lady Léonor, his mother. And I reminded Pedro that he and I shared the same dislike for royal courts, the fawning nobility.

Pedro insisted, "You will not forget, even in the wilderness, that you are a de la Cueva."

"I will be your queen," I told him. "Pedro, I am going to change the old customs. The first thing I am going to do is have chairs made for the ladies. And, whether you like it or not, we women will sit at your table!"

He looked dumbfounded. "You will dine with us? Beatriz, you won't like it. The language—our tongues are often loosed by wine and we speak of..."

"Women!" I cried. "So why can't we be present, to hear ourselves praised? Ah, Pedro—I've wagonloads of books, and these we will read aloud and discuss. A dozen of my favorite musicians travel with us; we will have music at supper, my lord, and dance afterwards.

"I have planned pageants and fiestas, and the theater—our dramas will not all be holy preachings, Pedro—no, we are going to laugh and enjoy ourselves."

My lord was not as pleased as I. "Women can be tiresome," he said, with his customary bluntness. "Witness those two wagon-loads of females behind you, my lady. I doubt I can get them safely across the ocean."

"Let them throw themselves overboard," I said lightly. "I will manage alone. And you forget Rosita. Her courage has not failed her."

"True," Pedro replied. "I envy the man who will have that one for wife. She mended the cloak I am most fond of, and I cannot see her stitches—it is like new. I thank you, Beatriz, for calling this to her attention."

I had not. I had not noticed Pedro's cloak was torn, nor did I know which was his favorite. Rosita had been swift to please my lord and I was jealous.

"Give me your clothes that need mending," I told Pedro. "I've little enough to do. I would be glad..."

"You?" He laughed and kissed me full on my mouth. "Keep your pretty fingers smooth, love; let Rosita do my mending."

Later, I asked Rosita about the cloak. She smiled, showing her sharp teeth. "You did not notice, my lady? He has a favorite cloak. He told me an Indian girl wove it specially for him, years ago. Those britches he uses for hard riding—they are remarkably contrived, and darned many times by someone whose fingers are cleverer than my own."

I wanted to ask Rosita more about the Indian girl, but I knew my jealousy would give her pleasure. I could see she wanted me to ask; she fidgeted, wanting to tell me something. I ignored her hints and told her to give me whatever of Pedro's needed mending.

Several evenings later it rained, and Rosita and I were shut in the stuffy wagon. Pedro would be late, I knew, because wagons were mired behind us and ahead. Rosita gave me Pedro's cloak; the hem, she said, was half-undone. I asked for needles and thread, and a strong light.

The cloak was faded, but its colors glowed softly. The weaving was close, different than any I had seen before. "Indian work," Rosita said, and she stroked the cloak lovingly. I pulled it from her hands. "I will take up the hem," I said, in a tone she recognized as one of dismissal.

I sat alone in the wagon, the cloak spread over my knees. Its outer side was patterned with stars and arrows, faded but still visible. I saw the stitched gold of a crown which would rest on Pedro's shoulder. Flowers or butterflies, I could not tell which, marched the length of the hem. I turned the cloak inside-out and I wondered at the weaving because the inside was all one color, a worn brown. I stood and wrapped the cloak about me. It was as long as my own *tapado* and warm as my lord's arms about me.

When I removed the cloak I saw, near where the garment would cover Pedro's chest, the pattern of two joined hearts, very faint. I sat closer to the candles and traced the red dye of the hearts. They were linked, and in their centers was some embroidery. Moving my finger slowly, I traced the letter P. in one heart. The other heart, I think I guessed it before I felt it, held the letter L. L for Luisa—the name Pedro whispered in his sleep?

My stomach churning, I clutched the cloak to me. L?...Luisa! The air was suddenly stale, I could scarcely breathe. I unlaced the flap at the back of the wagon and pushed it up, but the wind blew it shut again. The leather slapped my hands smartly. L ...for Luisa.

The cloak lay on the floor, and I picked it up gingerly. Luisa—she had fashioned this garment. It was his favorite cloak. When he wore it, did he feel her arms about him? I saw the torn hem, and the many patches.

"It is fit for burning!" I said loudly.

Deliberately then, I cut the cloak into small pieces and pushed each remnant into the coals of the brazier. The stuff smoked. There was a rancid odor in the wagon and the smoke brought tears to my eyes. I fanned the fire hot, and fed it all the cloth. It was slow to burn and I knew my hands and face were smudged.

"What in God's name?" Pedro swung himself into the wagon.

I stared at him. He was wet through, weary. "I had to burn your cloak," I said, or rather whispered - I was so afraid. "There," I pointed at the smoking brazier, "I burned it."

"Why? What possessed you?"

"It...I...it had..." I could not find the words and I began to weep.

"You had no right—why the Devil did you burn it, Beatriz? You could have waited. If you must do these things, ask me first! Bah! the wagon stinks!"

He stood above the brazier, rubbing his hands. "I'm starved," he said then. "Where is the girl Rosita? My horse slipped a shoe, I've tramped through mud—and come to find you muddle-headed, my lady, a cold fire, and I'll wager you've not thought of feeding me?"

"No," I admitted weakly, "I hadn't thought of food, my lord. I...I was trying to ...I sent Rosita away, and—I am sorry. Certainly there is food prepared—a bird, perhaps, roasted, and wine to warm you..." My words tumbled, senseless, and I pushed my hair back and knew I dirtied my face. My fingers were all charcoal.

"I'm sorry," I repeated.

"I'll fetch my own supper, Beatriz. Bishop Marroquin invited me to join him this evening, but I refused having grown accustomed to dining with you."

Pedro stared at me. "In God's name, why did you burn that cloak? Are you mad, girl?"

"Because it had initials, two hearts and the initials..." I began, but it was no use; he was gone. He did not return that night.

It was not until Seville that he joined me again. An agony of time! I did not eat. I hardly slept. I had not recognized, until then, my growing love for Pedro. My hunger for him was so intense it frightened me. And it was at this time, during his arbitrary absence, that I realized I could lose my lord. Such knowledge was like a dousing of ice cold water, and I resolved to keep my jealousy to myself. Doña Beatriz could hold my lord's attention, but that child in me, so starved was she for love—I would have to keep her hidden deep.

Rosita cleaned the wagon. Her eyes were mocking; she was impudent, lazy in my lord's absence. I pretended indifference. I said that the cloak had not been worth mending, that Don Pedro had thrown it away. She did not believe me. I began to make Pedro a new cloak.

I sewed by sunlight and candlelight, and I, who hated sewing, blessed the task I had set myself. It kept me from brooding. The cloak I made is velvet and lined with silk. It was done, even to the rich embroidery, when we reached Seville.

It is a fine purple cloak, the coat-of-arms of Santiago on its back, and I gave the saint yellow hair like my lord's own, curly stitches in golden thread. Inside the cloak, above Pedro's heart, I drew in ink, designing two hearts, linked: one with a P in its center, the other with a B. I did not wish to copy Luisa, only to show my penmanship better than her own uneven stitches.

Pedro received my gift with a show of pleasure I knew was not sincere, but I appreciated the fact that he did not mention that cloak I had burned. I showed him the initials and hearts. "Our own," I said.

"I am branded," he teased, sliding the cloak over his shoulders.

"I would fill your heart forever, my lord," I said meekly.

"Forever, Beatriz? That is a word for the young. I am past believing in forever. Tomorrow is enough." He stroked the velvet cloth. "Very fine," he said, "not suitable for hard riding, but good enough for our appearance in Seville. When we reach Guatemala there is someone there who will weave me a warm cloak."

"Myself," I said eagerly. "Somebody there will teach me to weave, and I will fashion you a garment large as a tent, soft as swansdown!"

He laughed and reached for my hands. "Your fingers are pricked and calloused," he protested. "The Indian loom is heavy, Beatriz. No, I prefer you as you are: your hands smooth, your skin like porcelain."

He bent to kiss my palms. The pulse in my wrists leapt to the urgency of his lips. "Too long away from you, *querida*," he said, his voice husky, wanting me.

Hard it was, but I held myself stiff. "It was you who chose to stay away, my lord. And I am not made of porcelain! You have but to ask—I will weave all your clothing if I must...."

He was not listening. His fingers loosed my hair. "You will give me a son, *querida*; that is all I ask of you."

CHAPTER 17

SEVILLE. I felt like a mole come from its tunnel underground into the full light of April's carnival. *Sevilla, La Magnifica!* I had imagined it exotic, rich, sophisticated, and I was not disappointed. The city is the heart of the Spanish trade route, the end and the beginning again of our treasured Carrera. Indie spices; coffee and chocolate and sugar; silver from Peru; gold, emeralds, pearls—the Spanish frigates and galleons unloaded their treasures in the harbor of San Lucar, to be shipped up the Guadalquivir River to Seville.

We left our wagons and provisions under guard outside the city gates. Pedro rode in beside my litter. His horse was decked in a saddle and bridle of rubbed bronze fittings, and Pedro himself wore that cloak I had made him, his ceremonial sword, and a red-plumed hat. Négri trotted smartly ahead of us on a small pony; he carried the banner of Santiago. Paco, with the other officers, rode just behind me. My twenty women, their wailing reduced now to mews and sobbing, had, each of them, her own litter. We made a splendid procession and, peering between my curtains, I saw many heads turn to look at us. I was eager to see everything. Impulsively, I pushed my curtains aside.

An Arab prince, trailed by his twittering harem—women enclosed in locked sedan chairs and litters—that procession jostled our own and I stared, open-mouthed, at the multi-colored silks, the jewelled crescents and stars, the giant black slaves. The Arab, riding close, leaned to look into my face. His dark eyes caught and held my own. I know he heard my sharp intake of breath because he chuckled and leaned forward from his saddle. I felt my cheeks blaze. Our procession halted with a jolt. Pedro rose in his stirrups and shouted an oath, and struck the Arab with the end of his reins, drawing blood. I thought there would be a street brawl, but the Arabs are vassals to Spain now and this man controlled his rage, sat erect on his horse.

"Cover your woman if you would keep her," he advised Pedro between clenched teeth, and spurred his horse forward.

Pedro dismounted. He pulled my curtains shut. Promptly I opened them again. We glared at each other. "I will see Seville." I said.

"And all Seville can ogle you? Mother of God!" Pedro swore. "Have you forgotten who you are?"

"I am your wife, not your slave," I said. "Leave my litter open, please. Do you want me to suffocate?"

A small crowd had collected about us. The people were curious, amused, expecting some comic opera argument between husband and wife. Pedro's face was white. I hesitated, then I saw a group of boys poking fun at Negri's deformity. I would not have that. I smiled sweetly at my husband. "I insist on my curtains open," I said, "but I will wear my *tapado* to please you. One eye, my lord? You will grant me permission to see Seville with one eye?"

"With one eye only, Beatriz," he agreed, and then, as I knew he would, he saw the humor of this and we proceeded on our way with much merriment.

Sunlight fell across our broad cobbled street like stripings of gold. Shadowed alleys spewed garbage. I saw sunburned seamen from the north, their hair in two long braids across their bare chests, gold rings in their ears. Sullen *Moroscos* leaned in arched doorways, curved daggers in their sashes and all of them wearing jewelled symbols of the Christian Faith. The Inquisition is powerful here and heretics seek to depart Seville for distant lands. Those who dare inquire about the foreign heretic, the German, Martin Luther, or those who are caught perusing Erasmus—they are submitted to trials of water, fire, and ropes.

I had never seen that grim stage where the only theater is scaffolds and human flesh burning—my parents had kindly kept me from witnessing the cruelty of the *auto-da-fé*. Now, I gazed with an admiration mixed with fear at the swarthy secret faces. I had been told of mosques built underground, and devil worshippers practicing their hideous rites in caves. Inscrutable eyes regarded me, and I stared back, fascinated.

A narrow street leaned to my left and I peered into its dimness. Women and little girls loitered at the edge of our sunlight, and I saw not a one of them had clothes to cover her. "Pedro, they are almost naked!"

"The Street of Whores," he told me. "Beatriz, a lady does not look in their direction."

"Why not? I feel no revulsion, only pity."

A muddy lane to my right, and I saw water and wharves at its end. I heard harsh shouts and a weary song chanted, it seemed, by a thousand doomed voices.

"The Slave Market, Beatriz," Pedro said. "You have a strong stomach, my lady. Do you still insist on seeing all of Seville?"

"All," I replied—because even ugliness was exotic to me; I had never seen it before. And, wanting to show Pedro I could face any horror as long as he rode beside me, I pushed back my hood so that I could look with both eyes.

The stalls delighted me. This one tinkled, bronze and copper. Another breathed enchanting perfumes, and still another showed gloves in all colors. We were to stay with Pedro's cousin, Don Juan Alvarado and his wife, and I hoped that Señora de Alvarado would take me to visit the markets. Was she like me? I wondered, or would I have to sit at gossip and cards? Would Rosita be the lucky one sent to buy laces and unguents? Rosita and Négri—how I envied them! I resolved that here in Seville I would do my own errands; after all, I would tell Pedro, this was the last civilized city I would see in a long time.

Just then our procession halted. Two friars had dragged a broken body into the street. They blocked our way and the two men fell to their knees, grasped at Pedro's stirrups, at my curtains. I saw, before I hid my eyes, that thing which they dragged: he was naked, charred, wrenched out of shape.

"Have mercy, sir!" cried one of the friars. "This is our friend. He is the very soul of all that is good."

Pedro hesitated, then his horse reared because the stench from that body was overpowering. "Why is he brought to this condition if he is your friend?" Pedro inquired.

"Jewish ancestory, sir. Like Christ Himself, his very goodness caused suspicion and jealousy. The weights have broken him, my lord." I heard a sob crack the young voice of the hooded friar, and his fellow prayed Christ's name aloud. "We took him from the refuse heap. But he lives, my lord! In the name of your protector, St. James, give this man comfort in his last hour."

I heard a strangled gurgle. It could not be from that flesh near dead? I looked, and saw the body move. "Pedro," I begged, "the least we can do is place him in a litter."

"Francisco. Négri," Pedro spoke crisply. "Clear the way for my lady and myself."

"Paco, don't!" I screamed, but my brother rode directly at the friars and their burden. He would have ridden right over them if they had not moved. I saw Négri rein in his pony. The frightened friars scrambled out of the way, and it—he—lay between myself and Pedro, a man spilled on the cobblestones. The crowd about us waited silently. Their faces were not friendly.

Pedro gazed straight ahead. "Forward," he gave the order, and I believe he would have ridden over that body if it had not raised its poor head and spoken. How had that mouth retained its tongue? And if there was a tongue, whence came the strength to speak? That moment I did believe in God's miracles. *"Señor,"* the man mumbled, "I pray you, finish me with your sword. For Christ's sake," the blind eyes whitened, "good sir, free my soul."

I saw the glint of Pedro's drawn sword. Quickly, I slid from my litter and knelt beside the wretch. "God bless you," I whispered. I did not want to touch him, but I leaned close so he would hear me. "God take you, good man."

Back again in my litter, I hid my eyes. I did not see the sword do its work, but I imagined peace like a silk curtain drawn across that face that was no longer a face. It seemed my body's strength drained from me.

Pedro closed my litter tightly. "We are near my cousin's house," he said, and his matter-of-fact tone kept me from fainting. I heard him give the command to move forward. My litter swayed. Negri's hand plucked my sleeve. He offered me a cut lime.

"Suck the sour, my lady," he advised.

I had no desire to see the sights of Seville again until I heard heavy gates open, and close safely behind us. Kind voices welcomed my lord and me.

Don Juan Alvarado bowed deeply and offered me his hand. I smiled, but felt my knees trembling as I descended from the litter. Don Juan gave me to his lady's care. Her name was Magdalena; she was stout, grey-haired, and exuding kindness; her skin shiny, unpowdered, and her lips, moist against my cheek. "You are pale, Doña. It has been a long journey. I am sure you are weary."

"I am, but—" Pedro's eyes caught my own, and he shook his head, meaning I must keep silent. I looked about me and remarked on the loveliness of the *alcazar*, the courtyard. It was more like a garden, and I sat gratefully on a marble bench in the trellised shade of jasmine.

Suddenly, there was a great racket at the door. A man's voice shouted, "Show us the lady who blessed the Jew!"

Don Juan looked askance at Pedro and myself. Paco and Négri moved to my side. My ladies whispered in a distant corner, and I saw Rosita regaling them with our recent adventure.

"Open up! Give us the lady who blessed the Jew!"

Rosita ran to me. She was panting from excitement, or fear, I could not tell which; her upper lip was beaded with perspiration. "You must go out, Doña," she whispered.

"Idiot!" Pedro raised his hand as if to strike the girl. "Beatriz, go inside. Magdalena, my lady is tired. I will take care of this."

But I refused to move. Pedro and his cousin stepped toward the doors, their swords drawn. "No, Pedro!" I cried, and would have run to him but Magdalena pressed me back.

Pedro lifted the iron bar and flung the doors wide. I saw the street outside and a raggle-taggle collection of beggars gathered. "Give us the Christian who blessed the Jew!" somebody shouted.

I heard a cackle of laughter and saw a gypsy woman, her black hair ragged, her finger pointing at me. I thought her body like a snake's; coiled, boneless somehow. Her painted mouth gaped, revealing broken teeth. "That's the one!" she shouted, gesturing at me.

"Silence!" Pedro thundered. The crowd huddled quiet. All but the gypsy who stuck out her tongue at me. I thought her a fiend from Hell.

Pedro's words were as crisp as that winter we had left behind us. "The lady who blessed the dying man is Beatriz de la Cueva de Alvarado, the wife of the Captain General of Guatemala. Do you dogs dare demand her presence? It is she, Doña Beatriz, who should command you gone!

"Beatriz," my lord beckoned me. "Come. Send the rabble away."

Pedro's eyes held mine, and I managed the distance between us, my head high and my face uncovered.

"Bid the wretches gone," Pedro said. "Tell them what you did, and why." He saw my paleness and slid his arm about my waist.

I looked full at the gaunt faces. Starved they were, and fearful, and I knew they would sell their souls for a trencher of bread. Only the gypsy wished me harm. I did not look at her, but spoke directly to the ruffians. "The sufferer begged release. I gave him God's blessing. Who would not do the same?"

"You are the Lady de la Cueva?" someone demanded.

"I am Beatriz de la Cueva, wife of the Conquistador, Don Pedro Alvarado," I replied, leaning on my lord's arm.

There were whispers then, and some grumbling. "The king's own family—she has noble blood—a Catholic lady, and he is a soldier, the King's favorite...."

The ragged crew stared at me, hesitating. Several of them bowed. I looked straight at them until, one by one, they slunk away. Only the gypsy remained. She glared at me.

She crept close, and I stood half-hypnotized. "That one you blessed—he kicked me from his doorstep," she whined, " he called me witch, and said I must repent. I cursed him, naming him Jew."

She grimaced at Pedro. "You know my story. Am I mad, my lord? It is your friend brought me ill luck."

Pedro stepped towards the woman. "Get out! Be gone

before I have you skewered by my men."

I did not want more cruelty. I tossed her a handful of coins. "Take these and go," I begged.

Her long nails plucked the coins from the dust. She looked full at me. "Remember my face, Doña," she warned. "You will see me again. It will not be forgotten that you blessed a Jew.

"Damn the proud soldier-conquerors!" she screeched, and knelt, groveling in the dust at Pedro's feet.

I was frightened. "For God's sake, leave us!" I cried.

"I will," the gypsy grinned, "but not before I lay the Devil's curse on you and yours." She began to scratch strange symbols in the dirt.

I fled. Magdalena took me up the winding stairway to my rooms. "Such a welcome, child," she clucked. "Such horrors! And our Seville is lovely, I wanted you to..."

"It is horrible, and cruel," I wept. "I hate it!"

Rosita came, her hands quick and hard as she helped me to disrobe. "Why did the beggar frighten you?" she asked. "You are Christian. An evil curse cannot hurt you, can it?"

"Of course not." I pretended to an indifference I did not feel. I turned gratefuly to Pedro who had entered the room.

"My lady is both kind and foolish," he said, and sat down near me on my couch. Rosita knew she was dismissed, but she lingered, listening, until my lord must order her to leave.

"I am so tired," I confessed, "and I am frightened. Pedro, it is all such a puzzle. I did as my heart dictated, and now they curse me for showing mercy."

He raised my head and touched the iced rim of a goblet to my lips. "Drink this and sleep." The wine was sweet, and its power moved like a heavy hand to close my eyes.

I heard Pedro explaining to me the vast distance between papal laws and Christian love, but his voice came from a long distance away. He sounded much like Tio Francisco, and I clutched his hand as I drifted on a tide of sleep. I dreamed a gypsy drenched with rain, yowling at my door, and Pedro holding me from going to her. I fought him, and I awoke, sweat-soaked, to find him still beside me, his hand in mine. I slept again.

The next morning I told Pedro about my nightmare. "Who is the woman? Why should I dream of her?" I demanded. "Pedro, she said you knew her story."

"She's a whore," Pedro said bluntly. "She attached herself to a friend of mine, but he wants no part of her. He loves another. Now she blames me for her misfortune."

"She cursed us and that frightens me," I said. "Pedro, I believe in witches. Perhaps she has the Evil Eye?"

"Witchcraft is forbidden," he said sternly. "Beatriz, you are too soft. Your head is filled with nursery tales. I would you were more reverent. It is the Blessed Virgin who should haunt your dreams."

"If God gives light," I said, "He makes a darkness too. Pedro, I imagine the dark full of fearsome things!" I held my lord close. "That woman—I know it is foolish, but she does frighten me."

He stroked my hair. "Show her your fear of her, and you will be forever in her power. Acknowledge her evil, Beatriz, and she can curse you. It is all in the mind, my lady."

He kissed me. "When you are afraid, speak Christ's name, Beatriz, and all will be well." He smiled then. "If you fear magic, little one, what will you do in New Spain where the Indians mutter of serpent-gods? It is there, Beatriz, that the demon shamans offer living hearts to stone idols."

"Dear God!" I felt my flesh prickle. "I do not believe that," I said. "Pedro, it is our Christian God they worship now."

"So they pretend," he told me.

CHAPTER 18

THE FOLLOWING MORNING I begged Pedro to take me with him to the wharves where cargo was being readied for our voyage. Paco and Négri accompanied us; the two gentlemen on horseback, and Négri and myself on mules. I rode sidesaddle and was veiled head to toe, but it was a pink sheer silk that I could see through.

"Today, Seville is rose-colored, "I told Paco gaily.

"It is full of pretty women," he grinned, and, riding through the streets, Pedro had to reprimand my brother many times. "Give me your attention," he told Paco. "There is much you must learn. Your days are mine until we leave."

"And my nights, sir?" Paco flashed. "I long to see the dark side of Seville. You promised me yourself."

I nudged my mule to ride between brother and husband. "Pedro's nights are mine," I said.

"Ladies do not go out after sundown," Pedro reminded me.

"Then you will instruct me at home, in your cousin's house. I am sure our sea voyage can be improved by a woman's touch." I spoke lightly, but Pedro knew my purpose.

He scowled. "Ill luck, the sailors tell, to bring a woman on a ship. You've twenty virgins to watch, Beatriz; it's there your touch is needed." He spurred his horse to ride ahead of us.

Paco saw me squirm with anger on my rocking chair of a saddle. "Beatriz," he said, "this man you have married, you cannot keep him like a lapdog. Release him to hunt where he will, the quicker he will return to you."

I glared at Paco, but just then we arrived at the wharves; Pedro ordered my brother to a distant errand, and the sight of the Guadalquivir River made me forget my anger. It was so wide that, if I had not been told otherwise, I would have believed it to be the sea. The variety of vessels afloat, docked, and careened, bewildered me. This estuary harbored galleys, barges, canoes—all manner of river and coastal craft. Sails fluttered like painted banners. Scarlet-patched canvas drooped. I saw long rowing boats, and the galley slaves chained to their oars. Free men shouted from aloft; they swung from rigging, hung from spars, or whistled at me from crows-nests atop the mast.

Many men called my lord's name. He dismounted, removed the rich cloak I had made him, and walked about in his worn britches and crumpled boots. I was quick to join him. "Show me the tall ships," I demanded.

Pedro told me the river is dangerously shallow in places, and the *galleones* and other large craft must anchor at the river's mouth, beyond a sandbar, in San Lucar. It was there, Pedro said, that the ships discharged their cargo and sent it up river to Seville.

Pedro explained the vast array of goods and how all was brought ashore. Silver ingots were weighed by the amount one man could lift in his hands, and this year, Pedro told me, Peruvian mines were sending more silver than ever before.

"My kingdom is poor in exports compared to Peru, to Mexico. Even the Indie Isles do a richer trade than Guatemala," Pedro said wistfully.

He explained then how customs officials make short shrift of smugglers, and that every passenger from San Lucar must have the correct papers and pay the boatmen before disembarking in Seville. "A tedious expensive business," Pedro complained. "I have arrived at San Lucar, rich beyond counting, then spent it all before unpacking.

"Is it fair, Beatriz?" Pedro demanded, "We officers must outfit our own vessels, recruit our own men. We fight the battles. Then, if we are victorious, we are ordered to return to Spain at our expense. To give the King his Royal Fifth, we must bribe his inspectors, reward the boatmen lavishly, pay harsh church levies. Do you deem this fair, my lady?" The river breeze curled Pedro's hair, and I saw his eyes suddenly old, flat blue like a becalmed sea.

I spoke gently. "Why do you persist in treasure hunting if you find the rewards unsatisfactory?"

He shrugged. "I know no other trade than soldiering. It

is my living, Beatriz."

Placing my hands on his shoulders then, I shook him gently. "Your living, as you put it, makes you more alive than any man I have yet to meet." And I kissed him in front of all that ruffian crowd, and he blushed, pleased and mortified as any boy.

"Don Pedro?" A tall gentleman greeted my husband affectionately. Pedro embraced him heartily, then turned and introduced me. "Captain Bernal Diaz del Castillo, my lady Beatriz."

I smiled. "The soldier who conquers with a pen," I said, and curtsied. "I have read all of your writings, my lord. It is Cortes you admire, but I thank you for your praise of my husband. You described that last battle with the Aztecs so brilliantly I lived it through your words."

"The lady reads!" exclaimed Captain Castillo, and his remarkable grey eyes swept me from head to toes. "Not only is she beautiful, but she reads." He bowed and kissed my hand. "Doña, read me, quote me, and my heart is yours!"

"We are old friends," I told him, and asked if he would be with us on the voyage. He replied that he had just lately arrived in Seville, some business for General Cortes, but he hoped I would welcome him some future day in Guatemala.

"Bring me books," I begged. "Pedro will not allow me half of what I want. I will give you a letter to my Uncle Francisco."

"A letter direct to Don de los Cobos?" Castillo's eyes twinkled, and he slapped Pedro's back. "This time you have bettered yourself, and the rest of us too. My blessings and congratulations."

"This time?" I wondered what the captain meant and would have asked him, but he suggested we follow him to the wharf's edge.

"I've a canoe piled with hides," he said, and he winked at Pedro. "*Amigo*, the bundle must be lifted carefully—no spill!"

Castillo's canoe was tied in the oily shadows, away from the other craft. He and Pedro jumped into it. I saw my

husband press the cargo of packed hides which looked
scrubby to me, of little worth.

Pedro chuckled. "What is it we must not drop, Bernal?"

"Hush." Castillo crouched on the skins. "Look beneath,"
he whispered. "Have you ever seen such fine
workmanship?"

Pedro lifted one skin and then another. "God be
merciful!" he muttered. "Is it all yours, Bernal?"

"Won fairly, and I mean to keep it. Help me get it past
the inspectors."

Pedro shook his head. "Impossible," he said. "They will
shake out each skin. They know all our tricks, Bernal."

I leaned from where I stood above them. "What is it?"

"Gold, Beatriz," Pedro told me. "An Aztec prince's
finery." He looked at Bernal. "You say it was taken fairly,
by yourself alone?"

Castillo nodded. "Mine, Pedro. Call it payment for the
history I write. Cortes and yourself, Pizarro and the
others—all of you wax rich on my praise. I am a poor
scholar, Pedro. The king does not reward his scribes."

"But Tio Francisco has bound your letters into books!" I
protested. "Your descriptions, Don Castillo, they bring
even that dull Court alive. I assumed you are always
amply rewarded."

"Assumptions are passed on as convenient truths, my
lady. I write history for my own pleasure. I am seldom
paid."

Pedro stood erect, rocking the canoe. "I would have you
keep this bundle, Bernal," he said.

"But how?"

"I will take it," I offered. "Pack it quickly on my mule. No
one will dare question a lady like myself."

Pedro swung himself up to stand beside me. "I forbid
you," he said. "Beatriz, you cannot ride out of here with a
king's worth of gold plate. It is too dangerous."

"I will take it," I insisted. "Pack it behind my saddle.
Négri, bring my mule forward."

Quickly, carefully, the bundle of hides was handed up
and lashed behind me. I slid Pedro's cloak around my
shoulders; it was long enough to cover the skins.

"A fine cloak," I teased Pedro, "but not fit for hard riding."

Calling Négri to follow me, I rode away wishing it was *Señorita* carrying me and my treasure. The mule plodded with agonizing slowness.

But I rode straight through—past the stout councilmen come to the wharves to strike bargains of their own; past the probing customs inspectors and the tax officials—straight by all of them. My face was discreetly hidden by my rose-colored silk, and my hands did not tremble on my reins.

I believed myself safely away when a woman's shout halted me. "That fine one there—she's got the king's treasure under her skirts!"

I saw the gypsy, hair veiling her face, her finger pointing. Négri pressed close. "Ride fast, Doña," he whispered.

"Halt there." A corpulent beetle of a man approached, bowing. "Your name, Doña?"

"Doña Beatriz de la Cueva de Alvarado," I replied, cooly. From the corner of my eye, I saw the gypsy slink nearer.

"A fine lady like yourself," the beetle buzzed, and his hand crawled across the bundle set behind me. "What brings you to the wharves?"

"My uncle's business," I said. "He is Don Francisco de los Cobos." I leaned back in my saddle, placing my hands protectively on my hides. "The king's private papers and maps," I said. I nodded in Negri's direction, seeing his black face gone grey, his mouth agape. "My man there," I said, "he will take these to Valladolid tonight. The king wishes it. Let me pass."

"Drag her down!" screeched the gypsy. She was so close I saw she had one blue eye and one black eye. The stench of her unwashed body revolted me.

"Beatriz?" Pedro, with Bernal close on his heels, thrust his way through the crowd gathering about me.

"My lord," I said, keeping my voice steady, " I carry the king's papers. Order this man to let me pass."

"I give the orders here," the fat one whined. "If you have

important papers, why are they hidden under common hides?" He struck my bundle, and I imagined the gold spilling, and Pedro, Bernal, and myself ignominiously arrested.

I sat straighter in my saddle. "The king will be angry that I am detained. If you value your life, let me pass, *señor*."

The gypsy seized my bridle. "Do not believe her!" She appealed to the crowd. "Yesterday this fine lady blessed a Jew. Today, she smuggles gold."

The woman would have pulled me down, but Pedro drew his sword, and Don Castillo's scowl caused the inspector to blanch. He held the woman off. "You are mad, wench, to accuse the Doña de la Cueva." He looked at me. "Give me proof of your mission, Doña, and you may pass."

Proof? I stared at him. His squinty eyes would not meet my own. I guessed then what he meant. He wanted money, a bribe. But I had ridden out with Pedro as simply dressed as possible. My silk *manta* covered a gabardine riding habit. I wore no jewels.

"Proof, my lady," the inspector insisted.

My wedding band was not enough. I looked from Pedro to Bernal and saw no more than hope in their eyes. The man's fat fingers fumbled with the ropes of my burden.

Then, yes! I remembered—I did have something. I reached inside my bodice and drew out Tio Francisco's emerald ring. I dangled it before the beetle's nose.

"This bears the seal of Santiago," I said. "Is it enough?"

His quick snatch at it proved the emerald more than enough. I lifted the chain from about my neck and gave both ring and chain into the greedy fingers.

The man fairly drooled over the gem. "I will keep this until I am assured the king has received his papers, Doña. Then I will send him your ring—my word on it!" he promised.

"Of course," I smiled, and I looked at that beetle-man so long and hard he fairly sank through the ground.

Viciously he turned on the gypsy and struck her face. "Liar!" he hissed.

"Yes, the two of you," I whispered, and I spurred my mule forward, longing to ride straight over the two vile creatures. But I knew I must get away with all speed and dignity.

Négri rode close beside me. "Your emerald," he breathed, "is your burden worth your jewel, Doña?"

"I carry Don Castillo's treasure," I said. "It was that gentleman's words convinced me of Don Pedro's worth. I owe Don Bernal a great deal. Spain, too, is in his debt. An emerald is small payment for a man who will be read through history."

I missed the weight of my emerald above my heart, but that night Pedro's ardor was like a crown of jewels awarded me. And my lord was jealous too. "Bernal's pen is his sword, Beatriz. He spills ink, not blood. Do you prefer that, my lady?"

"Prefer it to what?" I asked softly.

Pedro tightened his arms about me. "You are mine," he said. "I will not have you easy with other men. Sometimes your eyes are wide, your smile too sweet. Beatriz, I swear you would flirt with the Devil if he interested you!"

"Perhaps," I murmured. "My lord, your hands are devilish tonight. Oh, I adore you!" I flung my arms about his neck and pulled him closer. There were times I wished our passion might last the night long.

CHAPTER 19

"I WILL REPLACE YOUR RING," Pedro told me. We were enjoying a rare moment alone in his cousin's patio.

"It was my talisman," I said. "It cannot be replaced. The ring belonged to my uncle. I had refused to marry you, *querido,* and Tio Francisco gave me that ring to remind me he offered me a kingdom. The stone bears the crest of Santiago."

Pedro smiled. "You were a stubborn wench, Beatriz. I believed I had taken a shrew to wife. And now—"

"Now?" I asked eagerly.

"Just as stubborn, but equally intriguing." Pedro tucked a spray of jasmine in my hair. "Bernal finds you fascinating," he said.

"And you, Pedro, how do you find me?"

"Very young," he replied, "tender, but impetuous. I fear for you."

"I do not fear for myself," I retorted, irritated because Pedro seldom said he loved me. The thought nagged me that loving was something Pedro had put aside, years ago. Then I asked him, "Who is the gypsy so intent on destroying me?" Pedro had told me not to speak of her and the mystery was a persistent riddle.

"She is sent away," he said. "I found a captain whose wife was in need of a serving maid. The woman sails for Panama tomorrow."

"I dislike her face, Pedro. She has one blue eye and one black eye. She is pale enough to be pure Spanish, but her features are coarse."

"She is *meztiza,* of mixed blood, Beatriz. I remember her on Cortes's marches. She is a camp follower, and bad luck."

"Does she practice witchcraft?" I asked.

Pedro laughed. "Her art is old, but it is not witchcraft, Beatriz. She is a whore. Her name is Belial. She insists she was wed, some years ago, to a friend of mine, Captain Portocarreo. He swears she lies, that she is a tavern

98

woman wanting to better herself through marriage with a Spanish officer. There was a time, I remember, when Portocarreo found Belial bewitching. Now he calls her witch and claims she has set a spell on him."

Pedro stood, and began to pace the bricked path. He spoke more to himself. "I am aware Portocarreo courts the lady Léonor, in Santiago. She is a girl far too young for him."

"Léonor?" I asked gently, seeing my lord troubled, his thoughts distant.

He answered bluntly. "Léonor is my daughter."

I thought I had not heard correctly. I stood and caught him in mid-stride. "Your daughter?"

"Keep your voice low, Beatriz. "Here," he led me to a marble bench well away from the house. "Let us sit and I will tell you."

I sat as far from him as possible. I turned my back to hide my distress. "Speak, my lord," I commanded.

He sighed. "I pray you understand. I have half a century, Beatriz, and I have lived in places far removed from your own world. We might be the sun and moon, my lady."

"Now is that darkness when the sun and moon collide," I whispered, but Pedro did not hear me. His voice persisted, low and even:

"The year was 1519. I was full grown, Beatriz, and you were not yet born. I was in Mexico, with Cortes. He took that city called *Tlascala*. The *Tlascala* Indians had suffered under the rule of the prince, *Moctezuma*. They welcomed the Spanish as their liberators. Their chiefs swore allegiance to Cortes and promised to help us in the war against the Aztec king."

My lord's face softened; he looked younger, and his eyes were half closed. "Go on," I murmured.

"General Cortes insisted the *Tlascalans* b e c o m e Christians. The nobles and priests refused, saying their people would not desert their gods and would revolt if so ordered. The *Tlascalan* elders interceded and suggested that Cortes and his officers choose highborn women of the tribe for their wives. These girls, the elders said, could be baptised; they alone could embrace our faith.

"Politics, my dear," Pedro smiled at me. "We were weary of fighting. We needed allies. Many of us were wounded, all of us near starvation. Our own priest, Father Olmedo, reminded us that the fruit of Christian marriage is Christian children.

"Still, Cortes hesitated. He had a wife, a Spanish lady, who resided in Cuba. But Cortes, his officers, myself among them, knew we must marry or die, defeated in Mexico. We prevailed upon Cortes, telling him that a firm alliance with the *Tlascalans* meant certain victory."

"And certain pleasure for yourselves?" I protested. "It was not Christian, my lord."

Pedro smiled thinly. "It was most fortunate, my lady. Cortes chose the princess called Marina for his wife. She was intelligent, as well as beautiful. She spoke the Indian dialects, and without her as interpreter, I doubt we could have taken Mexico. Marina was Cortes' beloved companion for many years."

"Yes, yes," I interrupted, "I know about Marina. Brave and clever she may have been, but Cortes had a wife. He did mortal sin."

"You judge hastily, Beatriz," Pedro advised. "You were not there. What you call sin saved our lives. We were in desperate circumstances."

"All of you took wives?" I asked, and knew my voice trembled.

"Yes," Pedro said. "I was given the princess called *Teculihuatzin.*" Her Indian name sounded like the whirring of birds' wings, and I thought Pedro lingered over the soft syllables. Then, he said, "She was baptized Luisa, Doña Luisa."

"Doña?" I flared. "A savage dubbed lady? A black heathen, and naked I suppose, painted for battle! Who called her lady? You, Pedro?" I could not control my disgust.

"She was a chief's daughter," he said quietly. "She became my wife. She was not naked, nor was she black, Beatriz. If Marina was Cortes's star, so was Luisa my guide and comfort. She was born a noble lady, and brave."

Pedro's face looked haunted. He spoke more to himself

than to me. "I blame myself for her death," he said. "I told Luisa not to travel with me to Peru. But she insisted and I relented. She perished in the high mountains.

"It was my fault," Pedro repeated. "My lady Luisa said she must share all with me, but I should have ordered her to remain in Guatemala with our daughter."

I sat speechless, feeling my body slumped, drained of its strength. Pedro's words, his obvious sorrow, struck like fists pummeling my stomach. "You loved her very much?" I whispered, and covered my ears, not wanting to hear his reply.

Pedro grasped my hands. "I loved her then, before you were born, Beatriz. She made me happy. How could I not love such a woman? Luisa was brave and loyal, and the mother of my child."

"Léonor!" I spit the name.

Pedro nodded. "She awaits us in Santiago."

"She awaits you, not me," I cried. "I will see her in Hell first, the whore's daughter!"

I wrenched my hands free and stuck Pedro full in his face, raking his cheeks with my nails. I wanted to smash the complacent blue of his eyes. "How many halfbreeds have you fathered for the glory of God and Spain?" I hissed.

Pedro asked for understanding. But how could I understand? All I knew was that I had been terribly deceived. All I heard and understood was that Pedro loved another—Luisa, a princess and beautiful, brave, and sharing his victories and defeats. How I envied that Luisa, riding beside her young captain, *Tonatiuh*, Child of the Sun. And she had borne him a daughter. Pedro had named this child for his mother.

"I will never love your halfbreed" I promised, and would have walked away, but Pedro held me fast, forcing me to listen.

"She is your age, Beatriz. Léonor is very like you. She has your spirit. I left her in Portocarreo's care. He is old enough to be her father and will guard her with his life in my absence. But I have forbidden their marriage. Pedro Portocarreo is a veteran like myself. I promised Luisa, on her deathbed, that our daughter would marry a titled

Castillian, a man of wealth and noble breeding."

Before God, I hated this adored Léonor! "My parents did not consider you too old for me," I snapped. "Will you send your daughter to Spain, shopping for a husband?"

A new thought seared me then: "What is Léonor's dowry? Could it be the Kingdom of Guatemala? If so, you play a treacherous game, my lord."

He did not smile. "Léonor will choose for herself," he said "When she meets your brother, she will not look further."

I stared at Pedro. He sported his ambition with such blatancy it appalled me. Legend said my lord could be cruel, and I believed that now. For the first time I noticed the slump of Pedro's jowls, his thickening lips, the pronounced hook of his nose. I said, quietly, "You married me for Léonor."

"Beatriz," he appealed, "I married you because I need you. Because Guatemala needs a royal queen. You are not so stupid as to believe otherwise. And Paco?" Pedro shrugged. "The idea of your brother wed to my daughter—I must admit the thought has occurred to me." His fingers tightened like irons about my wrists. "Be reasonable, Beatriz. I intend to found a dynasty. Guatemala will endure."

I wrenched free. "Guatemala be damned!" I cried. And then I asked Pedro if my uncle was aware of these Indian connections. "I am your third wife," I said. "Truly, you are a misbegotten scoundrel!"

Pedro did not flinch, his face was frightening in its severity. "You've a tongue from the streets," he said. "Curses do not become a queen. See to your manners before you arrive in Santiago."

"I refuse to go to Santiago," I said. I stepped back, holding my head high. "I am going home, my lord. And Paco, he goes with me."

"No, little firebrand—" Before I could evade him, Pedro had me fast about my waist, held so close his buttons pressed, hurting my breasts. His breath smelled of tobacco, and I saw the blonde hairs of his moustache beaded with sweat. His lips nuzzled my ear. "No, you will not leave me,

Beatriz. You are proud as I am, my lady. You will not crawl home defeated—that is not like you." His mouth was hot on my throat. "Bury the past," he whispered, "Beatriz de la Cueva, my lady, my queen...."

Pedro's mouth stole my breath. His body swallowed mine. I struggled, trying to resist him. "Your daughter, Léonor - she will not be queen?"

"Not while you live, my love," Pedro promised.

But I would not be quieted. "Ask my forgiveness," I insisted. "If I am your queen, you should beg my forgiveness."

"For what?" His hands were in my hair. "It is your temper, your ambition that strike sparks between us. Perhaps we are too much alike? It has occurred to you, has it not, that I might die, that you will rule? I have read it in your eyes, that cold dream of yours."

I hung my head. "I have imagined you gone," I admitted, "and myself the sole ruler of Guatemala. Yes, we are both ambitious, my lord." I looked directly at him then. "But it is your deceit I despise. You should have told me about Luisa."

He cupped my chin. "You were not yet born, Beatriz. If I had known our future, perhaps I would have waited—celibate as a stout and gouty bishop."

He could always make me laugh. The scent of jasmine folded sweet about us, and the sounds of Seville were muted. "Praise God you are not stout—or a bishop," I teased, and moved into his arms. He lifted me and carried me inside and up the stairs.

The setting sun washed my couch red and gold. Luisa, I thought—but I have him now! I pushed Pedro's hands from me and undressed by myself, slowly, that he desire me. I let my hair loose and knew it soft about me, the color of sundown.

I knelt to remove his boots. My fingers trembled. It was oblivion I sought, a respite from that pain called jealousy.

I had learned how to please him and, when he slept at last, sated, I kept watch in the darkening room. Of course he had loved others, I told myself, I would never know how many and it was foolish to ask.

Luisa is dead—I repeated it over and over—she is dead. I knew I must not dwell on yesterdays; I resolved to think only of the morrow.

Ana came to mind, and I remembered her words. I hold the pearl in my hand now, I thought, there is but one path before me.

Pedro awoke then, and I smiled at him. "When do we sail?" I asked him.

"Within the week, Beatriz."

I shivered and he asked my why, and I said the sun had gone down, our room had grown cold. But it was a sharp foreboding that had chilled me. Seville had brought me excitement, it had dealt cruel surprises. What lay ahead? I wondered: Would I be brave enough?

I sat up abruptly. "I will not be stepmother to your Léonor," I said bluntly.

"You will be friends," Pedro told me gently. "My lady, you can afford to be kind to my daughter."

His eyes were blue on me. He asked no more than kindness and I was ashamed.

I swallowed hard. "I will be courteous to your child." I said.

He gave me a stern look. "Courteous, of course. And patient too, my lady. I have not met anyone who does not love my daughter."

Jealousy soured my mouth. I turned away to hide my tears. "Pedro," I murmured, "you ask a great deal of me. If I am patient, kind, forgiving—what will you give me?"

He pulled me down beside him. "I give you loving now, and a strong wind tomorrow, Beatriz, a calm sea and a fine ship."

And your love? I wanted to ask—do you give me all your love? But Pedro had slipped from my side. He was whistling, pulling on his boots.

CHAPTER 20

FORTY SHIPS AWAITED US in San Lucar. *Galleones, naos,* and the smaller caravels. Pedro had contrived another city, this time it was sea-borne. Horses and mules, cattle and pigs, sheep and chickens—three ships held all our animals and I called them Pedro's Arks.

Each of the forty vessels had building bricks and dressed stones as ballast. We carried wheat and oats, nails and needles, olives and oils, dried meats, candles.

"Is New Spain such a desert that we must bring even our own trees?" I asked, because I saw small fruit and nut trees being hefted aboard.

"Would we could afford twice as much, Beatriz!" Pedro exclaimed. "Every other one of my soldiers should be replaced by a carpenter, a bricklayer, a stone mason. Santiago lacks craftsmen. The Indians are ignorant of civilized living, and the Spanish landowners are lazy. We have no olive trees, no grape vines. Guatemala's soil is rich; there are *hectares* of *maiz*, but we must plant our own wheat and barley, and potatoes."

Pedro regarded me sternly. "I have warned you, Beatriz, the territory is unfit for a woman."

"I will make it fit me, Pedro. I am eager for the adventure. Yes, I am willing, my lord, but the others—" I glanced at the cluster of veiled women nearby. "Pedro, must I take them all on our ship? Their bleating will be the death of me."

"There is a vessel specially prepared for the women," Pedro said. "Négri sails with us, he will care for Paco and myself. And you will have Rosita. The space is cramped, Beatriz."

"Then I do not want Rosita," I said. "She prattles. She is always watching us. I will choose another, a quieter girl."

"Take whoever you like," Pedro shrugged. "I will miss the small rose, but—"

I tugged his arm to divert him. "I want to see our floating castle," I said. "Will you accompany me aboard?"

"Castle?" Pedro hooted. *"La Estrella* is packed bow to stern, keel to deck railing with food, water, and trade goods. Your chests alone take more than half our room!"

"La Estrella, the Star," I breathed. "It is a lovely name, Pedro."

"Her figurehead is a lusty mermaid, with red hair like your own, my lady." Pedro pointed at a tall ship. "See her there. Négri will help you aboard. I will join you later."

My Star. I thought her glorious, a floating island decked for a carnival. Our one room set squarely astern was stifling, but I discovered a small door which opened onto a little balcony the size of a chariot. I hoped I could stand there, tucked under the high afterdeck, the sea running steep under my feet.

I chose a woman called Petra to help me, and she and Négri set to the unpacking. I went up on deck to watch the excitement of our departure.

The *Carrera de India* is always dangerous. Pedro sailed well in advance of the hurricane season, but I knew we could be beset by both storms and foreign pirates. There were cannon spaced below deck, Pedro had told me; he sailed tight as a fortress. We were to move southwest, direct to the tropics where disease, hunger, and thirst would be our enemies. The wooden ships, I knew, were prone to rot and decay in the damp heat. Pedro's worst fear was for our horses; his greatest treasures were the pregnant mares we carried. I looked across the water at the *nao* that held *Señorita,* and I wondered how she fared. I prayed she would not sicken and die.

Bishop Marroquin and Paco joined me at the railing. "I am packed away in a cupboard small as a coffin," Paco complained.

"I fare little better," I retorted.

Bishop Marroquin smiled. "It takes getting used to. If the weather holds, you will not be uncomfortable."

A tall young man presented himself. His name was Hernandez, he told us, he was a navigation officer from the *Casa de la Contraction.* He knew wind systems, ocean currents, and compass variations, he said, and that he would be with us all the way to Puerto Caballos.

"You will teach me," I told Hernandez. "My uncle has shown me something of the stars and I would learn more." Paco shook his head. "My sister is a walking university," he complained. "She cannot get enough of learning."

"Can anyone?" I demanded. "I will ask Señor Hernandez to give a class each evening."

Paco struck his forehead in mock dismay. "I have enough to do, Beatriz. I have charge of the trade goods for Santo Domingo—the potatoes, cassava, and sacks of beans; the pottery, and silk, and saddlery—and the slaves. Do not give me stars too!"

"Slaves?" I was startled.

"Two hundred Africans," Paco told me. He pointed at a galleon at anchor in the harbor. "There—they are loaded like logs. I hope they last the voyage."

I was chagrined. "How can I sleep at night?" I asked, "Négri has told me how terrible it is—chained, blind in the darkness. I loathe slavery!"

Bishop Marroquin intervened. "I have seen to their food and drink myself, Doña. The slave trade is a rich one and a custom we cannot change. We can only improve the conditions of the voyage. The slaves were baptised yesterday. They are content, their lives in God's keeping."

"Content?" I blazed. "Bartered like Paco's sacks of beans? How are they content, my lord? No—I will not sail with slaves as cargo."

"But we sail now, Beatriz!" Paco shouted, and in the ensuing excitement I forgot the slaves. Later, the ships were scattered, and I could not mark which one carried the Africans. Too, Pedro and I found a happiness together on that voyage that kept me so content I did not inquire about our living cargo.

We had blue days; wet and dry days. Sky above us and water beneath; I remember the creaking of the ship's timbers, the salt wind and the delicious sense of freedom I enjoyed. I shed my stays and most of my petticoats. No need for headdress, or clogs, or even stockings. We played like children, Pedro and I. Our room was so crowded, we lay abed most of the time. Pedro forbid me to drink water and perhaps I was half tipsy from the wine we drank, but I was happier than I had ever been. Not a moment of sickness, and I was never afraid, not even in that one storm that clawed our sterns and almost caught us.

I learned the stars. Hernandez told me stories of whales and mermaids. Time lost meaning for me; I believed the ship's bells made a music for my pleasure, and because my hourglass would not stand steady I packed it away. When, between one day and the next, the water turned incredibly blue, and I asked Pedro Why; he told me we were not far from the West Indies Isles and Santo Domingo. I was surprised. More than a month had passed—I wanted much longer and I said as much.

"Don't you always want more?" Pedro teased. His face was bronzed, his eyes burned blue. "Time will not stand still, Beatriz."

"But you and I—we will always be close as this," I insisted.

I did not want to go ashore in Santo Domingo. We were to stay in the Governor's Palace, and Pedro told me I must dress in whatever finery I could manage from my chests. He said that word of his noble wife, Beatriz de la Cueva, must reach New Spain before we did. "I want it known, *querida*, that I have the king's blessing on any future ventures."

I obeyed my lord, but I was uneasy. That gypsy woman in Seville—Pedro had told me she had sailed for New Spain. "She is determined to hurt me," I said. "I feel her presence."

"She will not be here," Pedro assured me.

He was wrong. I saw the woman many times that next week. She was among the crowd on the wharf when the longboats rowed us ashore; her eyes drew mine as if she had some magic power. She hissed when I passed her, and I felt her hatred like a hand squeezing my heart. She would not be dismissed from my life.

But Santo Domingo, white-washed and pink in the blistering sun, diverted me. Trees bloomed with exotic flowers, and I thought the sky was made of birds. Flocks of parakeets preened and chattered like women on market day, and these small birds made such merriment that my own pair squawked miserably, and I released them from their cage.

The Governor's Palace was of Moorish architecture; the arched doors opened to the sea, to beaches I longed to explore. I swear, I should have been born a fisherboy or a wild sea bird! Why couldn't I take my bath in a sea pool, I wondered, and what would the governor's lady say if I suddenly shed my shoes and ran away across the sand?

But I was not free. I was Pedro's proudest trophy, and to please my lord, I behaved with that cool aloofness copied from my mother. To please myself, I sought out those few gentlemen who did not deem it beneath their dignity to talk politics with a lady.

Members of the Indies Council advised me as to the condition of Guatemala. Truly the kingdom was a morass of distemper, greed and treachery! The Governor of Mexico, Attorney Maldonado, and the Governor of Honduras, Don Montejo—both schemed to take Guatemala from Pedro. Indeed, Montejo had installed his own municipal government in Santiago; he had had the effrontery to write King Charles a miserable tale of my husband's desertion and debts.

Immediately, I wrote my uncle and our sovereign the truth, and I assured them I would advise my husband against violence. Letter writing was easy, but I knew I must convice Pedro that war was unnecesary. I reminded my lord that he carried the Royal Seal, the King's Grant, and that the Council in Santo Domingo approved him as governor general.

Pedro wanted Don Montejo's head. Too, he wanted to show off his Spanish archers, his fine horses.

"Montejo will not have Guatemala," he swore. "It is I who will have Honduras!"

"Buy it," I advised. "Do not spill more blood, my lord. This Montejo is badly in debt. Bribe him with gold and you will have Honduras."

Pedro regarded me with astonishment. "You should have been born a man," he said, and he asked where I had come by all my information.

"I listen," I told him simply. "You are too full of glory past, my lord. The battle is finished and you are victor.

Now, you must be watchman, guardian. Lay aside your weapons, Pedro, and use your ears."

I saw him finger his swordhilt, and I knew he did not like the role I suggested. Always the conqueror, always the gold lust, why did I believe I could tame him?

CHAPTER 21

IT WAS IN SANTO DOMINGO that Pedro returned me my emerald ring. "That fool doubted the stone's worth! He sold it as jade, Beatriz, and it found its way, on a sailor's thumb, to the market here. My lady—" Pedro bowed, and pressed the ring into my hand and kissed my fingers closed above it. I was both pleased and touched.

Those were lazy days in Santo Domingo, and I thought to write my mother of all I had seen and done. A few lines scratched, and I put my quill away. The heat was stifling, my sweat blotched the ink, and I could not find words to make my mother know all I was thinking and feeling. "We lay abed throughout most of the voyage, there was little room for doing else." I giggled, thinking of my mother's face when she read my words.

My skin was sunburned and my hair blown dry in the salt air. Rosita massaged me with oils. She resented my banishment of her during the sea voyage, and I remember a night when she was particularly cruel. She was helping me prepare for a party, brushing my hair quick and hard. Watching my face in the mirror, she said, " I am told my lord Pedro was once wed to an Indian princess . Could it be true, my lady?"

"It is true," I said, keeping my tone carefully matter of fact. "The daughter of that marriage awaits us in Santiago."

Rosita's face was dark with disappointment. "Don Pedro has told you then? And you do not mind?"

"My lord tells me everything," I replied smoothly, and I dipped my finger into the warm scarlet wax and painted my lips in a smile.

"You know about his other children too?" Rosita pressed. Her tug on my hair then brought my head back and I saw my white throat stretched, pale in the glass.

"That beggar woman from Seville, my lady—she sows a rich gossip."

"Yes, gossip!" I snapped. "Kitchen talk, Rosita, and I will

not permit it. Keep your tongue to yourself, girl, or I will leave you here to fend for yourself." I stood quickly. "Give me my fan. I will go down to the guests."

I could not leave Rosita fast enough, and I slammed the door shut behind me. It was not until I stood at the head of the stairs that I remembered my hair was not done, it was bare of the flowers and jewels fashion decreed. No matter—I would go down as I was, my hair loose as Pedro liked it. Yes, I would attend the party in my petticoats if I must! Rosita's chatter was a poison I could not stomach.

Voices reached me from the *sala* below. I clutched at the railing, thinking the marble stairs gaped steeply. I could fall. I heard someone laugh. Suddenly I did not want to go down, to meet people. Were they laughing at me? What did they whisper behind my back? Did they say, "Poor Beatriz who loves her lord so blindly, while he?..."

But I knew I must go down, my head high. Many times I had faced people just like these. Gossip had never hurt me. Breathing deeply, I carefully descended the stairs. My lord awaited me below.

"No jewels, Beatriz?" he asked.

I knew his eyes admired me. "The night is hot," I said. "I have a slight headache. Rosita annoyed me and I brushed my hair myself. I will set a new, a more comfortable fashion perhaps."

He chuckled. "A pretty fashion for the young. But some will gossip. They will say I am a miser, that I give you little for adornment. Some will be jealous and call you shameless, bold." He set my hand in the crook of his arm.

I shook out my fan and regarded him across the green feathers. "I have heard you called worse than shameless," I dared.

"Ah!" He grinned. "I am an ogre, *querida*. I eat young girls!" His mood was careless, and I replied in kind.

It was a pretty evening and I tried to push the gypsy and her gossip from my mind. I knew my loose hair, unadorned, caused some sensation because the ladies glared and gallants pressed about me. I indulged myself in flirting, so much so that Pedro was annoyed. He insisted we retire early. I refused, saying I wanted to dance the night away. I felt a great need to cause my lord pain.

Forcibly, Pedro took me from the company. Knowing many eyes were upon us, I stood halfway up the stairs and I said loudly, "My husband feels his gout, it is his age. Please forgive us."

One step below me, Pedro turned to face the company. "Forgive me," he said, "my wife is young, she has not yet learned a queen's manners."

I fled, and would have shut Pedro from our room but he entered close behind me. I wheeled on him. "I am not too young," I blazed, "and if I am, it is you who will age me!"

I stared at him, wondering if I dared accuse him outright. Had Rosita spoken true? "I must know," I said aloud. I did not want to cry, not now, but I felt tears on my cheeks. "Pedro, I don't know you!"

He was gentle then, winding his hands in my hair. "Knowing all, perhaps you would despise me," he whispered. He held my face that I must look at him. "You are troubled, Beatriz, What have they told you?"

I sighed, happy to have him close again. "It was servants' gossip, my love." I tilted my head, pretending to a smile I did not feel. "I am told you are a philanderer, a cheat, a liar, every lady's delight. You are..."

He stopped my mouth with a kiss. "I am your beloved," he said.

"God help me," I breathed, "you speak true." And I shut my eyes tight against Rosita's wink, the gypsy's grin.

"I am your beloved *now*," I repeated, stressing the last word, knowing it was all that mattered. But that insight frightened me and I clutched Pedro. "I want you forever," I said fiercely.

"I will have you now...and here...and here..." he whispered, his mouth on my throat, on my breasts.

CHAPTER 22

IT WAS APRIL 4, 1539—I remember that date because it was the first and only time in my life I have succumbed to sickness. It was Négri who nursed me then, and it was because of Négri that I found the courage to go on.

The coast of Honduras, New Spain—it was not the lush Paradise I had expected. Indeed, I think it is the very mouth of Hell. Pedro had boasted Puerto De Cabollos was a fine port; I cursed him for his stupidity. Red mud, swarms of stinging insects, trees with an oozing sap and roots that clutch, feed on air. The sun lay on me like sheep's wool, and thirst ached my throat.

We struggled for a footing on that compost heap of centuries—stench, rot, and decay. Walls of green jungle stood against us, and the sea we had crossed locked us in from behind. I believe it was the monstrous emnity of the land itself that struck me mute and shivering. I was certain that God had never set foot upon this land; ancient gods mocked us—in the roar of a tiger cat, the hiss of a snake, the sucking of the bog, the clenching roots of vines that devoured tall trees. Death is the name of the jungle god. I knew my soul shriveled, my bones melted.

The Indians who greeted us were not the beautiful trained creatures in Pedro's retinue. These men were bold naked, painted and tattooed in lieu of clothes, crafty in manner and servile to the extreme. A few among these held themselves aloof from us; they boasted many gold ornaments and decked their man parts with such arrogance I was revolted. My ladies prayed aloud and hid themselves in the flimsy shelters provided.

No sooner had we landed than I asked Pedro when we would depart. He told me there was no road out, one must be built to accommodate our caravan and he had sent for Indians from Guatemala. "It could take a month, Beatriz," he warned.

A month! No road out of this purgatory? I could not believe it. How far was Guatemala? Why was there no road, and why hadn't Pedro sent word ahead of us, months ago, to have the wilderness cleared? I had a thousand questions, but my lord was immediately preoccupied with the news from Guatemala and the provisioning of our party. I envied Pedro's cool proficiency in the face of what I considered to be utmost danger, but I knew he was accustomed to this God-forsaken place while I—I could not imagine anywhere on earth that did not have a road, a castle, fresh water, and gracious ceremonies of arrivals and departures.

I saw Rosita immediately defeated. "We have come to the end of the world," she moaned.

"The bottom of the world," I said. Because it was April, and spring in Spain. Here was a steaming inferno, eternal nightmare. I succumbed to panic. I lay on a pallet in a stifling tent, hearing my breath rasp. Truly, I believed, I would soon be a corpse like Francesca, buried and forgotten. My ladies refused to come near me, believing I was taken with plague. Rosita thought I had the pox; she feared for her own looks. It was Négri who remained beside me, night and day, and nursed me back to health. Négri gave me my first *mango* fruit; and, at his urging, I drank the sweet liquid from the coconut. Once, when I was strong enough to sit and hold a dish and I complained of the meat's toughness, Négri told me I was eating monkey meat. *"Mono del Rey,"* he called it, the king's monkey, and his courtier's mincing bow was so like Valladolid that I laughed. But then I wept. "I want to go home," I confessed, "Négri, *I must go home!"*

Négri bowed again, and I saw his owl-face serious. "I will fetch Don Pedro immediately," he said. "My lord must be informed of your decision. You will not be queen of Guatemala? You have changed your mind, my lady?" Négri shrugged. "It must be the cockroaches, big as mice, I agree, and mice do frighten ladies."

"I am Beatriz de la Cueva! I am not afraid," I protested.

"But my lady insists she will go home." Négri grimaced. He shrugged. "Well, you will not be the first woman defeated by this country."

"Defeated? Négri, I have hardly begun—how can I be

defeated?"

He grinned at me. "I was going to ask you that, Doña."

Pedro set two hundred men to open a trail wide enough for two mule trains. The labor was completed in twenty-five days. My lord warned me of the wearying trip overland; I would ride in a litter, he said, and we must travel hard until we reached San Pedro Sula. There, Pedro said, he would have Guatemalan Indians waiting to help us on the last stage of our journey to Santiago.

Twenty-five long days and nights—they blended, melted, dripped. A long, green jungle of hours in which my bones felt bruised, headaches racked me, and chills chattered my teeth. But I would not turn back; I did not complain.

No sooner were we settled in that wretched collection of hovels called San Pedro Sula when Don Francisco de Montejo, Governor of Honduras, descended upon us with a small company of soldiers. Don Montejo accused Pedro of treachery. He said my lord had deserted Guatemala. "I am captain general," Montejo wheezed, and he went on to say my lord trespassed in a territory that was no longer his. "You have abdicated," Montejo told Pedro.

I saw my lord bristle, and his hand go to his sword hilt. I stepped between the two men. I had been watching carefully and I saw Montejo boasted a power he did not possess. His clothes were ill-kept and his soldiers appeared half-starved. I thought this captain came more as a beggar; his eyes were shifty and he wrung his hands. He stammered too, in the manner of a man who does not know how to phrase his needs directly.

I looked straight at him. "What is it you want?" I demanded. "Is it money? Speak up, sir, my lord is weary. We have thousands of Spaniards and Indians in our retinue. Don Pedro is a busy man." I stressed the thousands, and I saw Montejo wet his lips.

"You come to bargain," I guessed. "Perhaps to sell Honduras?"

"Gold, yes," Montejo nodded, "and your Province of Chiapa, in Mexico. Then I will retire."

Pedro breathed heavily; I had sensed his signal, and a

gathering of men behind us. "My lord," I whispered, "this man can be bought. Hold your temper. We can profit from this."

I looked at Don Montejo and his eyes dropped before my gaze. "Retire, sir?" I asked. "What do you mean? You will retire to Honduras, or—"

"I will retire, Doña Beatriz," Montejo said shortly. "If Don Pedro pays his debts, I will give him all Honduras."

"Coward!" Pedro swore.

Montejo would not be ruffled. "Chiapa is wealthy. Honduras is—"

"The very mouth of Hell!" I exclaimed, and saw Montejo smile.

Pedro was stern in his anger. "It is blackmail," my lord said. "Why should I pay his debts? I will not be party to his greed and treason."

"Don Montejo wishes to retire," I said smoothly. "He needs monies, and that yearly revenue with which Chiapa will provide him. He has no intention of returning to his own appointed post, as you do, my lord. The Governor of Honduras is telling us that he will say nothing of any presumed indiscretion of yours if we will say nothing to the king of the sale of Honduras."

"*Por Dios!*" I clapped my hands to my head in mock dismay, "you gentlemen deal territories much as women play at cards!"

Pedro did not smile. "Blackmail," he insisted. "And what have I done that I must buy my way out of it? You are the traitor, sir. You sell your territory. Let us fight for Honduras, and for Guatemala. Let me win the territories with honor."

I turned my back on Montejo then and spoke directly to Pedro. "We can ill afford the loss of men and horses," I said. "Close this gentleman's mouth with gold. Be done with it, my lord."

Montejo interjected: "Don Pedro must do as I wish. I am privy to information that can destroy him."

"And what is that?" I asked cooly.

"Your husband has borrowed money to construct a fleet at the Port of Iztapa, on the coast. He has no intention of remaining in Santiago. He will desert his post again, and embark on a disaster similar to that endured in Quito, Ecuador. The king must be informed."

I was stunned. I looked to Pedro for confirmation on this charge. He replied, his voice flat: "I have our sovereign's permission to seek the Isles of Spice. I need a strong fleet. It is expensive. The iron must be carried overland from Vera Cruz. The money for all this," Pedro shrugged, "must be borrowed."

Don Montejo smiled at my discomfiture. "Your ambition is backed by a noble dowry, Don Pedro. Tell me, sir, will the lady Beatriz rule Guatemala, in your absence?"

Pedro flushed to the roots of his hair. " Damn you!" he shouted. Then, controlling himself, he seized my hands. He spoke directly to me, but I guessed he was telling all present. "It is said I married Doña Beatriz to improve my position at Court. But ours is a love match. Already, I am too much in my lady's debt to ever repay her."

Such gallant subtlety! I felt a rush of foolish pleasure and knew I would give my lord whatever he desired. There would be no borrowing between us. And, yes—my uncle was right: I had wed a scoundrel.

Pedro spoke harshly then, "Montejo, what will you take for Honduras? How much to get you gone from here?"

"Two thousand gold pesos, your Province of Chiapa," Don Montejo licked his lips," and one of your great estates in Mexico."

"Done," said my lord, sharply. He called for parchment and ink, and the contract was drawn and signed. Pedro threw the paper at Montejo's feet. "Take it, and get out of my sight!"

When Montejo had packed up his mules and departed, when we were alone, I embraced my lord. "It was a sweet thing you said before all the company," I told him.

"I might have killed the swine," Pedro replied. "It is politics, my lady; I want it known our fortunes, yours and mine, are firmly united. It is easier then—"

"To borrow on my name!" I blazed. His dry explanation hurt and angered me. "I will not finance your dreams, my lord," I said coldly.

"You've no choice," Pedro said. "What is yours is mine. It is the law, Beatriz." Then he was angry. He said I had no right to interfere with his affairs; my presence in the interview with Montejo, Pedro said, had cost us more than we should have paid. The man was base, Pedro grumbled, and without a battle all would say my lord had got Honduras unfairly.

"People always believe the worst of me," Pedro said, drily.

"Because you live by the sword. You are careless, my lord," I told him. "You must use your wits."

"I have conquered by my sword," he replied. "And I will not live by your wits, Beatriz."

Ah! I understood. It was I who had managed the bargain with Montejo, and in so doing, I had trespassed Pedro's territory. I had wed a proud man; in the future, I must keep myself behind the scenes.

"Pedro," I said softly, "you have won a victory today. You have enriched your kingdom with new territory, and not a drop of blood shed. A master stroke, my lord."

He grinned eagerly as any boy wanting praise. "You will tell the king how it was done, Beatriz?"

I did so that very night. I wrote the king, and my uncle, and gave all credit to my lord. Honduras was ceded without a battle, I wrote, not mentioning the new fleet planned and the vast amount of monies borrowed for another expedition. I believed that, once in Santiago, I could keep my lord beside me.

Pedro made a great story of Montejo's early retirement. He boasted of his kingdom that stretched now from Mexico to the Isthmus of Panama. I took advantage of his good mood. I asked my lord to reward Négri for the latter's care of me while I was ill.

"If it weren't for Négri," I said, "I would not be here, alive and well."

"And I would not have had Honduras so easily, my lady," Pedro said. His mood was expansive. "Montejo was impressed by your name, Beatriz de la Cueva."

"De Alvarado," I reminded him, and wanted to say that Montejo had been defeated by my intelligence, but I

119

refrained. Instead, I pressed that Négri be made a Soldier of Spain.

"A soldier, and my majordomo," Pedro agreed, and he made a grand ceremony of Negri's promotion. We feasted that night and toasted Honduras with raised cups. Pedro was praised by all present for his diplomacy.

It was Bishop Marroquin who lifted his cup in a silent toast to me. I sat quietly on my cushions, thinking how this land had frightened me at first. Indeed, it had given me a deathly fever. But now I knew New Spain was not so different after all. Everywhere men crawled for gold and titles, and such crawling made them stupid. I would stand erect always, I resolved, but just behind, never in front of my lord. And if what was mine was his, I would keep it so, as ours.

"Why are you smiling, Beatriz?" Pedro asked me.

I tipped my cup, licking the last of the wine. "Because I am queen of two territories. Because you have honored my Négri. And because," I looked about me at all the wine-befuddled gentlemen, "we make merry at a lean banquet in a wretched jungle thicket, at the bottom of a world that is topsy-turvy—and I find it all richer than Valladolid."

Pedro kissed me, then lay at ease, his head on my lap. Paco filled my cup from his own. For the first time, I thought of Santiago as home, and I could not wait to get there.

CHAPTER 23

SEPTEMBER 15, 1539. The sky was morning-glory blue and the air sharp scented with pine. We had climbed from the lowlands to the mountain's rim and now we descended into a green valley. I saw Santiago, small and perfect as a legend town, its castle, cathedral, and Plaza Real perched on the slant of a mountain, the head of which was wrapped in a *manta* of clouds.

We had been traveling for one long year, and I had come a lifetime away from all I had known. I had come safely through fever and deprivation and heartache. Was I wiser? I know I was less impatient, a whit less tender. I felt myself enclosed in a thin armor which would thicken, I knew, in the ensuing years and I was grateful for it. But it would never stifle my passion for my lord. I was one year older, one year married, and one year deep in love with my husband. My love for him was my Achilles's heel; thus, strange to say, my beloved lord was my most treacherous enemy.

Then, however, on the outskirts of Santiago, I was elated, victorous, feeling only a small unease which could be shed in the bustle of preparation. Pedro halted our caravan beside a steep-falling river, just outside the city gates. He said we must wash and dress ourselves in that royal finery we had kept in chests for just this day. I would ride into the city on a white mule, my lord told me.

I replied that I would not mount a leaden-hooved mule, but would ride beside my Captain General on my own mare, *Señorita*. "And she must be brushed to glistening!" I gave the order.

"You will not ride astride?" Pedro worried.

I reassured him. "I will ride as if I moved in the king's own progress, Pedro. All in Santiago must know your return with a bride *'de origen noble,'* of noble origin."

He gave me one of his rare smiles. "I will be proud," he said.

I wore green velvet. Rosita dressed my hair high, and set

121

my green-feathered hat at just the right angle atop my curls. Pedro brought me a gold circlet to wear instead. He stood behind me and I saw our two faces in the glass.

He set the small crown carefully on my head, and kept his hands there a moment. "I would I was just beginning," he whispered.

"But we are," I said, "we are at the beginning, my lord."

He shook his head, and I saw his face somber. "My victories lie behind me. You should have seen it—seen me then, Beatriz. Do you think I would have waited outside a city? No—in those days the gates were opened to me, soldiers knelt to me, the Indians carried me aloft on their shoulders."

Absently, he stroked my face. "Perhaps Santiago is not mine now. The gates will remain shut and we will have a battle on our hands."

I was filled with foreboding. The city ahead of us was strangely quiet. Was it a trap? There were many, I knew, who wanted Pedro's prizes. Did an army lie in in wait within that silent town? No, I thought, I will not have it that way! My lord must have what is rightfully his, what is mine now too.

I turned to him and held him close. "You are tired, Pedro. The city is quiet, like a man asleep, daydreaming, as I do when I wait for you and you are long in coming. Ah! my lord, it is high time you returned home. They are fools who do not greet you with trumpets!"

He straightened with an effort. "I am too old for trumpets, Beatriz."

"You are splendid," I insisted. "Now, go and change, you must look like a king."

But he remained dejected. It was with great effort then, I reminded him. "Your daughter awaits you in Santiago. Have you forgotten her, Pedro?"

I left him smiling, and went to show Paco my crown. "How do I look?" I asked my brother.

"A rose among thorns," Paco replied, with an amused glance at my surly ladies.

Soon Pedro joined us. He was tall as a carved saint, gilded in light silver armor. His ruff was so high I

wondered where he had managed to hide it until now.
He stroked the minute folds of the lace under his chin.
"Rosita washed and pleated this—God knows how! Bless
the girl, she has clever hands." I saw "the girl" smile, and I
noticed she sported a new rose-colored gown.
"Fetch the cloak I made Don Pedro," I ordered her.
I gave Pedro a hard look. "Why didn't you tell me you
needed a fresh ruff? I could have—"
"No, you could not have, my lady," Pedro teased, and he
spun me about, admiring me from every angle. "You are
perfection, Beatriz!"
He addressed Paco, "You are to reside in the palace with
Beatriz and myself."
And with Léonor, I thought. Pedro meant us to be all one
family. I wondered if my brother had been told about
Léonor. Paco is a romantic, and I thought it certain he
would fall in love with an Indian princess. I placed my
hand on his arm. "Walk with me a way." I said.
Paco and I strolled among the mules and wagons. He
bowed to my ladies and I heard their giggles. All of the
twenty maidens there, I guessed, would like to wed my
brother. Had he an eye for one of them? I asked him, but he
shook his head. "Like scared rabbits, the lot of them,
Beatriz. You have spoiled me. I could not endure a
mewling Francesca. I want a Beatriz."
Or a Léonor perhaps? Hadn't Pedro told me his
daughter resembled me in spirit?
"Paco," I spoke seriously, "the Indian girls are beautiful.
Don't disgrace our family, I beg you."
He bent double with laughter. "From what I have seen,
the Indian maids are overwhelming in their nakedness. I
dislike their smell, their swarthiness, and it is plain to see
they are not immune to insect bites. No, Beatriz, you need
not fear, your brother will not spawn halfbreeds." Paco
turned serious then:
"This new world excites me, Beatriz. There is
opportunity here, a man can be himself. Look."
He turned me about and I saw the valley at our feet, the
broad cup of it furred with forest and the rim jagged but
softened with clouds.

"Our town there," Paco pointed, "Santiago is well-watered. It is set in a fertile land."

I gazed across the valley, up at that volcano called *Fuego*. I saw flames, smoke, and a drift of ashes. For a moment the earth under our feet pulsed like the skin of a giant drum.

"I am afraid, Paco," I admitted. "It is said old gods dwell in the fire of *Fuego*. It is the very pit of Hell. And," I continued, pointing at the peak of the mountain on which we stood, "this monster is called *Agua*. It does not spit fire, Paco, it holds an ocean of black water. Pedro tells me that if the sides crack, there will be a killing flood." I shivered. "Our kingdom is precarious, Paco."

He smiled at me. "Our Captain General ordered Santiago built here, Beatriz. You must trust him. I do."

"Yes, I must," I repeated softly.

I heard bugles behind us, and my lord's voice ordering all into line.

"Paco," I clutched my brother's arm, "he has a daughter. Her name is Léonor, a halfbreed, and—"

Paco was striding towards the caravan. He stopped and turned, and winked at me. "I did not think my lord Pedro had been a monk all these years," he said, and caught my hand to hurry me. "Come, my sister, they wait for us."

We rode forward. The city gates remained closed against us, and the silence from inside bewildered me. It was not until Pedro had announced himself several times that the gates swung wide.

I saw immediately that Santiago was smaller than I had expected. Indeed, I saw no more than a small fortress; a few cobblestoned streets; adobe huts, several grim stone edifices pretending to be palaces, and the skeleton of an unfinished cathedral.

Pigs grunted, roosters crowed. Stout city officals in shoddy robes stood silently before us. Scruffy, grizzled veterans in outmoded armor spat and cursed, did not salute my lord. I saw hive-huts, all thatched with reeds. I had believed I was coming to another Valladolid; I had dreamed of another Seville. But this shambles, Pedro's Santiago—it was hardly made, it was cruder than a mountain village.

Pedro guessed my dismay. He rode close to me. "I have left it all for you to design, my lady," he whispered. "Try to see it as it will be."

As it will be, for me to design—the thought pleasured me. I smelled bread baking. I saw a pen of fat cows and I thought of cream. I noticed again the freshness of the air, and I heard the crystal splatter of falling water. I could see then, through my lord's eyes, how our city would be. Pedro pointed out the towers of three completed convents, Bishop Marroquin's small leper hospital, and the roses planted thickly in the central plaza.

Flutes and drums sounded. I thought the gaiety a trifle forced. Those hoarse shouts from the assembled soldiers were no more than that accorded any captain, and I sensed a real hostility emanating from the cloaked dignitaries who waited on the steps of the Captain's Palace.

Pedro dismounted and climbed the steps alone. He greeted a scowling gentleman who loudly announced himself as Gonzalo de Ovalle, the new alderman, and spokesman, he said, for the city council.

Ovalle did not bow. "What right have you to enter here with an army?" he asked my lord.

From my horse, I scanned the faces of those gathered to greet us. There was little disapproval of Ovalle's rude manner, and I sensed few were genuinely pleased with my lord's return. Quickly then, I dismounted and went to stand beside Pedro.

"Show them the King's Seal and the Royal Orders," I whispered, because Pedro's hand was on his sword.

"The city is yours," I reminded him quietly.

Pedro gave Ovalle the papers. "Read it aloud, sir," he commanded.

The document was long, but the words precise. By the time Ovalle was finished his voice was weak, and all within hearing distance knew my lord was captain governor; that any man who stood against Pedro would be fined 100,000 *maravedis.* Ovalle gasped when he read this, and Pedro chuckled at the gentleman's acute discomfort.

A portly figure intruded. He snatched the King's Order

from Ovalle's hands and made as if he would tear the papers in two.

"I am sent to try you," he told Pedro. "You deserted this post several years ago, Captain Alvarado, and the Council of the Indies became concerned. I found your capital in a sorry state, sir."

"Who are you?" my lord demanded.

"Attorney Maldonado, a poor civil servant sent to do his duty." The gentleman bowed. His lips smiled, but not his eyes. "I am interim governor of Guatemala. The post was vacant..."

Pedro interrupted—"And my palace?"

"I live in the castle—yes." The lawyer bowed again.

"Not so poorly now, I'll wager," Pedro snapped. "It is you then, with the help of that rabbit Montejo and with this jackal here—" he glared at Ovalle—"you who dare to usurp my authority. Where are my brothers? Before God! I'll have all your heads for this treason!"

My hand on Pedro's arm, I spoke gently to him. "Sir, there is no need for violence. These men are beneath you. Show each of them the Royal Seal, and—" I turned to smile graciously at the assembled company, "please introduce me, my lord."

Pedro guessed my intent. With royal dignity, he drew me forward. "Permit me, gentlemen, to introduce my lady wife, Doña Beatriz de la Cueva de Alvarado. And her brother, Don Francisco de la Cueva."

Our name was enough to make this crowd obsequious. I curtsied with such cool aloofness I might have been standing in the great Court at Valladolid. Paco performed likewise, his eyes fixed somewhere above the bowing heads. Moustaches and beards grazed the top of my proffered hand. I looked directly at each gentleman, and I knew that not a man among these would dare to speak against the name De la Cueva.

"Bring the ladies forward," I reminded Pedro.

"Ah, yes!" Pedro appeared bemused by our royal behavior. "We are thrice blessed," he announced. "I am captain general by your sovereign's command. I have been given a royal wife, and our gifts to you are twenty noble ladies, brides for my most loyal officers."

One by one, Pedro brought my ladies forward. Each of them, blushing and cowering, was immediately surrounded by men in uniform?

All are well-pleased, I thought, and turned to take Pedro's arm. "Show me our palace?" I asked. Then I whispered, "You see, how easy it is, my lord? A show of dignity, and power. And," I giggled, watching the gentlemen slaver over the ladies, "the promise of a bride perhaps. Your homecoming is done, Pedro."

He spoke grudgingly. "It is your presence, not mine, Beatriz." Then I saw his eyes widen in delight. A small figure was running swiftly towards us. Pedro dropped my hand and stepped forward.

"My daughter!" he exclaimed. I had never heard his voice so warm.

The girl was slight, her skin so dark I hoped it was sunburn. She had a pixie face, her hair blown every which way. I saw her skirts were divided for riding astride, as I did. We were much alike, Pedro had told me many times.

With wet eyes, he presented Léonor. She slid her arms about my waist. *"Mamacita,"* she whispered.

I did not like her boldness...I put her away from me. "At least you could have combed your hair," I said sharply, unkindly. I might have been my mother speaking but I could not help myself.

Pedro's arm was tight about the girl; he wanted me to love her as he did but, long before, I had resolved I would not. Did she resemble her mother? I wondered. I had to admit the girl was pretty.

"Your father's homecoming," I continued, "have you no gowns for such occasions, child?"

She blushed, and smoothed her skirts. "I—I was so excited, I forgot everything. And then I was late, I always am. *Mamacita*, forgive me."

I inclined my head coldly. I spoke direct to Pedro. "There must be a *fiesta* tonight, a celebration. If I could see the castle, the kitchens, there are servants, I suppose?

"If you will attend me now, my lord?" I stretched out my hand, but Pedro had eyes only for his daughter.

"I am tired," I said, sharply. It was true, I was feeling a great rush of weariness, of defeat. Despite my resolution to be kind to Léonor I had failed. Now I knew Pedro was angry with me.

"Your rooms are ready." His face was closed against me. His arm was firm about his daughter.

I tried to make amends. "We will see you later," I said, inclining my head to Léonor.

She ignored my gesture. "Of course you will," she said brightly, "I live in the castle with you. I will attend the *fiesta* this evening and dance with my *querido.*" She kissed Pedro, plainly taunting me from the shelter of his arms.

It was Négri who rescued me. "There are refreshments," he reminded me. "Your rooms are prepared, Doña." His face held such distaste, I doubted his words.

I took the attorney's arm, and, with my ladies, I walked the short distance to the castle.

"A pretty girl," Don Maldonado mused, "you must not be harsh with her, Doña. She is young, she lacks a mother's guidance."

"She needs a husband," I replied.

The attorney nodded. "There is not a gentleman present who would not wed the lady Léonor, if she would agree."

A merry voice spoke behind us. "That beauty you speak of—she is waiting for me!" Paco was breathless, eager. "Beatriz, you did not tell me. Who is the lovely in the scarlet gown?"

"She is my lord's halfbreed daughter." I knew I should not speak so, but could not contain myself. "I did tell you, Paco."

"Don Pedro's daughter? Beatriz, you are unkind! I will go and escort her myself." Paco hurried away, and I was left to enter my castle on a stranger's arm. It was grim and dark.

I saw bats hanging, high against the vaulted ceilings. Pine needles had been hastily spread on the stone floors, but the stench was of soldiers, leather, vermin droppings, and stale wax.

My dismay embarrassed Don Maldonado. "You were not expected," he said. "It has been years since a lady lived here."

"I doubt there has ever been a lady here," I retorted, trying to keep my voice steady. "My lord had an Indian wife, and the daughter is not much better. Ugh! It has the stink of animals."

Not even the fires blazing in my rooms could warm me. It had been such a triumph, my own victory, entering Santiago. Now Léonor's presence had poisoned it all. I was angry, and more than a little ashamed of my rudeness. Rosita helped me bathe—there were drowned flies in my water bowl—and to change. My linens were damp, and I could not decide which of my gowns to wear. I chose the warmest, which was the least becoming, and Rosita smiled a cat's grimace, buttoning me up the back. When I was despondent, she was gleeful. Whatever demon made me keep that girl, I do not know.

Pedro did not come to inquire if I was comfortable. I did not meet with him again until the banquet that night, and then he was occupied with Léonor—a fatuous father teaching his daughter the new dances from Spain. Paco, too—I saw him completely bewitched.

I sat lonely, at the head of the table, beside Pedro's empty chair. Nothing pleased me as it should have, not the snow-ice brought from the top of *Agua*, nor the sparkling wine made in an Indian village nearby. These last were luxuries I had not expected, but I paid them no mind in my black mood. Jealousy does not improve my looks, and I knew I appeared sallow, as sinister in my gloom perhaps, as a storybook stepmother.

Portocarreo sat on my left. He was greying, but lighthearted, a true gallant with his curled moustaches. He claimed a dance or two with me, but his eyes seldom left Léonor's whirling figure. I guessed his gaiety forced, inspired more by the wine than the company. Gently I asked him what troubled him.

"A woman," he confessed. "She arrived not ten days before yourself, Doña Beatriz. Her presence makes me uneasy. Some say she is a witch."

"Belial?" I guessed, and my heart froze. Somehow, I had known I would not be rid of the gypsy.

Portocarreo stared at me. "You know her? How?"

"She intrudes on my life also," I said. "My lord has told me she seeks vengeance. Is it true? Did you play with her affections?"

He shrugged. "She pleasured me a night or two. I promised her nothing. Now she will wed me, or send us all to the Devil."

I leaned closer. "But you will wed another," I said softly. "It is Léonor you have chosen. I can help you, sir."

He stiffened, his black eyes narrowed, and in the set of his shoulders, I saw the soldier behind the gallant's mask. "My lord's daughter is forbidden me," he said.

"Don Pedro is my sworn comrade. I will not move against his wishes, and it will behoove you, Doña, to follow my way." He left his place at table, not waiting for my reply.

I was ashamed; I sat alone, feeling myself an island in a sea of merry-making. Would no gentleman dance with me? Certainly not Bishop Marroquin who took Portocarreo's place beside me. He spoke kindly, urging me to smile, but his eyes followed Léonor's twirling figure. "A sweet thing to see," he murmured. "She worships him as her mother did."

My spoon dropped from my fingers, clattered to my plate. It seemed all present turned to look at me. "I have had enough!" I cried, and stood abruptly, almost overturning my chair.

My voice too shrill, I summoned Négri, ordered him to light a torch. "I will retire," I announced. Pedro did not trouble himself to wish me goodnight, and not a man or woman present asked me to stay.

That first night in Santiago, I slept alone in a vast curtained bed, the mattress of which was straw, and mouldy. The *fiesta* sang and laughed under my floorboards. It was Paco's voice I heard, and my lord's baritone in reply, and then a girl's high voice. The night was still, hot, and I tossed restlessly.

I heard the dancing music stop, and Léonor began to sing. Pedro's voice joined with hers, but their song was foreign, a strange aching chant that held their listeners silent and rocked me, somehow, half-asleep.

There was wind, and rain. The latter fell like hail. The hinges of my shutters whined, and the curtains about my bed lifted wild as a woman's skirts in a dance. Far away, I heard Pedro and his daughter singing.

I think I dreamed. I saw white arms and whiter hands fling my curtains aside. Who was it wished to look at me? I pulled my bedcovers over my face. But the presence was certain, insistent, until the singing faded and I slept.

CHAPTER 24

CLANGING BELLS awakened me. I remembered Bishop Marroquin had said he would celebrate Mass in the cathedral. The space beside me in bed was empty. Where was Pedro?

"My lady, he went late to bed," Rosita told me. "I asked him not to disturb you." She smiled, set my tray of chocolate beside me, then crossed the room to kick the dead coals of my fire back into the grate.

"A primitive place," she said, wrinkling her nose. "I thought the castle walls would fall, there was such merriment last night. I danced my feet raw."

I guessed the girl had basked in the attention of men who had not seen a white woman in years, and I warned her now against such gentlemen. "We must find a husband for you," I said.

She looked at me, mischief in her black eyes. "One like your own, Doña. I would not wed a lesser man." She pursed her lips and blew a kiss into the air.

I thought her rudeness intolerable. I had spent a restless night. I reminded myself that I was mistress of a castle now, there was no need for me to depend on this impudent creature.

"Rosita," I said, with some coolness, "my lord tells me I have more than enough maidservants now. The ladies with me—they are ill-at-ease. You will be mistress of their wardrobes, and," I smiled because the idea pleased me, "the first lady wed, you will leave this castle with her."

Rosita scowled. "You will rue the day you send me from your service, Doña. It is cruel to discharge me without reason. I will not forget. Don Pedro—he says he cannot manage without me."

"I give the orders here," I said, but her face showed such malice then that I was frightened. I lost my temper, and gained an enemy. "I dismiss you now," I said. "On your way out, send me several of the new girls that I can instruct them."

Rosita was humiliated; I should have shown more patience, but her arrogance was insupportable. She sent a dozen thick-haired Indian girls to wait on me, and stood giggling in the doorway, gloating over my dismay when I glimpsed these untutored barefoot wenches.

I dressed by myself, my every move scrutinized by black eyes. I guessed these girls regarded me as some mystery descended from the sky. So many of them, silent and pressing close about me. I saw one sniffed my petticoat, another fondled my boots. One was quite hypnotized by her face in my looking glass. When there is time, I thought, I will teach these girls to bathe; their hair must be braided and they should wear the same color garment. They must wear something! I resolved, because many of the girls were naked from the waist up. I realized I was giving them as many covert glances as they were staring openly at me. That thought made me laugh, and my laughter earned me furtive smiles.

Somehow I made these girls understand that my room was to be thoroughly aired and my mattress burned. Speech was impossible, but I caught one girl using my hairbrush and managed to move both her hand and the brush to my own head. She understood and my hair became her task thereafter.

I chose a gown of blue velvet and a pearled cap of the same color. My emerald glowed. If my lord was at Council I wanted to join him there. I knew I must apologize for my ill temper of the night previous. Too, I was anxious to meet Pedro's brothers. I summoned Négri to show me the way, and passing through the long hall and down the stone stairway, I planned the tapestries and Turkey carpets I would use to brighten this grim castle.

Négri knocked on the tall door, flung it open, and announced me: "La Doña Beatriz de la Cueva de Alvarado."

It was a somber room, a soldier's room with one carved chair drawn up to a broad table. The men present were speaking in low voices, and they turned in surprise when Négri announced me.

My lord, splendid in purple and a short furred cloak near

the color of his hair, greeted me formally, and asked me to wait outside. "There is a small terrace which receives the morning sun," he suggested, and told me he and his brothers would join me presently.

I smiled as if I had not heard Pedro. "If you sit at Council, I am interested," I said, ignoring his frown.

Then I addressed the gathering. "Good gentlemen, my lords, I would know your names and titles that I can name you correctly, and your positions, for our sovereign king."

Pedro appeared dumbfounded at my boldness, but Paco stepped forward, admiration and amusement in his eyes. He introduced me to Pedro's five brothers: Diego, Jorge, Gomez, Gonzalo, and Juan. I could hardly tell these gentlemen apart because each of them resembled my lord, being fair of hair and broad of shoulder. Jorge was the tallest and Juan, I believed, was the youngest. He looked near my own age, and his manner was such that I was glad I had chosen a bright blue gown.

Bishop Marroquin showed me to the one chair. I sat down and settled my skirts about me. "Proceed, gentlemen, I do not wish to interrupt."

There was an uncomfortable silence, then my lord mumbled something about their business being all completed, and the others nodded sagely. I guessed immediately that, as men do, the Council had been summoned, the great door closed—not for secrecy, but for the sake of comradeship, male talk, mutual assurances of heroism and victory. Overgrown boys come together, I thought, to relish old battles, to renew bonds and confidence.

I leaned forward. "If your business is done," I said, "perhaps there is one among you who will tell me about the Indian people. I confess, I am at a loss. Should I fear them? I do feel an unease in their presence. The Indian language is foreign to me, and their customs are most strange."

The Alvarado brothers stepped near the table. "We do fear the Indians, my lady." They spoke almost in unison, and I hushed them with a smile.

"One at a time," I suggested gently. "I want to

understand. Jorge?" I looked up at Pedro's giant older brother and wondered that this man feared anyone, anything. "Are you afraid, Don Jorge?"

"All of us are," he admitted. "But the Indians must not guess our fear. Any weakness shown, and their thousands will wipe our scarce hundred from the face of New Spain."

Diego spoke: "We hold the Quiche and Cacique chieftains prisoners. My brother should have them killed."

I sensed discord, and I suggested, "If my lord kills the leaders, won't their people be angry?"

Pedro looked at me gratefuly, nodding his head.

"Doña," Jorge spoke again, "every year before we conquered Mexico, more than two thousand five hundred Indian slaves were sacrificed by their priest and kings, to their idols. The blood sacrifice, my lady—it is most horrible!"

"Suffered by our soldiers too, when they are taken in battle," Pedro interjected.

"The blood sacrifice?" I asked.

Jorge nodded. "We have all witnessed it, my lady. A stone knife, the breast sliced wide, and the heart torn living from the flesh."

There was silence for a moment, and I knew each gentleman present relived those horrors when they stood helpless against the Indian strongholds, at a distance but not far enough away that they could not hear and see the sufferings of their comrades taken in battle.

"But they are worse than animals!" I exclaimed. I turned to Pedro. "Perhaps you should kill the heathen kings?"

He shook his head. "I hold them hostage. While there is peace, they live. The first sign of an uprising, a hint of unrest—the Indians know I will kill their kings."

Young Juan clenched his fists. "Your lord is too kind, my lady. Our royal prisoners live better than we do—holding court, waited upon! I have seen them drunk on incense, dressed like courtesans."

Pedro interrupted. "Enough!"

But Juan persisted. "And that other—the one who hides in the caves on *Agua's* slopes. He is both witch and priest, Pedro. Why do you let him roam free? It is rumored he eats human flesh! Hundreds go to him for cures, for spells. He wields power, Pedro—we have warned you."

Again my lord shook his head. "Precisely because of his power he is free. If the witch was taken, all of us would suffer."

"A real witch?" I asked.

Bishop Marroquin leaned forward. "Doña, believe me, a strong faith flourishes here. This talk of witches—it is ridiculous, and forbidden. Warriors are become farmers now, the blood sacrifice will be soon forgotten.

"We build churches," the bishop continued, "and many Reverend Fathers baptize and instruct. The natives attend Mass. Indian and Spaniard live in peace, and it is that way we must direct our prayers, my lady." He looked sternly at each gentleman. "And our thoughts. Idle talk sows the Devil's seeds," he warned.

"You speak true," Pedro said, but his voice held doubt. "I insist on peace. I have given the Indian nobles power over their own people, and there are several of these who have shown themselves assiduous as ourselves in keeping law and order."

I smiled. "It seems the Indian gentlemen appreciate power and wealth as much as the Spanish dons."

My remark drew chuckles and a nodding of heads. Pedro sent pages for wine, and our talk became lighter. I told Pedro's brothers about the fat Montejo and that man's ceding of Honduras to my lord without a battle. I made the tale amusing, and Pedro's brothers were gallant, so attentive that Pedro himself must follow suit.

I insisted on pouring the wine. All present said that it was a new and delightful innovation to have a lady at the Council table. I mentioned the king again, and Tio Francisco, and I said I would write immediately and name each gentleman present, stating his loyalty to my husband, to Santiago, and to Spain.

"And no more talk of witches," I promised Bishop Marroquin, and told him also I would ask the king for monies for the Church. I saw the bishop was well pleased with me. Indeed, as always, I basked in the gentlemen's attention. I would attend all Council meetings, I resolved,

Pedro must accept me as equal.

I asked if the two dissenters, Maldonado and Ovalle, had fled. Pedro said he had ordered their departure. "They go to Mexico," he said, "to wait, and pounce again when and if Santiago is undefended."

"That will never be!" I cried. We raised our cups.

"Viva Santiago!" we shouted. Bishop Marroquin beamed at me. "The lady is a true soldier," he said. "God will bless you, Doña."

"God has blessed me," I replied, looking directly at Pedro. Then I asked, "There is nothing here to frighten me then? The woman, Belial?"

"She is gone," Pedro said. "Portocarreo complained of her presence; he said you were concerned too, my lady. Early this morning I sent her off in a caravan bound for the coast."

Was Belial gone? I doubted that. "Perhaps she will not come back," I said. I reached for Pedro's hand.

Jorge warned me: "Take care, Doña. Do not venture from the castle. Whatever you need, send for it. Indians wait in ambush. All is not as tranquil as my brother and our good bishop insist. Pedro has been away too long." The tone of Jorge's voice showed his displeasure with Pedro's absence.

"Your Captain General has returned, with a queen," I reminded Jorge. "We bring the king's blessing, and peace."

"So be it." The young man smiled. "I note your curiosity regarding witches, Doña. You must stop your ears here; I am told the very air is laden with spells." He winked at me. "Love spells, my lady."

Pedro frowned. "Jorge, and Beatriz too—must I forbid you to speak of what we are hard put to abolish? The walls have ears. If the Indians discover there is one among us who leans towards the old gods, we are lost."

"We only tease, my lord," I said. But I knew myself curious, wanting to know more of these ancient rites.

"I forbid it," Pedro repeated sharply.

"Do not forbid me anything," I said lightly. "Forbidden fruit is a temptation."

I smiled at Jorge, and took Juan's proffered arm.

"*Caballeros*, will you show me the gardens?"

All were eager to do the honors. I was shown a balcony with a view that caught my breath.

Valleys and mountains. Our castle spanned a rocky gulch, the sides of which were planted with pine and fruit trees. Looking up I saw the crevice cutting deep and dark to the top of *Agua*. "If this gulch should fill with water, we would be swept away," I said.

The morning was sun-blessed, and all the valley at my feet was green, but I felt a brooding fate, a heavy, patient waiting. Did the volcano above me really contain a bottomless lake? I pictured the water black, and wide watching eyes rimming the volcano mouth.

"Could the volcano overflow, in rainy season?" I asked.

"It could, but it won't, Doña," Jorge answered me. "We have dammed those streams which flow from *Agua's* lake. It is centuries, the Indians say, since water filled the gulch below us here. There is no danger."

No danger? I felt my perch precarious, but dared not argue the bland assurance of these conquistadors who settled castles and townships where they willed.

Pedro approached us. "Are you pleased, my lady?" he asked, slipping an arm about my waist. "Will you stay awhile?" he whispered, teasing. "I swear, last night, I thought you ready to depart."

"You did not come to see if I was gone," I replied. I strolled with my lord apart from others. "My night was ghost-ridden." I said. "Rosita tells me you and I sleep far apart."

He pulled me close against him. "It is I who would haunt you, and you who put distance between us." He frowned. "Rosita is a gossip and oversteps herself. Why do you tolerate her rude behaviour?"

"I thought I needed her," I admitted, "but I dismissed her this morning." I chuckled. "She left me to the ministrations of a gaggle of geese."

"You are mistress now, Beatriz," Pedro told me. "Select your women with care. And now, *querida*, see there—my daughter approaches, and on your brother's arm. Will you show them this morning's smiles?"

He looked so anxious that I kissed him quickly, then turned to greet Léonor. Her fingers on my brother's wrist looked brown against his white skin. They were leaning close, caught up in some foolishness. I frowned.

"Doña," Pedro spoke earnestly, "you promised to be kind. She is but a child. You have told me yourself, many times, what it is to want a mother's love."

"We are too close in age," I reminded him. But I saw his face when he looked at his daughter, and I relented. "Perhaps," I said hesitantly, "perhaps someday we can be friends. Give me time, Pedro." Time to forget whose child she is, that is what I meant. I knew I could not forget.

"*Mamacita,* good morning!" Impulsively, Léonor spread her hands to me.

"You may call me Beatriz," I replied, managing a smile. And we walked together: Paco and Léonor, Pedro and I. We wandered down the broad stairs to a sheltered patio. I admired the orange trees in their red clay tubs, and Pedro fashioned me a blossom crown. Paco repeated the mock ceremony for Léonor.

We make a pretty tableau, I thought, it is a new tapestry stitched here, in Guatemala: The Captain General and his noble lady, the Spanish don and his Indian paramor. God keep her just his paramor, I prayed, but my heart jumped like stitches dropped when I saw Paco serious, mute and clumsy as a love-sick schoolboy.

CHAPTER 25

I KEPT MYSELF BUSY that first year with the refurbishing of my castle, and then the town itself. Pedro said I must not meddle with the castle's outer walls, six feet thick, but I had his permission to do what I wished with the dank labyrinths inside. I wanted my rooms scrubbed clean of ghosts, past lives—I determined on grandeur and gaiety.

Yes, I was busy, and thanked God for it! I had arrived in a primitive land; earthquakes and volcanos, drenching rains and a merciless sun. Loneliness circled me, relentless as the packs of wild dogs that roam *Agua's* peaks. I learned to live with the threat of plague, of Indian uprisings. Day after day, *Agua's* waters gathered above my castle. The very air was heavy with foreboding. Other women would have left; so many noble ladies pine for home, but this is my kingdom and Pedro is my beloved lord.

Belial returned, as I knew she would. She sticks like a burr to Santiago. Pedro forbade her entrance to the castle grounds, but I was always conscious of her malevolent presence. She lived on Rosita's charity—God knows, those two made strange bedfellows! They were drawn together by their desire for revenge on Pedro and myself. Rosita became the whore of a wastrel captain; she watched the man drink himself to death that she might have his gold.

I did not wish to brood; I kept my days full. I designed my nights to keep my lord amused: fiestas and masques, music and fine food. Pedro permitted me to attend the Council meetings, and several hours of each day I devoted to letters to Spain.

I trained my Indian girls, and brought in menservants too. Mother would be proud of me; often I have wished she might visit and see what I have accomplished. But I was lonely. I would not befriend Léonor; I kept her at a distance, hoping Paco's infatuation would fade.

My failure to conceive became an obsession. I kneeled at my Virgin's feet, asking Her why I was not with child. I had tried all measures, and still I was not pregnant. I sensed

Pedro's impatience. He will cease to love me, I thought, he will seek a new wife.

Several of my Indian girls had learned my language. Sometimes, beset with loneliness, I would urge these girls to tell me the forbidden god-legends. It is all folklore and superstition, much like the tales Ana told me, and I saw no harm in it.

Agua is inhabited by phantoms, my maidservants whispered, there are magic spells to be had on *Agua's* peak. The mountain spirits are kind to lovers, the girls said, giggling, covering their mouths with their brown fingers. A witch lives on *Agua*, they said; he grants the heart's desire, if you dare, my lady....

I shook my head. Witches are devil-spawned, I knew that. But a prayer to the old gods, a prayer whispered in the name of love? Pedro need not know. I resolved to ride with him there, to the top of *Agua*. Perhaps the gods would bless us.

One early morning Pedro and I rode to *Agua's* summit. The sun stood high above our heads and Guatemala stretched green to the horizon. We dismounted, and I held tightly to Pedro's arm. The crater gaped at our feet, a black lake with no bottom to it.

"It is awesome," I whispered, eyeing the slick water where, I supposed, the gods slept, listening, their eyes wide.

Pedro tossed stones into the lake. His eyes were on the horizon, and he said ours was a kingdom worthy of sons. "When will it be?" he asked longingly.

"Soon," I vowed loudly, hoping the gods heard me. Then I said, wanting love-words, "Are you content, my lord?" He must love me here, I wished—let the gods see us!

"I have what I want," he said brusquely. But I knew his eyes admired me. I unpinned my veil and let my hair blow loose.

I turned my back to the dark water. "We are alone," I whispered. But my scalp prickled. What gods did I invoke? I wondered; I felt one step closer to a terrible Unseen.

"Pedro, hold me!" I cried.

He drew me quick against him. "I would have you now,

Beatriz—the sky above, and the sun on you. There is a wildness in you this morning...."

We embraced on that high peak. Our horses grazed nearby. We were alone in a blue space, above the world. "It is magic," I whispered, "we will make our child here, Pedro." I thought the deep waters blinked and I knew the gods listened.

Pedro's hands were in my hair. "You make the magic, Beatriz." He held my face close to his own and his broad thumbs moved against my throat. "I will spread my cloak, *querida*. Are you bold enough?"

I took his cloak from him and spread it on the grass. "Love me," I invited him, and I lay back and let the sun fill my eyes.

He kneeled, straddling me, and pushed my skirts above my waist. "Wanton," he muttered, his voice thick. He rolled my stockings down and caressed my thighs. I felt the mountain wind across my belly and I shivered. Pedro's love—I felt such ecstasy I knew the gods must wake.

"Your breasts—in the sunlight," Pedro murmured, and he undid the laces of my bodice, pulled my gown low.

"My one love," I whispered, then his tongue was in my mouth and his weight on me, and when he entered me I felt such joy. I remember the glint of the sun, the silence broken then....

A ribald cackle of laughter froze us where we lay. I opened my eyes and, behind my lord's shoulders, I saw Belial. She stood above us, her hands on her hips, her toothless jaws exposed in her broad grin.

"The bull and his cow, come to rut on *Agua*," she giggled. "Do you seek the old spell, Captain?"

Pedro stumbled to his feet, his face scarlet. "Be gone, woman!" he shouted. I saw his eyes flick to his horse, to the dagger in his saddle.

I scrambled erect, clutching my dress to me and feeling shamed somehow—such scorn in Belial's eyes. I knew I must look like a servant girl and I was remembering that humiliation when my uncle had ridden in on Alonso and I.

"How came you here?" I demanded. Because it was a morning's ride and I knew the woman had no horse.

"Someone near here." She smirked. I thought her manner furtive, and I wondered who lived in this forsaken spot.

"An outcast like myself," Belial answered my unspoken question. "He calls himself wise."

Pedro wheeled on me. "Beatriz, I forbid you to speak to this woman!" He glared at Belial. "I will have you flogged for trespassing. It is forbidden to come here."

Belial cursed. She spit at Pedro's feet. "You can't hurt me, not on this mountain. Take care, soldier, the rocks have ears."

Pedro moved quickly. He drew his dagger from his saddle and seized Belial by her hair. He flung her to her knees and set the knife's edge to her throat. He might have killed her, but I stepped forward. "Don't, I pray you, my lord. Do not have her blood on your hands."

I don't know why I spoke so because it would have been better if Belial had died there. But she was evil; I knew she would haunt me. "Let her go," I begged Pedro.

"As generous as she is fair." It was a voice, soft, behind us. I turned and saw him, black-haired and tall, and dressed in white. There were blue stones on his hands and the sun's radiance was on him like fire. His appearance was startling; I had never seen so exotic a man.

"Let the woman go." His voice was low but it held such authority that Pedro released Belial.

"Who are you?" my lord asked.

"You know me," the stranger replied.

He gave Belial a glance that erased her smirk. "I sent you for herbs, not gossip," he told her. He was not unkind; he spoke as if he reminded a servant of chores she had forgotten.

To my surprise, Belial curtsied. Then, after a withering look at me, she scurried away.

Pedro addressed the stranger again: "You are the one who lives here? Yes—they have told me of you. You live beyond the law."

"I live here," the man repeated, and he made a gesture as if our meeting was terminated. He behaved like royalty, and I sensed Pedro's unease.

"Wait—" my lord blustered. "Do you have permission to live here? I am Captain General and..."

"Yes." But the stranger was looking at me. I felt he read my soul. He spoke directly to me. "You lead your lord too far," he warned. I blushed; I knew he guessed my purpose in coming here.

He nodded somberly. "Have patience, my lady. The gods move in their own time."

"Yes," I whispered. I felt this man harbored a thousand secrets. I wanted to touch him. I stepped forward. "Sir—" I said urgently.

He avoided my hands. "Not yet," he said, "perhaps never. It will be your choice, my lady." He turned and walked from us.

"Wait!" I cried.

"Beatriz!" Pedro's voice intruded sharply. He stepped between me and the departing stranger.

"But I want to know!" I entreated. "Pedro, that man is not Spanish or Indian, he is from another world. Let me speak to him, please!"

"He is a hermit, a beggar," Pedro told me. He was scowling. "Some say he is a witch. This is a cursed place, Beatriz, it crawls with odd creatures. Let us mount and ride for home."

I obeyed. My head was spinning. "What was Belial doing here?" I wondered aloud. "Do you know that man, Pedro?"

"I know of him." My lord pressed close to me. "*Agua's* slopes are host to Satan's creatures. Beatriz, you will not ride here again. Do you understand? I forbid it."

I nodded. I was but half-listening. My mind was on the stranger, the blueness of his stones, his radiance—I had longed to touch him. "Who is he, Pedro?" I persisted.

"Speak of him again and I will have him hunted down, burned! Beatriz, are you listening?"

"But Belial," I said, "it is she who is evil, Pedro—not that man." I smiled. "He said it would be my choice—if we should meet again."

"You will not, by God—you will not!"

Pedro's shout caused his stallion to rear. My lord tumbled to the ground and sat there speechless, looking up at me, his mouth slack with surprise. I had to laugh. I dismounted quickly.

"Oh, my dear." I helped him to his feet, and hugged him close. "I angered you, I am foolish, forgive me." My lips sought his. I smoothed his beard, his hair, set his cap straight on his head.

"There, there," I soothed, until he smiled. He chuckled. "We were interrupted, sweet lady."

"Yes, rudely," I agreed, and I laughed too. "We were a pretty sight, my lord."

Pedro helped me mount. He was shaking with mirth. "The Captain General and his lady—caught with their britches down!" He was back in his saddle again, riding close to me.

"Pedro, for shame!" I admonished, and spurred my mare forward and raced my husband home.

We rode with a clatter into the courtyard. Pedro lifted me down and carried me inside. The servants stood open-mouthed.

Pedro bounced me on the wide bed. "The sun has burned you in odd places," he said, and we collapsed in gales of merriment.

Later, many times, I was to recall that stranger on the slopes of *Agua*. He had seemed kind, I thought, but if he had to do with Belial he was evil. Why did I wish to see him again? He said I had led Pedro too far—what did that mean? A warning, perhaps?

Yes, it was dangerous to seek the old gods. If I believed in witchcraft, I would be vulnerable to its spells. Ana had told me so; not to stray from the path, she had said that too.

CHAPTER 26

THERE ARE SOME who say my lord spoiled me. I know I
kept him by my side. I think he came to love me.

True to my resolve, there are chairs enough in each room
that all may sit at ease, and it is still fresh wonder to me
how the conversation is improved when ladies need not
crouch on pillows looking up at the gentlemen. I have but
one dining hall; I seat my guests with care, and Don Bernal
has told me that it is the ladies' wit and beauty that supply
the leavening for what might be otherwise ordinary bread.

Always deferring to my lord, I had Santiago's alleys
transformed into streets and avenues. Indians and slaves,
merchants and guildsmen, all have well-defined limits for
living and working. I wanted the laws clear. Paco showed
a talent for this, and it was he who set the prices for goods
and services. Those who cheat are whipped in public.
Loiterers and beggars are discouraged. Dueling is
prohibited, all arguments being brought before the
Council.

I wanted the nobility of Santiago to be easily recognized.
My lord agreed; he said the horse must be a sign of rank.
On pain of 100 lashes and banishment for one year to the
mines, no mestizo, mulatto, negro, whether freed man or
slave or Indian, can ride a horse. It seems a cruel law but
our Indians are surly, sometimes openly rebellious, and
only a member of the soldiery on horseback can control
them. The Indians believe the horse to be a god-creature
and the white-skinned warrior on his back to be invincible.

There was one problem with this law however: Léonor is
a *mestiza*. Would she be forbidden her white mare? The
devil in me wanted it so, but Bishop Marroquin reminded
me of the many illegitimate children begotten by Spanish
nobles and their Indian women.

"Let those who are recognized by their fathers have all
rights and privileges," the bishop said, and Pedro and the
others were quick to agree with him. I wondered what
would happen if all illicit relationships were punished by

the death penalty? I knew few gentlemen would be left alive in Santiago!

I have held firm to those traditions of Old Spain that are most pleasing. Our days begin with holy music. Each dawn the bells of the convents and churches are struck in assigned order, and the soft or sonorous chords echo past noon, and again to mark the Angelus. I like the splash of fountains, the echo of bells.

I asked Pedro for a room of my own where I might keep my books and my globe. He gave me the top of the highest tower, and it became my sanctuary, presided over by a Virgin whose dress and bearing resemble that of a Spanish noblewoman. I love her dearly, from her blue *manta* to her pointed slippers. It is she who has heard my whispered confessions, my fears, my prayers. There are times I have turned her face to the wall. Because she will not give me that one miracle I beg: I must give my lord a son.

I have spent body and soul to please my husband. It was months before he spoke again of the Seven Cities, or any further explorations. I planned masked balls, street theater, *fiestas* of all kinds. Our Holy Days were made splendid by processions, carpets of flowers on all the streets; the Holy Images paraded in their jewels and velvets.

There are those who say I was extravagant. I was accused of vanity and greed. But it behooved me to have people believe I had naught in my head but plans for the next carnival. I moved about freely, conversing with knight and traitor alike. Many times I nipped treachery in the bud and Pedro praised me for my insight.

It was I who wrote the letters to Spain. I translated Pedro's blunt demands for recognition into elegant phrases. I signed my lord's name and I used the seal of Santiago. Carefully, I kept Pedro's image untarnished.

In almost three years I had but one letter from my mother. This was soon after I had arrived, to thank me on behalf of twenty mothers for the marriages of their daughters here, under my auspices.

"The girls will be happy," my mother wrote, and she hoped I was not rebelling against that fate endured by all married women—*"enceint,"* she used the French word for pregnant, misspelling it.

I wrote her back again, woman-talk. I told her of my castle, my own small court. I wrote of my dismissal of Rosita and that impudent girl's subsequent behavior: she became the mistress of a ne'er-do-well captain, and when he drunkenly discarded her, she took his gold and established herself in a fine house. "An inn," I told my mother, "where the gentlemen play at cards and are served by Indian wenches." I did not tell my mother Rosita became mistress of a brothel. Nor did I admit to myself that my lord was said to visit that house. That was tawdry gossip put about by those who would destroy me.

I told my mother that Pedro had a "cousin," a girl near my own age. "Léonor is amiable," I wrote. I said nothing of Paco's increasing fondness for Pedro's "cousin."

I wanted to paint a bright picture for my mother. I did not write her that I had failed as a wife, that I was not pregnant. It was difficult, that letter, and I did not trouble myself to write Mother again. It was only in postscripts, in Tio Francisco's letters, that she sent me her love. I know Uncle invented those words.

I began to wonder if Pedro was too old to have a son. He was twice my age and, though we shared one bed, he came late to me and was often more enamored of sleep than myself.

I remember that April night, the end of Carnival. I thought I had never been happier. We were merry with dancing and wine. I wore a gown cut low in the new fashion; Don Bernal had brought it from Spain, and he had just told me he planned to live in Santiago.

There was a loud knocking on the outer doors and all the company stood still, their heads turned to see what fresh surprise I had planned. I felt uneasy somehow, waiting for Négri to announce our unexpected visitors.

Rosita entered and I turned on Pedro angrily, believing he had invited the girl. Before I had time to reprimand my lord, I heard a familiar cackle of laughter. The gypsy stood behind Rosita—Belial, ragwrapped, swaying in her drunkeness. I screamed when I saw her and buried my face against Pedro's shoulder.

"Heathens, all of you!" Belial shouted. "You and your wicked lord be damned to Hell!" she cried. She came so close I smelled her foul breath. "Barren woman!" she hissed. "You are cursed, Beatriz. Your fine lord sows his seed where he wills."

Leering at Pedro, she thrust a bundle into my arms.

"Will you take his bastard, lady Beatriz?"

I heard Rosita's giggle. Boldly she addressed my lord. "Would this brat were mine, I'd have you hard then!"

Both women departed, quickly as they had come, and I swear the two are devil-spawned because not a gentleman there, not even my lord, dared detain them.

Pedro touched the bundle I clutched in my arms. "We will retire, Beatriz," he said quietly.

I followed him. I felt my burden's furtive movements and, before we unwrapped the rags, I knew what I would find.

She was too small, half-starved and filthy. She had a pale fringe of hair, and blue eyes. Her skin was white and I knew this was no gypsy's daughter. "Whose child?" I whispered, and I guessed his answer before my lord spoke.

"Mine," he said bluntly.

"She is not a year," I said, knowing my voice trembled. "Oh, my lord, could you not wait until we had our own?"

He would have comforted me but I did not want his hands on me. "No, Pedro—I will die if you touch me!"

Mustering what dignity I could, I told my lord to return to our guests, to tell them I felt unwell, that I would not dance again that night.

Alone then, I knelt above the baby and gave way to tears. I felt racked, broken in two. The child made no sound, but her small hands tangled themselves in my hair.

"The babe is hungry. She should be fed, my lady." It was Bishop Marroquin. He urged me to my feet.

"Take her away," I begged. "There is a convent where they will care for her. Take her now, please!"

Roughly I pulled free. The child cried out and reached for me. The bishop smiled. "She has chosen you, Beatriz."

"I have not chosen her," I said bitterly. "I want no child

but my own. Remove her, I implore you."

Bishop Marroquin bade me sit down. He gave me the child to hold. As soon as she was snug against my breast, she stopped wailing. I felt her fingers curl tight about my own. "I will not have her," I said.

The bishop knelt beside me. "For God's sake keep her, my lady. She was given to you with a curse. What will her life be if she is left so? Pity this small soul. Only you can save her, Beatriz."

The bishop's voice was gentle. "Receive this child, Beatriz; accept with love. Forgiveness is the gift you will bring to our Lord's altar."

"It is a sin to lie," I said. "I will never forgive Don Pedro. I am his queen and he has shamed me."

Anger choked me. "Forgiveness! It is mewly-mouthed preaching, my good Bishop. It is a lesson to keep women in their place. Would I be forgiven if someone placed my child by another man in Pedro's arms? Would my lord forgive me? No! I would be punished."

My anger disturbed the baby and she gave a sharp cry. I rocked her gently, gazing down at her. A week of good milk, a little caring, and she would be rosy and plump. Would she have her father's sun-gold hair? I wondered. Her small mouth opened and I held her close before she could utter a cry.

"I do not wish her harm," I said. "But, Bishop Marroquin, my distemper will poison her days. Give her to the Franciscan Sisters."

He shook his head. "You will keep her with love, Beatriz." He made the Sign of the Cross above us, then left us alone together.

I sat stiff, the babe quiet in my arms. I felt a thousand pains—my reason and emotions all entangled. I wanted to kill Pedro. For a terrible moment, I thought of killing his child.

My arms began to ache. The baby whimpered, and I removed her damp clothes and wrapped her in my silk shawl. But she would not sleep. Without forethought, as if I had a dozen children of my own, I undid my bodice and pressed the child's mouth against my breast. Her lips worked for the milk I did not have.

Then the thought came to me: If I play mother to this little one, will God relent and send me my own? If I could forgive Pedro, would God forgive me? My sins were many. I had cursed my marriage. I had imagined my lord dead and myself ruler of Guatemala. I had given myself to another before my marriage. I did not honor my parents. And—oh, mortal sin!—in my heart, Pedro was my one god.

I felt I drowned in my multitude of sins. For the first time I knew the soul's terror. I clutched at the small life in my arms.

Can I forgive my lord? I wondered. I had managed to accept Léonor. Could I live with this child too? I must take one step at a time, I thought, and I felt my fears recede. I began to know what I must do. I knew this child would haunt my days unless I looked on her with love. And a jealous woman is not pretty to behold—I would lose my lord's respect. I am queen, I told myself, I can afford forgiveness.

I relaxed, and the baby slept. She was snug in my arms and I was glad of her warmth. I don't know when it was that Pedro came for me. He moved on tiptoe, uncertain of my mood.

I beckoned him near. "She sleeps," I whispered. Then I said, "Her name is Anica." I know not where that name came from, but I knew it suited her. "Anica," I said again.

"You are not angry?" Pedro asked.

"I am wounded, my lord," I told him cooly.

He made a move to embrace me but I recoiled, feeling a distaste I could not conceal. "Not until I am healed," I said.

He swore he would see Belial caught and hanged.

"Leave the woman alone," I said, "she cannot hurt me anymore. What is done cannot be erased." My voice was steady and I was proud of my control.

Pedro looked at me intently. "You are greatly changed," he said, and he touched my shoulder, and left his hand, too heavy there.

I winced. "Please, my lord."

Then I said something that dropped Pedro's mouth open,

that reddened his face to the roots of his hair. "The child's mother—she is cared for?"

Pedro nodded, shamefaced. "But it was nothing, Beatriz—a night, and too much wine, I was befuddled and..."

I sat straight, clutching the baby against me that he would not see my hands. I wanted to claw his face! Instead I spoke softly. "We will not speak of this again, my lord."

"Never!" he swore. "Never again, Beatriz!" And his tone was so fervent, so sincere, I prayed my disbelief did not shadow my face.

CHAPTER 27

MY DIGNITY AND sweet manners in the ensuing days surprised everyone. Pedro kept the distance between us that I insisted upon, and I saw he regarded me with new respect.

I believed I had made a pact with God. If I kept Anica, God would give me my own child.

It was not easy. I wondered that I could walk about and smile as if nothing had happened. Now I understood those masks I had mocked at Valladolid; without such masquerades, humanity would dissolve in its own tears.

Jealousy is contemptible. Yes, I felt my passion indecent. Common sense told me I was Pedro's wife. What matter if he dallied with another, a slut whose name and face he would not recall? But I was hurt. I could not endure the thought of another woman in my lord's arms. I tried, but I could not forgive Pedro his indiscretion.

The baby Anica thrived. I could not deny her hunger for love. Her midwife was a pleasant Indian girl, too docile for Pedro's taste. I wondered about Anica's mother. Was the woman one of Rosita's whores? Paco has told me the girls in that brothel are from all walks of life, that not a few are beautiful.

"But you love Léonor," I told Paco, and I asked him why he must visit Rosita's house.

"It has nothing to do with loving," Paco said. "There are two kinds of women, Beatriz, and both are necessary to a man."

"One woman cannot be all things?" I asked. I wanted to know what Pedro found in another that I could not give him.

Paco shrugged. "A man has hungers, Beatriz. Call a brothel evil—it is a necessary evil."

"Garbage!" I exclaimed, and laughed aloud at Paco's startled face. I would have told him women suffer the same hunger, but young Juan came looking for me then, and I went off with him.

"Flirt!" my brother called after me. I tossed my head and pretended I did not hear him.

I wanted to hold my lord close again. But I had kept him at a distance and now I was proud. I wished him to come to me. Of course he would not; he was withdrawn, angry.

Paco spoke true: I had become a flirt. I smiled boldly, laughed too loudly. I played with Juan, and Pedro's other brothers, and with Don Bernal whose palace is not far from my own. There were nights when the loneliness in me drove me to stay awake until dawn, gambling and dancing. When Pedro accused me of conduct unbecoming to a queen I smiled mockingly. I pretended I did not care, though my body cried out for my lord.

I turned to outside diversions. I found release in bloody spectacles: mock Indian battles, or starved mountain beasts set against others of their kind.

"Fighting is not theater," Pedro chided. "Beatriz, you have grown cruel."

"Perhaps I have caught your disease, my lord," I said lightly, and would have left him if he had not grasped my hands.

"I leave within six weeks," he said.

Six weeks? I stared at him. But he had told me nothing! All this while he had been making plans and I—I had pretended he did not exist.

"But you cannot go, not yet!" I cried. "I need time, my lord." Yes, I thought, time to love him again.

"Time for what, Beatriz?" he asked and his voice was cold. "Oh, you play my gentle lady in public, but your door is locked against me. Your tourneys disgust me. As for your gallants—many of them will ride with me, young Juan included. Bernal remains behind to prattle love legends. You will be content, Doña."

"But I am not, Pedro! It is you I love, only you!" I longed to embrace him, but he stood distant, proud.

"Listen," I pleaded, "God has promised me that if I keep Anica, He will give us a child. God has heard me, Pedro!"

He spoke sternly. "God does not make bargains, Beatriz."

I stepped forward. "Believe me, I have forgiven you," I

whispered and, with those words, I felt myself melt, soft again. "I do forgive you," I repeated.

Pedro was unbelieving. "You would possess me, Beatriz. It is one mood, then another." He looked long at me and there were shadows on his face. "*Por Dios!*" he muttered, "I'd like to see you a woman grown!"

"But I am," I chattered, "I am changed, Pedro. You cannot leave me now."

He looked searchingly at me. Then he was matter-of-fact. "There are things I must settle. Paco wishes to marry Léonor. You will agree to this, my lady?"

"Anything," I said eagerly. "Pedro, we will have a grand wedding. It will take months to plan. You will help me." I was catching at straws.

He shook his head ruefully. "You are generous today, my lady. Yesterday, if I had suggested this marriage, you would have thrown the soup at me. What has changed your mind?"

"The threat of your departure overwhelms me," I confessed. "Oh, Pedro, try me! Stay, and see our son born!"

"In six weeks, and you not pregnant yet?" he taunted. "Unless—" his face clouded, "you return me some of my own medicine? Beatriz, if any man has touched you, I—"

"You will kill him?" I asked. I thought he had relented, but he stepped back from me. " No, Beatriz, all is not forgiven."

His rejection hurt me, and I took refuge in anger. "You want me on my knees!" I blazed. "My lord, it is you who are changeable, not I."

"Why must we hurt each other?" he asked. I saw his age fall full on him then. I wanted to roll back the years. "Let us begin again," I begged. He shook his head, and I saw he was not really listening to me.

Quickly then, before I changed my mind, I left Pedro and sought Bishop Marroquin. I told him I had given my consent to the marriage of Paco and Léonor. "God will bless me for this," I said.

The bishop regarded me gravely. "You seek to make a bargain of some kind, Beatriz. God will not be bought."

"He will give me a child," I insisted. "There is forgiveness in my heart and I have confessed my sins. God must forgive me now. That is your own teaching, good Bishop."

I knelt at his feet. "Always I have needed proof of God's love. If He gives me a child, I will know He is kind. Otherwise, I must believe God is cruel."

Bishop Marroquin put his hands on my head. "You must learn to accept whatever God gives."

"It is never enough!" I exclaimed. I covered my face to hide my shame. "Pedro leaves me now. He is angry. If God gives me a child—"

I wept, my head on the Bishop's knees. "I have endured so much. My courage fails me. Good Bishop, confess me. I acknowledge all my sins."

He stroked my hair. "All, Beatriz?"

"All but one," I whispered. "I place Don Pedro first, before God in my heart."

The Bishop sighed. "Idolatry is mortal sin, Beatriz."

Loving is sinful? I wondered. I must accept whatever ill befell me? Bow the head and bend the knees—it was a teaching I could never understand.

I stood erect. "I would sell my soul to keep my lord beside me!"

"Yes, Beatriz," the bishop said, and the pity in his eyes frightened me. "I understand, child. But be careful. There are those unlike yourself—they would condemn you for those words."

"Small hearts—devil take them!" I snapped. I saw his face stern then, and would have called my wild talk back.

"The walls have ears," the bishop warned.

"Oh, but I am tired," I sighed, "tired of holding my head high, of pretending—yes! tired of forgiving. My good bishop, I confess, I am weary of loving. I wish my heart cold as Pedro's own."

"He needs you, Beatriz," the bishop said, gently.

"Not in the way I need him," I protested. I knelt then, wanting a blessing. "Give me something to hold to," I begged.

CHAPTER 28

MY BROTHER'S BETROTHAL TO Léonor was publicly proclaimed. There was feasting and dancing, and a keg of wine stood at every street corner. All were merry except myself. Pedro's infidelity still cut deeply, and I could not think beyond the fact of his leaving me.

For days we had largely ignored each other. We were at dinner one evening, the officers and their ladies crowding the long table. Pedro was speaking of Léonor's betrothal. "The nobility of Old Spain withers in cousin wed to cousin. Here we make a new world, Beatriz—the best of Indian and Spaniard,"

He chuckled and nudged me. "Your blue blood is cold, my lady, it needs a peasant's heat."

"As you have melted me?" I parried, and slipped my hand into his under the table. I wanted his affection again.

But he withdrew from my touch. "There is one you have melted." he said carelessly. "I swear our guest, that young Mexican, Captain Luis Carlos, cannot take his eyes from you." Pedro nodded in the direction of a dark-haired officer.

I had noticed the young man, and his glances in my direction. "He looks a mere boy," I said. "Pedro, will you dance with me?"

He shook his head, made some excuse. "But Luis there—he is lately from Mexico. He will teach you the new steps, Beatriz."

I protested, but Pedro insisted. He summoned Luis who bowed gallantly and offered me his arm. He moved gracefully as a court noble and I told him so. Luis said he had been in Valladolid last year, and he proceeded to show me the latest fashion in dance. Soon I grew breathless. I told Luis I was anxious for news of home, and I asked him to bring me an ice.

"Wait for me," he told me. "I have messages from your family. Perhaps we can walk in the garden."

I looked through the crowd of dancers and saw Pedro

deep in conversation with several captains. I knew they spoke of the explorations so imminent now. Suddenly I wanted no more talk of departures, ships, and golden cities. I wanted my youth again, to treat lightly of that entanglement called Love. Yes, I decided, I would like to walk in the garden with this handsome officer.

The garden was misted, scented with ginger. I saw the faint paring of a new moon in the sky. Luis and I strolled the brick path and he told me of Tio Francisco.

"He is old, wary as a fox. He spoke often of you, Doña. Your uncle wonders if you found the kingdom he promised you."

I hesitated. Then I said, "Should you return to Valladolid, tell my beloved Tio I have my kingdom but—"

"But?" Luis pressed.

"I am hard put to defend it," I admitted.

Luis slid my hand into the crook of his arm. "Guatemala is yours?" he asked.

"Mine, and Don Pedro's," I replied. "But tell me of yourself, Luis. My lord says you are lately from Mexico." I glanced at him. "You are a Spaniard?" I thought his skin swarthy and his manners not quite refined.

He flashed me a smile. "If I tell you I am part Indian, will you run back to your castle, Doña?"

I pressed his arm. "We are all part Indian here, Luis. This country toughens us. Tell me, you are a conquistador's son?"

"Don Pedro knew my mother," He answered. "She was Luisa's friend."

He brought our stroll to an abrupt halt. He gripped my arms. "I did not think to find such a young woman," he muttered.

His hands were powerful and he stood too near me. "What do you mean?" I asked.

"Don Pedro's wife—when they told me, I thought her to be plump, a matron near his age. You—you are young and beautiful."

"Yes?" But I did not understand. "When who told you what, Luis?"

"Come." He pulled me down the path, to the end of it

where a low wall edged the ravine. We were deep in shadows—too far from the castle. "I would go back," I said, suddenly frightened.

He spoke in a low voice. "I have come to take you away. Do not be afraid, little Doña, I am no pirate. There are those who want you safe in Mexico City. I am to escort you there."

"Mexico City?" I swallowed to keep my voice steady. "I will not leave Don Pedro. Why should I? Who wants me, Luis?"

He gripped my wrists. "They want Guatemala—and you are Guatemala, Beatriz! We are to ride tonight—now, my lady, I have a caravan waiting."

"It is a kidnapping!" I exclaimed.

I saw it all clearly. They would take me to Mexico City, hold me for ransom. Pedro must pay for my return.

I stared at Luis. "Do you believe my lord would give them Guatemala for me? No! He would not! He would march instead. And see you—all of you, Luis, who plan this madness—hanging by your necks!"

He ignored me. "You must come quietly, Doña. I would not like to hurt you. But I am ordered to take you."

"And well paid," I flared.

His hands hurt my wrists. I glanced about us. Never have I felt so alone! No one would hear if I cried out. I struggled in Luis's grasp. "I will pay you more, much more—if you will let me go!"

"Come softly now," he said. He twisted me about, held me with one hand and pulled a scarf from his pocket. "I must bind your eyes."

I ducked and squirmed. But I knew my struggles useless. I thought quickly. I slumped against him. "I—I think I am going to faint," I said.

I heard him swear. He released me a moment. I turned about, pulled his sword from its scabbard.

"Ha!" I cried, and I set the swordpoint to his throat, driving him to his knees.

I saw his face, pale. The sword was heavy in my hand and I wavered. He thrust forward, his hands on my skirts. I heard something rip.

Luis was on his feet. "Give me that sword, Doña," he demanded. He grasped the blade and I pulled with all my strength. I cut him badly and he howled with pain.

But still he pressed forward. I grasped the hilt with both hands and drove the sword at his stomach. The blade slid smoothly in—I think it was the force of Luis coming at me. He staggered backwards. His heels caught on the wall and he fell. He tumbled backwards into the ravine. I stood there, numb, the sword bloody in my hands. I was weeping.

I heard footsteps and I spun about. I thought it was more kidnappers. But it was Juan, Pedro's brother. I dropped the sword and flung myself into his arms.

"Look what I have done!" I cried.

"Pedro sent me to look for you," Juan said. "But what has happened, Beatriz? I thought I heard scuffling. Your dress—who has done this to you?"

"It was the young captain," I blurted. "He was going to kidnap me, Juan. And hold me for ransom, in Mexico City—and Pedro must give them Guatemala, he said. And I killed him, Juan, I took his sword and I killed him! He fell—over that wall." I pointed where I did not want to look.

Juan strode to the wall. He stared down into the ravine. "If he fell there, Doña, he is dead now." He returned to my side. "I do not understand—Pedro give them Guatemala?"

"Never!" spoke a deep voice behind us.

"Pedro!" I cried. I ran to him, and stumbled on the fallen sword. He caught me. "What is all this, Beatriz?" he asked.

"Luis—he brought me here, he said he was going to kidnap me. He tried to put a scarf about my eyes and—and I pulled his sword. I killed him, Pedro."

I clung to him, the words pouring from me. "Luis said you would give them Guatemala for my safe return. Would you, Pedro? Would you have given your kingdom for me?"

"I would have had their heads first!" he exclaimed.

I managed a smile. "I told him so—that you would see them all hang!"

"And you killed him?" Pedro shook his head in disbelief.

"You pulled his sword and killed him?"

"She is brave," Juan said. "Most women would have fainted."

I laughed. "Yes—that is what I pretended, to be a woman—that I was faint and foolish. Then I drew his sword. Yes, I pretended—"

"To be a woman?" Pedro guffawed. "And what else are you, Beatriz?" His arms went round me.

"Your own lady, and that is different," I said, my eyes closed. I savored his embrace, I had been so long without it.

"True courage," Juan said. He picked up the sword, examined its blade and wiped it on the grass.

I shuddered, remembering how easily that blade had slid into the captain's flesh. "He came at me," I stammered. "There was nothing else I could do."

"What should you do but kill the bastard!" Pedro exclaimed. He broke from me and paced the path. I saw his limp pronounced; he looked so tired.

"Luis's mother was your friend, and Luisa's," I said softly.

"I cared for him like my own son," Pedro told me. "Indian bastards—turncoats—abound in this country now." He sighed. "It was not like this, in the beginning. I swear, these territories have bred jackals!"

I nodded at Juan and he withdrew. I took Pedro's arm and walked with him. "Luis was young, impulsive," I said. "Don't blame him, my lord. Treachery begins in high places. It is the Spanish captains who plot against you."

Pedro's mood was dark. "They were my friends." He smacked his fist into his palm. "My friends—now they would steal my wife, take my kingdom!" He gave me a sharp look. "The traitor didn't hurt you, did he?"

I shook my head. "He frightened me, that's all."

"That's all?" Pedro asked gently. He stroked my face, closed my eyes with his fingers. He kissed my eyelids. "Indeed, you are brave, my lady."

Behind his head I saw *Fuego* spin ribbons of fire. The mist had lifted and I could not count the stars in the sky.

"I am brave because I love you," I whispered. I heard a

rumble and I felt the earth tremble under our feet. "So little time left us," I murmured, "Pedro, you will leave me to earthquakes and kidnappers?"

"Because you will stand firm against them all, *querida*," he said, his face in my hair.

No, I cannot, I wanted to tell him, I am afraid without you. But that was foolish woman-talk; I could pretend to courage. "Yes, I will kill for you," I whispered.

Then the enormity of what I had done struck me hard, and I shuddered. "Don't tell anyone about this," I pleaded. "They will say I flirted with the captain, led him on." I was thinking of Belial, Rosita—the evil they would spread.

Pedro hushed me. "It will be our secret, Beatriz. I will let it be known young Luis left suddenly on a secret mission and..."

"But you will bury him, Pedro—he cannot just lie there, forgotten!"

Pedro held me close. "Child," he murmured, "woman-girl...who are you? You wail for a proper funeral when you should be knighted. Do you know you have saved Guatemala?"

"You would have given them your kingdom for my sake?" I asked. If that were true, I thought, that would be my knighthood! "Would you have done so, my lord?"

He hesitated. Pedro cannot lie directly to me. "I would have fought them all—and had Mexico City for myself. There's a kingdom for you, Beatriz!"

I touched the glint of his hair. Yes, he must fight—it is his way. And he would leave me, time and time again. His arms were hard about me now. "You are brave, my lady."

"Yes—oh, yes!" I lied.

CHAPTER 29

LÉONOR WAS RADIANT. We had become friends, but she had never dared speak openly of her love for my brother. Now, speaking of their marriage, we were close as sisters. She asked me why, when I had first come to Guatemala, I had so disliked her.

"I am jealous of your mother," I confessed. "Léonor, do you believe in ghosts? There are nights—I swear your mother haunts my bedchamber."

Quickly Léonor made the Sign of the Cross. "Mother was never unkind, Beatriz. Father is happy with you, and all Mother wished was Father's happiness. If she comes, she comes to bless you."

Léonor hugged me in her impulsive way. "Doña, you see too many ghosts. It is not healthy."

I looked at her face. Her eyes held a sparkle I envied. "What keeps you so content?" I asked.

"I am loved," she replied simply. "God loves me, and Paco too. And Father of course—and now you love me, Beatriz. What more could I want?" She spread her hands to the sunlight falling full into her lap.

"I always want more," I confessed. "And what I have I will lose, Léonor." I was near tears, thinking of Pedro. "I want a child now, a child will keep my lord with me."

She shook her head. "You have wed a Knight of Spain. His departure—there will be many, Beatriz, it is in his blood. Pray not for the child, but for his safe return."

But I ached with foreboding. I had begged Pedro for his promise that if I became pregnant, he would wait my nine months with me. To no avail—Pedro's heart was set on the Seven Golden Cities. His army stood ready to depart. He had folded his maps and strapped them into saddle bags. The provisioning was almost done. Far away, months behind our mountains, the tall ships awaited their captain. My heart was heavy, and my sleep disturbed. There were nights I dreamed my lord dead, calling for me, and I unable to go to him.

I grasped Léonor's hands. "Dreams are prophetic. If Pedro leaves now, he will not return."

"Such talk!" Léonor rose abruptly from her chair. She hitched her skirts and knelt to blow upon my fire.

"*Mamacita*, the afternoon is chilly, and your room too dark." She settled down beside me again. "Beatriz, be sensible. Only God knows the hour of our death."

"But Ana told me," I persisted, "Ana could interpret dreams. She saw the future in a crystal. She told fortunes in the lines of a hand."

"Ana?" Léonor asked.

"My old nurse. She was a wonder, Léonor." I pulled her near and spread my hand. "Look, it is all written there. Ana said I must make a choice. I might take the wrong turning, she warned. Yes—it is all written before we are born!"

"Foolish and forbidden," Léonor scolded. Then she saw my tears and relented. "I have dreamed, too," she said. "Yes, I dreamed a man like Paco, long before he came. Beatriz, our heads are full of dreams, it is a way girls have of making things seem true."

I remembered Alonso. He had stepped out of a picture book. Yes, I thought, and been taken from me. God would take Pedro too.

Léonor could not comfort me. At last, to quiet me, she said she, too, could tell fortunes. "Let me read your happiness, *mamacita*," she said. But first she went to make certain my door was locked.

"Speak in whispers," she admonished, bending over my hand.

"Yes," she said, tracing a line, "a choice to be made." She hesitated. Then, abruptly, she placed her warm hand on my cold palm. Her brown eyes probed my own. "A choice, yes—a man at the end of a path. It is not Father. But you give him gifts...." She shook her head, and sat silent.

"So?" I said bitterly. "I have made the wrong choice. Even now it is decided? Léonor, help me!"

She shook her head. "It is the past I see, Beatriz. I cannot see your future." She put my hand away from her. "We are behaving like children. Only God knows the future."

"It is you who pretend," I said sharply. "My hand

frightens you, Léonor. My future is black, isn't it? Or perhaps it is not there? *La Sin Ventura*, the Hapless One—am I she, that one without a future?"

Léonor would not answer me. "It is cold," she said, and pulled her shawl about her shoulders. Her lips were pinched tight, and I knew I had angered her. I knelt beside her. "Léonor, help me to keep your father here!"

"But he is a conquistador," she said. "Do not deny him his life, Beatriz. You must be brave, as Mother was. Wish him Godspeed and a safe return. Give Father your blessing."

I buried my face in her lap. "I am not brave," I said.

She lifted my face, wiped my tears with the hem of her gown. "Beatriz, *mamacita*—I have admired you so! Since the day you came here—I have wished to be like you."

I stared at her. "You—you have wished to be like me?"

She nodded. "Your manners, your beauty—the way you walk, Beatriz, your head high. Your ease with all the gentlemen, yes—you are always graceful. We all remark your courage, *mamacita*. And Father adores you—he has told me so many times." She sighed. "I am a clumsy brown-skinned bumpkin beside you, Beatriz."

"Hush! Hush, little one." I embraced her. It was my turn to dry her tears. "Paco worships you, and your father too. Your manners? Léonor, I have longed to be free as you—sunburned, without a care."

We held tightly to each other then. "You do help me," I whispered. "Léonor, teach me how to love."

"God gives love, Beatriz." She stroked my hair.

"And takes it away," I insisted.

A clap of thunder startled both of us. A shutter blew wide as if rude hands pushed it. A gust of wind snuffed the candles beside us.

"Ghosts," I whispered, "Léonor, listen!"

"I will make light again," Léonor said. She brought a burning stick from the fire and lit my tapers. She closed and bolted the shutters. "There now," she said briskly. She smiled at me. "I have something to give you," she said.

She removed a small crucifix from about her neck. She slipped the chain over my head. "It was my mother's," she said. "I want you to have it, Beatriz."

I felt the cross fragile between my fingers; the small pearls were set deeply in the gold. I let it drop, and it rested just above my emerald.

"I have been given a kingdom, and a cross," I said. "Will I be safe now, from hauntings, Léonor?"

"God will bless you," she said, and she kissed me. "Walk straight," she whispered, "look neither right or left. There is one who will tempt you to stray."

"It is in my hand?" I asked. Ana's words had been much the same.

Léonor laid a finger to her lips. She touched the cross. "I wish you good night, *mamacita*."

CHAPTER 30

THE WINDS OF THAT MARCH blew cold, and rain kept us indoors much of the time. "Just a few weeks more," Pedro told me. "Three mares must foal. Then I will depart."

I clenched my fists. "Horses be damned!" I cried. "Mares drop foals. Pigs, sheep, and rabbits give their litters. Only Beatriz fails to fulfill her task. Why, why?"

He was weary of the subject. "God's will," he said flatly.

"Then God is cruel!" I cried. I gripped the stone parapet of the balcony where we walked and my hands slipped on the mold. I felt the dampness of the air and the mountains rising close about me. "It is a tomb here, Pedro."

"It is your kingdom," he reminded me.

"I do not want Guatemala, Pedro. You are the only kingdom I desire. Stay, and govern as you should, my lord."

He shook his head. "Captain Pizarro prepares to invade Peru. I am told that upstart Ponce De Leon moves north of Mexico. It is rumored some stumbling monk has found the Golden Cities. I cannot stay at home, Beatriz. *"Tonatiuh"* is not so old he has become your lapdog." He sighed. "This is an old argument, and one you cannot win, Beatriz." His lips brushed my cheek and he left me.

My lord forgets love as easily as he sheds his gloves, I thought miserably. It was gold he craved, and conquering new lands. He will never need me as I need him. I knew nothing would delay Pedro now except the promise of his child.

I turned and looked straight up, and saw *Agua's* peak shrouded. Pedro had had the lower slopes burned. I recalled the blackhaired stranger. Did he really converse with the gods? I wondered.

I had forbid myself such thoughts. It was *Agua* frightened me now, its lake swollen with the rains. Was the stranger gone? What magic did he practice? Often, for no reason at all, my thoughts went to him. I could never recall his features, only the strength and surety of his being. I felt he held the key to a peace I sought. I stared up at *Agua*. Mist from the god-mountain soaked my slippers.

I knew I must not let my mind wander. I have always been curious. When I dared broach the philosophical question of God, or gods, only Don Bernal did not frown. Pedro, of course, forbade me such talk. And he is right—he and the other conquistadors have fought long and hard to establish our Christian God here in New Spain.

I began to pace the balcony. Still my mind dwelt on the puzzle. My maid servants had told me of prayers answered, wishes granted. Was it myth, or true magic? Indian gods or Christian God, I reasoned, both dealt favors or pain.

Suddenly Négri called me. "Doña, the woman Rosita is here. Will you see her?" His face evidenced great distaste for my visitor.

It was on the tip of my tongue to tell Négri to send Rosita packing, but curiosity prompted me to say, "Bring her out here, Négri."

She appeared, resplendent as a peacock, all her misbegotten jewels and laces displayed. "Doña," she fluttered, and would have knelt and kissed my hand but I thought her soiled, and I stood away.

"Rosita?" I wondered what on earth the woman wanted—except my husband. She had let it be known far and wide that she still thought Pedro the finest man alive.

"Ah, but I envy you, Doña," Rosita purred. "Your castle, your fine gown—and this balcony, it opens like an altar to the gods!

"See—" Rosita pointed, "straight ahead, across the valley—that is Fire. And up above us, the lake of dark water."

She giggled. "The giants sleep, praise God! Do the volcanos do your bidding, lady Beatriz? Does your lord believe he has put all evil to rest under his sword?

"A bloody sword," Rosita whispered. "And he goes forth now, to conquer again. What will you do, my proud lady?"

"Why have you come?" I interrupted. "My lord Pedro would be angry if he knew you were here." Always this painted whore had dominated me, and for the thousandth time I wondered why. I should have turned my back on her.

As if she read my thoughts, Rosita stepped nearer me. "I have come to help you, Doña Beatriz."

"What can you do for me—you, the mistress of a brothel—you are trouble, Rosita. I will not speak with you."

But I did not summon Négri. I said, for no reason at all except it was much on my mind, "It is God's will I have not conceived."

Rosita pointed to a bench at the far end of the balcony. "We will sit there," she told me. I obeyed her, and she produced a fan wide enough to hide our faces. "I bring a forbidden secret," she whispered.

Her musky scent enveloped me. I wanted to run, but I sat, paralyzed, and the whisper of Rosita's silks was like the movement of snakes.

"I know a witch, a shaman," Rosita said. "He can give life or take it, Doña. It is said he can change the color of a child in the womb." She tittered. "My Indian girls want fair-haired boys, and not a one has been denied her wish. Listen, Doña—he has brought twin girls from a barren granny. He has destroyed the seed of many a burdened woman."

I shuddered. I made the Sign of the Cross betwen Rosita and myself. "Only God can give or take a life," I said. "Your words are the mouthings of a heretic, Rosita."

She persisted. "You want a child, Doña?"

I nodded, "I would give my soul!"

"Yes," she breathed. "You must give a great deal of gold, Doña. All your jewels perhaps." She eyed the chains about my neck, the rings on my fingers. "Your emerald?" she asked.

"I have it," I said, unable now to conceal my curiosity. "Rosita, this shaman's powers—you do not lie?"

She shook her head. "Come with me tonight," she urged. "There will be a moon. It is not far from here. Set a candle in your window. When the castle sleeps; I will fetch you."

She stood, and her jewels caught the sun, blazing like fire on her neck and wrists. "Yes, Doña?"

"I am frightened," I whispered. "Witchcraft is forbidden.

The punishment is death by burning. But if," I faltered, "if your shaman can..."

"He can, I swear it, Doña. Tonight—" Rosita was gone. Just the heavy odor of her perfumes left behind, and one black feather dropped from her fan.

I ground the feather under the heel of my shoe. Back and forth, back and forth—I paced that balcony until my heart beat slowly again. I heard the easy laughter of Pedro's brothers. From the garden, Paco called Léonor, and a bird's trill answered him.

An Indian girl sang in the kitchen, and I thought I heard dried corn slide into a kettle. In a distant field, a sheep called its lamb. A rooster crowed. Good sounds and echoes, I thought and felt myself sliding slowly, far away. Could I come back again?

I heard my lord's voice, impatient. "Where is my lady Beatriz?"

"Here, *querido*, dearest," I whispered, and would have run to him straight away, but I hid myself instead—feeling a great shame.

CHAPTER 31

THE WATCH HAD CRIED the midnight hour when I set a small candle in my window. Wind doused the flame; again I lit the candle and again the wind insisted. A sign? I was reminded of that errant altar candle at my Wedding Mass. I tried again, and this time the flame stayed.

My maid servants snored on their pallets outside my closed door. Négri had come earlier to bring my lord's Good Night, and the message that he, Don Pedro, would sleep at Don Bernal's palace — the two gentlemen were reviewing plans for the forthcoming expedition. For the first time, I blessed my lord's imminent departure and all that kept him from my side this night.

My window showed a silvered sky, and I cursed the moon's brightness. I slipped on my boots and made sure my *tapado* was at hand, and my satchel of gold pieces. Any moment now, Rosita would scratch on my door. Unless this was one of her miserable jokes? Was it a trick? Perhaps Rosita had already informed the bishop that Doña Beatriz had consented to visit a witch? No — I had paid her nothing, she had no proof.

A cat's scratch at my door then. "Yes?" I barely breathed the question. Rosita whispered, "Come quickly, Doña."

The halls were dark rivers of shadows and I followed Rosita past the huddled shapes of servants and guards. I walked on tiptoe, my boots in my hand. My hand found the stair railing and, feeling for the first step down, I stumbled and cried out; Rosita hushed me.

At the bottom of the stairs I paused. Have I made the right choice? I wondered. I hesitated, glanced behind me. A finger of moon striped the steep stairs white. A ghostly Ana beckoned. Then Rosita called sharply.

The great doors swung open at her touch. I saw the steps flooded with moonlight and I drew a deep breath, and ran—down the steps, across the courtyard to the gates. I saw two horses saddled, waiting in the shadows. "Come, Doña!" Rosita was mounted, waiting for me.

Señorita whinnied and I touched her muzzle. The moon slid behind a cloud and I blessed the darkness, and wondered at the absence of guards. Rosita whispered, "Wine dulls the soldiers. Hurry, Doña!"

I mounted. Just as I picked up my reins, the moon moved bright as day. A voice froze me. "Doña Beatriz?" I heard Belial's laughter. "Where does my lady ride, so late at night?" I saw the flutter of her shawls. Her fingers snatched at *Señorita's* bridle.

Panicking, I raised my whip and struck the woman hard, twice. She gurgled, and fell. I thought I had killed her. There was no time to look. Rosita urged me to follow her.

We rode quickly between the shut houses, the bulked silence of the convents, the cathedral whose spires pierced the moon's belly.

"Ave María!" I breathed, the churches left behind me, and the Bishop's Palace, and Don Bernal's dark windows. Soon the cobblestones ended, there were no more dwellings, and *Señorita's* hooves thudded on a dirt trail.

I recognized the path. It was here I had ridden with Pedro. He had forbid me to travel it again. I bit my lip and kept my eyes staight ahead, riding in Rosita's dust.

"Ride, Doña!" She whipped her horse to a gallop. I kept close behind her because my head spun dizzily. I rode clumsily as a rag doll.

We rode straight up the slope of *Agua*. Once, *Señorita* stumbled. I almost slipped from her back. Rosita looked back at me. "You are afraid!" she jeered.

I waved her on. We splashed through a stream. We climbed; then, abruptly, we descended into a narrow chasm. Huge boulders cast misshapen shadows. A fire flicked, suddenly, from the dark, and *Señorita* shied, almost throwing me.

"We are here, Doña." Rosita's breath came hard as my own. She flung her reins to a tall Indian whose presence startled me. He was naked except for a gold shaft like a dagger between his thighs. He reached to take my reins and his hands gave a strange heat. I flinched.

Rosita mocked my fear. "He is not the witch. Give him your horse, Doña. He and I will wait outside. Unless you are afraid to enter the cave alone?"

I hesitated. Even now I could change my mind. Perhaps it was Rosita's taunting that made me raise my chin, square my shoulders. "I will go in alone," I said, and turned to face the jagged opening in the cliff.

I walked blindly, through a short tunnel. So silent it was I imagined death like this—dust, quiet, and darkness. I simply walked forward.

Then I saw firelight. I stood at the threshold of a room carved round as a globe. Slowly I walked toward that fire, to the man who stood waiting there. He spoke softly. "Welcome, Doña."

Of course! I had known it would be he. Swiftly I closed the space between us. I smiled. He was wearing his white tunic; I saw the blue stones on his fingers, and his hair dark and heavy.

"I came," I said, feeling suddenly shy, childish.

He nodded. "You have chosen."

"It was not easy," I said breathlessly. "I would walk through Hell to give my lord what he desires."

He smiled. "To have what you desire, Doña."

I blushed. "I have brought you gold," I said, giving him my satchel.

"Sit here with me." He indicated a pile of silk cushions.

I sank down beside him. I could not take my eyes off him. "You are not Indian," I said. "You are an outcast, but you have the manners of a gentleman. You are a shaman—yes. Tell me, who are you?"

He spoke so low I must lean forward to catch his words. "I am Master of Dreams. I keep the keys to Paradise. I am whoever, whatever you wish, Doña, at your service.

"Now —" he spread his hands, "tell me your desire."

He spread a thick rug across his pillows, and he motioned me to sit nearer. "Your desire," he repeated softly. His eyes slanted, more gold than brown, and so seductive I could not look away. I drew a deep breath.

"I am barren," I confessed. It was strange, in his presence I felt no shame. With him there was no reason to pretend.

It was then I heard Rosita's giggle, and a man's murmur. Rosita gave a small yelp of pleasure. I made to rise to my feet. "This is a wicked place," I said.

He made no move to keep me there. "Whores, too, have their desires," he said. "I attempt to provide all answers."

He gave me a deep look then. "You are too afraid to seize your own dream, my lady?"

"I am here," I reminded him, and I sat still again. We were silent a moment, then I could not contain myself. "But can you give me what I want?" I demanded.

"What do you want?" His voice was kind, almost moving me to tears.

"My lord's love," I said. "If I give Don Pedro a child, I will have his love forever. Can you do this for me?"

"Love forever, or a child?" the shaman asked.

Was he mocking me? I wondered. I spoke angrily: "A child of course!"

He did not respond, nor did he remove his gaze from me. I found his quietness soothing. He gave no hint of evil intention, and I wondered at his claim to witchcraft.

"Is it magic that makes life?" I asked. "Perhaps it is not God at all?"

He smiled then. "Who is your god, my lady?"

"My lord, my husband," I whispered.

The shaman flexed his long fingers, and I thought the blue stones were like pieces of sky fallen into his hands.

He said, "It appears your god cannot give life."

He reached to lift a cup from the coals. "You will drink this. It is brimful of life."

I put my fingers to the carved rim. It was hot, and I hesitated. "You will not hurt me, sir?"

Gently but firmly he held the cup to my lips. Obediently I swallowed all the amber-colored liquid. Was it God's wine, I wondered, or the grapes of wickedness? I drank it down, tasting both bitter and sweet.

Almost immediately I was drowsy. I stretched my eyes wide open, fixed on the shaman. I had been frightened, but now I relaxed.

From out of a deep softness I heard his words: "Shape your desire from your dream, my lady. I am with you. Tell me of your pain."

"A child," I whispered. "My lord will love me then. He

will not leave me if I am with child." I clutched the shaman's hands because my head was spinning.

"Speak truth," he said. "Your desire is love."

I thought he scolded me—like the others, he would tell me I was too greedy. I gripped his hands. "I will lose my love!"

"No," the shaman said, "love cannot be lost."

"I will throw it away—yes, I am careless, sir, Ana said so, and Mother too, that I want too much! I have sinned. I wanted a crown, I have wished my lord dead." The words poured from me.

The shaman sat silently for a long time. Then he said, "Name your beloved, Doña."

"Don Pedro," I whispered, and I felt that name through me, coursing with my life's blood.

"Your sun and moon," the shaman said, his voice like an embrace. I knew he understood me.

"I cannot lose the sun and moon," I said, smiling through my tears.

"Of course not," he agreed.

"It is my love gives me life," I said. And then I asked him. "I am not wicked to feel so?"

I felt the wine's glow fading. "I would sit here forever with you," I said. "Is it your potion lends me peace?"

"The mixture clears the head, Doña. Magic is truth, and truth is magic."

He leaned forward. "My lady, there is no forever. Hold to the moment only, and rest content."

"Yes—yes!" I understood what he meant. "When I am confused, I will speak love's name until I feel it through me."

He nodded. I thought his eyes saw deeply into my soul. He stood, and raised me to my feet.

"And the potion?" I asked. "I will have my desire?"

"You have what you came for," he said simply. "Search your heart, my lady, what you want is written there."

"But your potion," I insisted, "it is more than mere wine?"

"Whatever you wish. What you believe, so be it, Doña."

I held tightly to his hands. There was such life to him! It

was all so uncomplicated. I sensed he moved through many different worlds, and judged no one, and understood all. I did not want to leave him.

Did he divine my yearning? Because he said, "There are no goodbyes, Doña."

I did not understand and I told him so.

He repeated the words: "There are no goodbyes. Whenever you wish, think of me and you will return here. What you have known is yours to keep."

I understood. Remembering can be magic, he was telling me that, what has been mine is always mine. I said, "You are wise, not evil."

"I am devil-spawned," he said. But his eyes were full of mischief and I knew he teased. Then he was serious.

"Not a word of this," he warned, "if you wish, you could destroy me."

"I could never hurt you!" I exclaimed.

"No, it will not be you," he said slowly. Then, with a gesture that held such tenderness in it tears started beneath my eyelids, he smoothed a lock of hair from my forehead.

His hand on me, he hesitated. Then he said, "I ask you to take care of yourself." He pressed my hand to his lips. "Do not weep for me."

What did he mean? I had a sense of wrenching loss. "I cannot say goodbye!" I cried.

He put my hands from him. "You take what you need with you, Doña."

"Yes—yes, I will!" I said, knowing with a rush that I could not forget him. And I knew also that I had what I had come for.

"Love, or a child?" he had asked me. I knew now I held the one, and the other must follow. If not—so be it. All this time I had held my desire, right in my hands, in my heart. Was it the potion or the shaman who had shown me truth? I did not know, but I was certain gold was a small price to pay for all I had received. I wanted to give him something I treasured.

I removed my emerald and my crucifix from about my neck. "Take these," I begged, "please. In memory of me." I gave my jewels into his hands.

He flinched as if my gifts scorched, and dropped them on the ground. "Your jewels mark me," he protested.

"Keep them," I insisted and, before he could answer, I left him quickly. I did not look back. I returned through the tunnel without a thought of darkness or death. My heart exulted. I knew I had my lifelong wish.

"Pedro!" I spoke love's name aloud.

Eagerly I stepped outside—to find the moon gone and a greying sky. Rosita and her horse had vanished. *Señorita* waited alone. I should have wondered then if some evil was not brewing, but I felt refreshed, excited. I mounted quickly and turned my mare's head towards home.

I fairly flew, seeming to know the trail surely. I knew I would not fall. Santiago was still dark, its streets deserted. I believed I was home safe, and no one to guess my secret. The shaman's magic had made me a child again. I believed the world good.

I saw a torch burning at Don Bernal's gate, and I urged *Señorita* until her hooves clattered on the cobblestones. The castle loomed like a storm cloud. Were the guards sleeping? And Rosita? Her raw desires attained, did she sleep?

It was when I reached the gates that Hell itself spilled like an avalanche upon me. Belial waited. "The lady Beatriz comes at last!" she shouted.

Her cry brought soldiers to swarm about me. Torches blazed. The castle doors opened. Pedro descended the steps two at a time. "Beatriz, in God's name where..."

"She has been with the witch," Belial screeched.

Pedro grasped my stirrup leather. "Where have you been? I returned early and found your bed empty."

"There is mud on her!" Belial shouted. "She has lain with the shaman. Do not touch her, my lord."

The woman fluttered between Pedro and myself. He pushed her from us. She would not be stilled. "The devil-lady struck me with her whip. I tried to stop her, to warn her. Hah! See how I bleed for my pains!" She lifted her blouse.

I saw the welts I had inflicted on the wretch. What

wickedness she spoke! Then I saw it all clearly: it was a plot, Belial to sound the alarm, and Rosita to lure me where I should not go. I sat limply on my horse, staring down at the acccusing faces.

Pedro put his hands to my waist and I felt his fury through his hold on me. "Dismount, go inside," he muttered, "I will come to you later."

Fatigued, I clutched at my lord. "It was for you I went there," I whispered. "Indeed, sir, there is no harm done." He must believe me, I thought, if he loves me he will believe me.

His eyes were flat blue, merciless. "You were forbidden, Beatriz. I would not have believed it, but Rosita summoned me—" his words were like gloved hands slapping me—" she said you rode past her inn, galloping wildly, and she went after you. She dared not go where you led her, Beatriz."

I was aware my body trembled as if I had fever. "Rosita lies," I said.

Pedro's voice thundered above my thin protests. "Whorehouse or Devil's fire? Which one tempts you, woman? I am told this shaman traffics with all evils." He almost struck me.

"They would turn you against me, my lord. Look at me!" I begged.

Pedro's face was grim, closed against me. "Cursed be that day I took you to wife," he said.

I looked about me and I saw that there was not a man or woman there who failed to hear those bitter words.

CHAPTER 32

"SHE HAS LAIN WITH THE SHAMAN." Belial's words. There was none in the castle dared accuse me outright, but I knew the gossip was vile. I kept to my rooms. I recalled that long-ago time when the girl, Beatriz, had loved a young Alonso and that love had been branded sin. I did not weep now; I waited for those close to me to come, demanding truth. They must believe me.

But Léonor did not answer my summons. Anica was removed from my room. My maid-servants were cowed, frightened of being near me.

Négri served me, his face ashen and his eyes filled with tears. "If you had told me, my lady, I would have gone with you, and had you home safe—no one the wiser. Why did you follow Rosita, Doña?" Négri said. "She is evil."

Bishop Marroquin persisted. "Why, Doña, why?"

"Because I would give all I have, my soul if I must, to give my lord a child," I answered.

"We must save your soul," the bishop said earnestly.

I stared at him. "Holy Father, you cannot believe that I..."

"God help you, Doña," he prayed.

I stood accused and convicted. From my tower room I watched Belial; her fire blazed bright beside her makeshift shelter near the gates. I knew she mocked me—even in the rain she stood, her head thrown back, her tattered hair streaming, her laughter like a crow's cawing.

My lord came to me at last. His questions hammered at me. He was deaf to my truth.

"Why did you do it? Where is this shaman, Beatriz?" His voice was harsh and his hands hurt my shoulders.

"Give me the witch, Beatriz!"

"What will you do with him, my lord?"

"Burn him," Pedro said. He leaned above me, his face heavy with pain and anger both. His fingers circled my throat. "I could kill you," he said hoarsely. "Confess: did the shaman touch you, Beatriz?"

"You have been drinking," I protested, "Pedro, you have

not changed your clothes since—since—"

"Since he had you—like a whore, eh? Rosita has confessed her visits there. Speak, woman!" Pedro slapped me twice, the flat of his hand bruising my cheeks.

"A cup of wine," I whispered, "there was some talk of you, my lord, no more than that, I swear it!"

He shook me, my hair fell loose. My gown slipped. His weight pressed me to the floor. He crouched above me, tearing at my laces until they snapped.

"The truth," he rasped, "a cup of wine, loving talk—what else? Was it good, Beatriz?"

"No more than that," I gasped.

"Bitch!" he moaned. I thought he would strike me again. The pressure of his lips on mine forced my mouth open. I tasted blood. Then he slumped, heavy on me, and his face changed from fury to grief.

"Why? Why?" he asked me. A sob broke from him. I stretched my arms to him.

His hands were rough, probing as if he sought the shaman somewhere hidden in me. He tore my clothes from me. He bit my breasts until I cried aloud. He spread my thighs and entered me, so slow and deep I felt him through me like a knife. He stayed, unmoving.

"Why, Beatriz, why?" His voice broke.

He lay full on me. His balled fists thrust behind the small of my back, lifting me to him. Tears between us, and blood. Sweat on my tongue, sour wine in my nostrils. I hurt, and then the pain left me, and I swung high to meet his passion. He knelt. I locked my knees about him. I swear there was no space in me that did not know him then. He gave a great shout. I felt ripples through me and I held to him, not wanting him to leave me.

"Stay, love," I whispered. And, this time he did. I do not know how long we lay entwined there, on that hard floor.

"Pedro—my lord," I breathed his name over and over again. This is the spell, I thought, his love like warm wine, filling me.

It was he who moved first. His eyes burned into mine, and I thought I had him back again. I sat, and reached my arms to him. He stood naked before me and I stretched my hand that he might help me rise.

"Pedro?"

His laughter mocked me. "In truth, you are bewitched," he said, "I've never known a lady take so to rutting." He spat the last ugly word, turned his back and left my room.

CHAPTER 33

FOR FOUR LONG WEEKS I heard the hunting horns and the dogs. I knew that every hut and cave was being searched for miles around. Pedro rode day and night; his brothers too, and Paco mustered his own hunting party. The net must close on its prey, I knew that—the shaman and I would be brought face to face.

Near the end of that time, in the fifth week, I felt ill. The food Négri brought me—it was like swallowing raw fish, and I vomited. Dogs and horses in the courtyard below and their stench made my head ache. I prayed to my Virgin, prowled my tower room and prayed again asking refuge for my Master of Dreams. I would not call him witch or devil.

I mourned, dry-eyed, for the hunted man, and for the love I had lost. The shaman is wrong, I thought, nothing would be the same between my lord and me. Ana had predicted true: willfully I had discarded the pearl, I had lost God's path.

A blood-red sunset, the end of April. It was Négri who told me they had found the shaman. My jewels buried in the sand floor of his cave convicted him. Rosita had confirmed his identity, Négri told me, and Belial had pronounced the shaman evil. Both women swore by all that is holy that I had begged a potion, a visit to the witch.

"Rosita invents—she knew the trail to the cave blindfolded," I said. "Belial has poisoned my lord's mind."

Négri said, "Rosita will be whipped. They will burn the witch. Don Pedro insists you will be present at the execution."

"I will not be!" I cried. "Négri, I would rather die than stand there looking on at such a spectacle!"

He touched my sleeve. "My lady, you will stand there—like the queen you are. It is you who must accuse the witch of evil.

"Doña," Négri pleaded, "your lord is like a wild man. His mind is crazed with ugly tales. If you do not attend, they will say you are afraid. Such talk will brand you guilty."

I was seized by cramps. Négri summoned my maids. I went to bed, pulling the heavy curtains tightly around me. "Leave me," I ordered. I heard the door close.

I lay still, my eyes wide. My cramps subsided. I folded my hands on my belly, as if to keep the pain from entering again. I must think—think of the fire tomorrow, of the shaman approaching....

I must think—his face. I saw it clearly before me then, that heavy hair, his golden eyes. Not a hint of reproach in those eyes.

"You do not blame me?" I think I spoke aloud.

He shook his head. He spoke so softly I held my breath to listen. "We will meet again, there is no ending, Doña. Remember that."

My cheeks were wet with tears. I lay quietly, not wanting to lose the image I had conjured.

"You will die," I said. "It is my fault."

"You blame yourself, sweet lady. Always you blame yourself."

I raised my hands to the shadow of him. "I will never see you again!"

I saw him smile. "You have forgotten so soon? When you want me, think of me. It is that simple."

"I am thinking of you," I said

"Thus, I am here." He spread his hands, and I saw that glint of blue I would remember.

"Promise?" I asked. "We do not lose each other?"

"We never lose each other," he replied.

"You give me my forever!" I sat up in bed.

"My lady, I give you the moment."

"Oh!" I flung myself back against my pillows. "You speak in riddles!"

"If you wish," he said.

He was leaving me. I saw only shadows.

"Stay!" I cried. I shut my eyes and thought hard on him. "I want to know if you are afraid. Tell me you are not afraid of tomorrow."

He came again. "How do you see me, tomorrow, Doña?"

"Not afraid, not you—not ever afraid," I said.

"It is all as you feel it," he said. "I am going now. You will let me go."

He was not a ghost. I conjured him real as the hand I hold now before my face. I knew he would not be afraid of death. Perhaps he did not call it Death? He gave other meanings to words.

I wanted sunlight then. I pushed my curtains back. I slipped from bed and stood, barefooted, on the floor. I thought of Pedro. I felt his agony, his love for me. I would stand there with him tomorrow. Because I loved him I would do his bidding. And someday, my lord would see me clearly again.

"It is a kind of magic," I whispered.

I knelt at my window, the sun on my face. "I won't forget, will I?" I asked the blue sky.

CHAPTER 34

I HAD PRAYED FOR RAIN, but that day dawned cloudless. Fever had come on me in the night, and my limbs ached. Two silent maid-servants brought me a scarlet gown. "Not that one," I said.

Her eyes downcast, one of the girls explained Don Pedro wished me to wear that dress. I was to wear my rubies too, she said, and the golden crown used only for state occasions.

I nodded, and stood numbly for the stays and petticoats, the stockings and brushed boots. Without a word, I offered my face for the white powder, the paint brush, the warm pink wax.

The very ritual of dressing lent me strength. Hair oil, and the pins and combs. Lace at my throat, and a ribbon tied. My fan, my prayer book, my rosary, and a small vial of camphor lest I faint.

When my lord knocked, I was ready. He was in somber black, enlivened only by the gold cross about his neck, the glint of his short sword. Unsmiling, he wished me good day, and offered me his arm. "We will walk together to the Plaza," he said.

Black banners shrouded the trees. The tall Virgin from the Cathedral had been placed on a makeshift altar. Her round glass eyes looked directly at the stake which was piled high with dry wood. I wondered where the pigeons had flown, and I missed the preening rustle of doves. Someone had stoppered the fountains.

All my Court were present; I felt their eyes on me, and I longed for a veil. Léonor wore the mourning yellow, and I blessed her courage. She pretended not to see me.

I looked for Belial, but did not find her. Then I heard a cackle above me and I looked up and saw the woman sitting astride a wall nearby.

"Devil's whore!" she screeched, pointing at me. Pedro gave her a look that silenced her; his face was flushed, and I heard titters from the crowd.

"I will not dishonor you, my lord," I whispered, and I climbed the steps of the pavilion prepared for Pedro, myself, and the Council. There were two chairs and Pedro offered me one. I shook my head. "I will stand beside you," I said.

An interminable time it was until a trumpet sounded, the priests said prayers, and Rosita was brought before us. Her blouse was torn, knotted about her waist, and she crossed her arms to hide her naked breasts.

Ignoring me, she knelt to Pedro. "Forgive me, my lord," she whispered.

Bishop Marroquin stepped forward and raised Rosita to her feet. He kissed her on both cheeks, and then told her to kneel again. She crouched at his feet, unmoving, throughout the long Mass. It was when the bishop offered Rosita the wine that she moved. She knocked the cup from his hands. She pointed at me.

"I am ignorant and poor." she cried, "It is she who should be punished."

Without a word Pedro recovered the chalice; he summoned the guards. The soldiers dragged the struggling Rosita to a post where they chained her cruelly, exposing her back.

I wrenched off my cloak. "Let me cover her," I begged, and would have run forward, but Pedro held me back.

He gave me the chalice. "If you must weep, fill this cup with your tears," he said.

I shut my eyes. I heard the whip's whistle slice fifty times. I thought Rosita fainted, she was so still. I did not look until it was over, and Rosita taken away.

Pedro was looking at me. "She is brave," he said. I could only nod. He took the chalice from my limp fingers. Then he spoke sharply to his soldiers, giving orders to bring the witch.

So many people crowded there, but their sighs were as one gust of wind when the shaman was brought into the center of the Plaza. I felt dizzy and bit my lip hard, and tasted blood.

He wore his white tunic, unadorned. I saw the turquoises on his fingers, and his hair was as I remember.

He resembled a carving I had seen once, gracing an antique bowl. Again I puzzled on the history of this man: he seemed to own no time or place, belonging to all times, all places.

His bare feet were hobbled with a chain and his hands bound, but he walked strongly forward and kneeled before my lord.

"May I speak?" he asked.

My heart quailed, I forgot for a moment that this prisoner was my friend; I imagined the tales he might invent. In that instant I saw clearly what he had taught me: what I believed him to be, he became: now he wore a witch's face. Then I saw him clearly again.

He smiled at me. "You will learn, my lady."

Pedro's hand slapped to his sword hilt. Again the shaman smiled. "Patience, Don Pedro, I will not be long."

Pedro cursed. Bishop Marroquin mumbled a prayer.

The shaman raised his head, and his voice rang strong to the far corners of the *Plaza*. "I am the future—take heed! Don Pedro, Conquistador, put by your sword. May your lady beware the dark waters!"

There was a hush over all. Then Pedro shouted, "Burn the witch slowly, in Hell's own fires!"

The shaman bowed. Bishop Marroquin spoke quietly to him, but he shook his head, his face serene. He looked at me. "I have no need of Christian blessings."

Alone, unsupported, the shaman approached the stake. He did not flinch when he was strapped. A soldier lighted an oil-soaked torch and looked to Pedro for the command.

My lord asked for the Holy Bible. He placed the heavy book in my hands. "Tell us, Doña Beatriz. Recognize the prisoner. Is he man or witch?"

I looked at the bound shaman. I spoke direct to him. "He is everyone, each of us. He is what you believe him to be."

"Witchcraft!" Pedro exclaimed.

He leaped down the steps and snatched the torch from the soldier. He touched the flame to the dry wood and it caught, ravening.

The shaman slept. I swear he slept long before the smoke swallowed him, and the flames. I saw his face, still and quiet. It was his own magic. He discarded his body before the fire consumed it. I felt his flight: a soft, certain release.

I stood and watched until it was all done, even the stake charred black. I knew my shaman had eluded pain—he was gone to another place. I felt no sorrow or horror, only relief.

Pedro touched me. "You feel nothing, my lady?"

"It is over," I said. I saw a singed turquoise in the white ashes of that fire.

Pedro took the Bible from me and I felt my hands numb from its weight. He kissed me, cool on both my cheeks. He said, keeping his voice low, "If it had been otherwise, you would have begged me to abstain. You are not so unkind, my lady. If the gossip ran true, you would not have permitted his execution."

"I have told the truth, Pedro," I said, and I fainted.

When I regained consciousness I found myself in bed, my ladies all about me. There were bowls of hot water, and more bowls packed with ice. From my waist down I was frozen, bound in cold cloths. "Why? What happened?" I murmured.

Léonor wiped my face. I smelled her cloth sweet, scented with lime. I saw she had been crying. "What is it?" I asked. "Am I hurt somehow?"

I glimpsed the blood-soaked rags before Léonor could hide them. "Am I bleeding?"

"You have miscarried, *mamacita*," Léonor said. "It was scarcely a month, Beatriz. You have lost the child."

CHAPTER 35

MAY 19, 1541. I had not yet recovered from the loss of the child when Pedro summoned the Municipality of Guatemala and announced his departure. He named Paco as interim-governor. Being unwell, I did not attend that meeting but my brother told me about it. I sent Négri to summon Pedro to my chamber.

"Why didn't you name me Interim-Governor?" I demanded, when my lord and I were alone.

Pedro gave me a half-smile. "When a Captain General must leave a woman in command—that is the end of the Empire, the finish of Captains General everywhere."

His remark angered me. "I am not just any woman, my lord. I am Beatriz de la Cueva de Alvarado, your wife, and queen of Guatemala. Or so it was you promised me."

He nodded heavily. "I did promise, many things...."

He looked so weary I ached to comfort him. But he avoided me. "I asked only peace, Beatriz. You have brought me passion, torment .."

"And love," I whispered, but he appeared not to hear me.

"You were a girl," he murmured, "an impulsive girl...."

"But old enough to be your given wife," I flared. "Old enough to voyage with you into another world—do you remember, Pedro, how hard it was, and strange to me? You did not consider me too young to sit at your table, matching my wits with your gentlemen, and conducting those tasks concerning your kingdom. Indeed, I recall, you were proud of me.

"My lord," I continued, "for more than two years I have tended your affairs. I have cared for your daughters as if they were my own. Placing my soul in jeopardy, I conceived your child, and lost that child.

"Am I too young, Pedro?" I demanded. "Once you praised my intelligence, you said I was beautiful. It was I you chose to be the mother of your sons."

"It was not wise to seek the shaman, Beatriz," Pedro said. "Santiago is rife with ugly rumors. The Indians gather openly, they are hostile. They say a Christian queen has forsaken her God for theirs. I have told you many times, we must be united in our efforts to erase the old beliefs. Beatriz, have you forgotten you are wife to a Conquistador, a Christian knight?"

I spoke softly. "I would pass through Hell to give you your desire. I am a woman in love, Pedro."

"A foolish girl," Pedro scoffed. "You have placed us all in danger."

He turned from me and went to warm his hands above my fire. I heard him mutter, "Dear God, I would be gone from here!"

I went to stand behind him. I placed my arms about his waist, and pressed my cheek against his unyielding back.

"I am frightened now," I said. "Bishop Marroquin says our child is in Limbo. Unbaptized, our child wanders, Pedro, forever shut away from God. Am I to blame, or you, my lord?"

He faced me square. "Was it the Devil's child, Beatriz?"

"Ah! There is the crux of all our misery—your infernal jealousy! Pedro, have you forgot? We made that child, you and I—in this room, on this very floor, my lord!"

He looked at me, and I knew he remembered. I saw the struggle in his eyes. Perhaps he does not want to remember, I thought, for some reason of his own he must blame me for what is both our faults.

I remembered the shaman's magic, and I asked Pedro, "How do you think of me, my lord, how do you see me?"

He scowled. "I try not to think of you at all, Beatriz." He put me from him. "Dress yourself, my lady, and come down. There is much to be done."

In public, Pedro pretended all was well between us. He lent me his support in those ensuing days when I must face the Court—their prattling tongues, accusing eyes. There are those, even today, who will not kiss my hand for fear of touching evil. Some call me "harlot." I am accused of heresy.

Léonor was cool towards me. Even Paco had deserted me. I think Bishop Marroquin believed me. But then the good bishop sees no evil in anyone.

One night, as Pedro was leaving my bedchamber after a perfunctory kiss, I delayed him. "It is unkind," I protested, "why bother with a kiss at all?"

"The castle has eyes and ears," he replied. "If it should reach Spain that there is trouble between us, the Crown could withdraw its support. I need you, Beatriz de la Cueva. It is your name will hold Guatemala while I am absent."

"My name! That was all you ever needed," I cried bitterly. "I have lived a masquerade, Pedro! You have pretended since the beginning."

It was then I asked him the whereabouts of my jewels: the emerald and Leonor's crucifix. "I want my own returned to me," I said.

"Your jewels are become the Devil's tools," he told me. "I have locked them away."

"And your heart too," I said.

Day upon day, the distance grew between us. To remain queen of Guatemala I needed Pedro, thus I pretended too. I was docile, devoted, and seemingly enraptured by my lord's boasting of his eighty ships, his several hundred horses, his thousand soldiers. My heart was nigh breaking, but no one guessed my pain.

"You leave me undefended," I told Pedro. It was the end of May, the night before his departure for the port of Acajutla where the fleet awaited him. "How long must I rule, alone, without you, my lord?"

"You forget you are Beatriz de la Cueva. You have the king's ear. My people will respect you—they must, for their own good." He gave a hearty yawn and then, to my amazement, he flung himself across my bed.

I said nothing. I didn't want to frighten him away. I pulled a cushion near the bed and sat upon it.

I leaned my head back, near his hand. "I could lead your army, Pedro," I whispered. "Together we will find the Seven Cities."

"No—" his hand was on my head and I scarce dared breathe. "Santiago has need of a noble queen." He stroked my hair. "I will send you a sheet of gold for your mirror, *querida.*"

The endearment came easily to his lips, and I wondered, as always, at my lord's ability to slip in and out of loving moments. And myself? I felt my body soft again, and my cheeks hot.

"My duty lies here," I whispered. His rough fingers were smoothing my cheek. "I will do what you ask. But—oh, Pedro—" I seized his hand, "if you would send for me!"

He lay silently. I held his fingers to my lips. I wished we could stay like this forever. The fire crackled; I heard the wind in the castle walls. Tomorrow would be cold. I shivered. "I feel winter already," I said, "and you not yet gone."

I knelt beside the bed. I wrapped my hair about his wrist, binding him tightly. "You are my prisoner," I teased.

He sat up. "Come here, beside me."

We lay across the bed, my head on his arm. I dared not speak. My lord had not been so gentle in many days.

"Beatriz?" He raised himself on an elbow and looked down at me. "Will you love me tonight?" His words came slowly. I did not remember his ever asking me like this before.

I hesitated. Perhaps he was feeling sorry for me?

"There is no need to pretend now," I said. "You must be weary, my lord. Tomorrow is..."

"Tomorrow be damned!" He pulled me close to him. "I will always want you, Beatriz."

And never love me whole—but I did not say that aloud. It was our last night, and only God knew how long it would be before his arms held me again.

I embraced him, pressing myself the length of his body. With tongue and lips I sought to memorize every inch of him. I closed my eyes to feel the moment—ghosts of yesterday, spirits of tomorrow, I would not permit them near.

"My sun and moon!" I whispered. "Dear God, I love you!"

He called me his dove, his fox—"My mistress, my own, my darling...my Beatriz...."

My breasts rounded under his hands. When we were fully joined, he rolled over. I rode his body, my hands on his shoulders, my knees locked hard about his hips. His yellow hair, his throat, his chest—I thought him beautiful and I told him so. "My lion," I whispered.

He pulled my face so near I thought I would drown in the blueness of his eyes. "Beatriz, you have been mine—you have been all...."

I heard the thud of his heart. I felt my belly soft and the hardness of him filling me. "Pedro—love!" I cried. And I turned, taking him with me, wanting his weight on me.

I saw his face above mine; it is engraved thus on my heart. And his words then:

"My lady," he said. "Conquistador's lady!"

Those words covered me like a queen's mantle. I raised my head to receive the crown. Conquistador's lady—the phrase erased the ugliness that had been, and my despair. Pedro saw me clearly at last.

"No goodbyes," I whispered, "only good night, Godspeed."

Behind my closed eyelids, under Pedro's kisses, I saw the shaman and I smiled. I had it all to keep. When I wished, I could take love out, like a book ...Conquistador's lady.

Pedro slept in my embrace. I lay quietly, marking the hours, hearing the night go out with the tolling of the hermitage bell. The watch changed below my window and I heard the watchman's shout: "All is well—all is well—"

Every man but the old veterans and the youngest boys would march with my lord tomorrow. I wondered if there was one among the soldiers, one who yearned to shout: "We abandon Santiago. All is not well!"

Yes, tomorrow would dawn fearsomely. But my lord had told me—I am a Conquistador's lady, his own, his all.

CHAPTER 36

IT WAS A PALE MAY DAWN with the threat of rain when my lord rode out of this valley. He rode at the head of 850 soldiers, and each of these men assigned battalions of Indians.

My face was bright as a spring flower, Pedro told me, embracing me for the last time. We stood alone a moment under the great arch of the castle's doorway.

I cupped his face with my hands, looked deeply into his eyes. "When you think of me, see me then as you do now," I begged.

"My own brave lady," he murmured.

His eyes, blue as that May dawn above us, looked at me with yearning tenderness. "By God, Beatriz, will it be written that we loved each other?" He touched my face as if he looked upon it for the first time.

My heart was full to bursting. "Godspeed, my dearest lord."

We descended the steps and, when he mounted, I held his stirrup leather for him. He leaned low from his saddle. His gloved fingers traced my brows, came to rest on my lips. I heard the stallion's heartbeat near my cheek. "God keep you, Beatriz."

When he was gone, I climbed the long stairs to my tower room. I watched until the last banner vanished behind the mountaintops. How long, I wondered, until my lord found Cibola, or the Eastern Indies?

I leaned on the stone parapet, not wanting to turn because months of dark time gathered at my back. I felt those months—palpable as living, hairy beasts. Loneliness would eat me alive if I permitted it. Without my lord, I could lapse into melancholy; my fantasies would lead me to the edge of madness.

Yes, I, Beatriz, knew myself well. That melancholy in me, deep, dark—it could flood my eyes with tears, suffocate my thinking, wither my flesh, stiffen my bones. My lord would return to a rheumy granny, a maudlin queen. It must not be so!

Months I must conquer, perhaps a year or longer. How to hold the wolves of empty time at bay? I could cling to this window ledge, consider falling, brood on death. Given time enough, I might even enter a convent. That thought made me smile. Once a little skinny girl had thought to close the door on life, shut herself tightly in a nunnery. "Never!" I spoke aloud. Pedro would not have left, loving me, if I'd been shrewish, moping. I would prove myself the woman he believed me to be.

Abruptly I turned my back on the stark mountains. I clapped my hands, summoning Négri. I would meet with my brother immediately, I said. There were but two of us now, even Bishop Marroquin was gone with Pedro. I knew I could help my brother hold the kingdom safe. In our presumed weakness lay our strength; there are many who consider Paco a weakling because of his noble birth. For myself—they see me Woman and thus spineless.

My first letter from Pedro is dated June 4 of last year. He states he has arrived at the port called Purificaçion, in the Province of Jalisco, Mexico. All his soldiers and Indians survived the march overland, Pedro tells me with some pride, and the voyage to Jalisco was favored by fine winds.

Pedro's only complaints concern the activities of the Viceroy of New Spain, Don Antonio Mendoza, who is already engaged in a search for the Seven Cities of Cibola. Don Mendoza and another captain, Vasquez de Coronado, have penetrated the Gulf of California, a territory Pedro considers his own.

My lord wrote that Mendoza was proposing a joint expedition, that Mendoza hoped Pedro would defer the voyage to the East Indies. Reading this, I surmised that Mendoza was short of funds, that he needed Pedro's arms, men, and monies. I was disturbed because I have never believed in the Seven Cities; it is the Eastern Indies that must be secured for the Empire.

Pedro wrote that Mendoza had suggested a formal contract with the clause that all expenses would be shared equally. Had my lord forgotten the Royal Fifth always assigned to the King?

I wrote him immediately, reminding him of his responsibility toward our Sovereign who had made this expedition possible. Pedro did not reply, and I wrote again begging him not to be tricked by foolish tales of cities made of gold.

In early December, a special messenger brought me a letter from Bishop Marroquin stating that my lord had signed a contract with Mendoza on November 29. Pedro had agreed to a partnership of twenty years duration that was binding to heirs and successors in case of death. Too, Pedro had ceded to Mendoza one-half of his profits from the projected voyage to the Eastern Indies! I was aghast, especially when I read that our old enemy, Maldonado, was present at the signing of the agreement.

The bishop also told me that my lord had moved on to Mexico City and was so captivated by that capital that the bishop doubted any expedition would be soon forthcoming. I remembered what that young Captain Luis (God rest his soul!) had told me of that Mexican city—all the beautiful women there had lovers. Was my lord so captivated then, I wondered; I knew he would forget me.

I did not share this news with Paco or Léonor. I did write Pedro an angry letter asking him if he had become both spendthrift and fool? And I told him, not mincing words: "If you should die, I will not be bound to the Viceroy." I reminded Pedro of Maldonado's past behavior, and I said that I distrusted any gathering in which that gentleman was present.

Should I have played the role of loving, trusting wife? Because Pedro lingered in Mexico City, writing me only occasionally. His letters describe the sophistication of the Court there, its wealth and luxuries. He was thoroughly enjoying the company of old comrades-in-arms. He sent no gifts, and asked little concerning my health or the welfare of his kingdom. "Paco will govern well," Pedro wrote in his blunt hand, and that he hoped my conduct was becoming to a lady in her lord's absence.

Oh! but his carelessness angered me! Pedro might leave me here forever, I raged, and none the wiser. I would not write my uncle condemning my lord's behavior; it would not be the first time Pedro was accused of abandoning his kingdom and I knew King Charles would be displeased. I kept my fears and loneliness to myself.

Bishop Marroquin returned to Santiago. His silence as to Pedro's activities distressed me. "Be patient, Doña," the bishop advised. "We must pray our lord's swift return."

I am not patient. I refused to turn my Court into a mourning nunnery. If Pedro diverted himself in Mexico, I would do the same in Santiago. I created many diversions, partly to hold my loneliness at bay, and also hoping my lord would somehow hear of his own Court's splendor. I wished to lure him home.

I rallied a company of boys, those Pedro had left behind; I dubbed them knights and set them to mock battles against Indians. All wore cotton padding in lieu of armor; there was no blood spilled. I believe I trained a stalwart company, and these same youths kept me merry through the long nights. The older women, wives like myself but staid and plump—they frowned on my behavior. I hoped the gossip spread like brush fires, all the way to Mexico.

I have always enjoyed masked balls. I do not permit the death's head, and anyone masquerading as a witch is denied entrance to my fetes. I did contrive costumes and themes from Indian myths, and the pageantry was such that I am criticized for what some call my "demonic behavior."

My halls were a bright haze of candles. I wore a painted mask to hide my despair. I knew my eyes were woebegone, but Bernal swore I was still the most beautiful lady in New Spain. Write my lord and tell him so, I wanted to say. But I am proud.

Later, there was cruel gossip from Mexico. It was rumored my lord had taken an Indian mistress. And I heard too that Pedro had resigned his position as Captain General of Guatemala, that he sought to be Viceroy of the East Indies when and if he discovered those islands. I closed my ears to such vileness. Truly I believe many of those rumors were put about by Rosita; she was never contrite and, I am told, she never ceased plotting my downfall.

I was thankful that the city's problems diverted me. We had no surgeon, and few able-bodied men. I assigned Indian girls to sweep the filth from our clogged gutters. I ordered contingents of boys to patrol dark plazas and alleys at night. Lately, Santiago has been ravaged by packs of wild dogs; these creatures have been bold enough to snatch a child from its cradle. There have been enough omens and portents to create real panic, and many of the nobility have left my city.

Paco warned me: "That wretch, Belial, she walks about crying doom and destruction on us all. She insists Santiago is delivered to a witch-queen."

"Only fools believe that woman's wild talk," I replied, and when Paco asked my permission to have Belial silenced, I refused. The gypsy is part fiend, her ghost would bring ill luck on my head. Too, I want no more killings.

I struggled to keep my kingdom whole. I reminded those who would desert of their oaths as Knights of Santiago. And reminded them too of the gold Pedro had promised them. Many were swearing they would have my lord's head. A certain Don Gonzalez presented himself in formal audience to demand I repay him the sum he had lent Pedro. I paid him from my own diminishing stores and, because he is a grizzled veteran and I have few such men left, I promised my payment would be kept secret—he would receive twice what he had lent when my lord returned.

The Indians are surly. Their secret faces frighten me. My lord was their god-figure and they are confused now, sheep without a shepherd.

It is the weather I fear most of all. We are either mired in a stifling heat, or drenched by rains. Corn and wheat fields are flooded, the land erodes. Our winter will be a thin one. The farmers predict starvation.

One night in June a storm split the heavens, shattering my shutters. Water poured across my floor, dousing my fire. The candelabra fell with such a crash I awoke believing an enemy had invaded my chamber. Négri knocked, but I was too frightened to answer his call. Then Léonor came, and I was so glad to hear her voice I forgot my fears.

"Sleep with me," I begged her. She had been distant since the shaman's execution and her father's departure, and I had missed her companionship. Now the cold night thrust us together, and we shared my furs.

I asked her if she had forgiven me. She replied that she had been angry at first. "But when I saw your face, Beatriz, that terrible morning—when you lost the child—then I forgave you." She kissed me. "I pity you. Oh, *mamacita*, your love is such—it breaks like water from a dam."

I hushed her, not wanting talk of water bursting loose. *Agua*, with its full lake, was always on my mind.

"Santiago is doomed without Don Pedro," I said.

Léonor tried to cheer me. "Soon Paco will celebrate his Name Day," she said. "I have promised him a fete, and a *piñata*—that clay pot stuffed with gifts."

It is an Italian pastime she spoke of: a clay pot swinging on a rope, and each guest has his turn to break the pot with a stick, spilling its contents. Each participant is blindfolded, and his flailing at the pot above his head provokes much merriment.

Together in the candlelight, Léonor and I planned the *fiesta* and who would attend. I noticed the storm had abated. My windows revealed a night star struck and clear.

Barefoot, I went to my casement. "That storm came on so suddenly," I said. "Its thunder was that of a hundred horsemen. I thought a battle had begun and Death himself rode over me."

Léonor came to stand beside me, her arm about my waist. "It is June," she said, "the rains begin early. Father has been absent for a year. Will he come soon, Doña? I will not marry Paco until my father returns."

I turned to look at her. My own troubles had so beset me I had almost forgotten Léonor and Paco. They had been patient. Now I saw Leonor's face wan as my own.

I embraced her. "Pedro will come soon," I said, and with those words my heart felt lighter. I smelled pine fragance on the wind from the mountains; I saw a falling star.

"Léonor, do you know what I am thinking?" I whispered.

I leaned on the sill to see more of the heavens. "When our

piñata cracks, when the jewels are spilled, another guest will appear. Don Pedro will come then, Léonor. Just at the right moment, the doors will fly open and he will stand there...."

"His hands full of gold!" Léonor was caught up in my fantasy. "Yes, *mamacita*—we must plan a royal *fiesta!* "

"My lord's homecoming," I said. "It is our secret."

I leaned far out, gulping the fresh air. Another star fell and I followed its arching flight until its light died. I remembered the old tale: A falling star marks a hero's death. I shivered. That storm from nowhere; a clutching at my heart; the dying star. I held to Léonor.

"But he is coming home," I insisted. "Pedro will come before winter."

CHAPTER 37

THIS WOULD BE MY LAST FETE before the winter rains came in earnest. I wished my brother's betrothal to Léonor publicly proclaimed, and thinking on this, I wondered at the strange interweaving of lives, each thread drawn precisely to create this tapestry called Guatemala.

Was it God's design, or happenstance that, in two successive generations, Spanish and Indian would blend bloodlines? This could not happen in Old Spain, but it was permitted in the New, in the Colonies.

I had been shocked, yes—horrified—by Pedro's Indian wife, their *mestiza* daughter. Now Léonor was my constant companion and, with all my heart, I approved her marriage to my brother.

That June, I remember now, I felt a page turned, a chapter closed, a knotting of threads and the tapestry almost completed. It was with Don Bernal I could discuss these feelings. "I am changed," I told him. "I feel a weariness and a resignation I have not known before."

"It is old age, Doña," he teased. "You are all of twenty-two." He inspected me closely, his black eyes mischievous. "Amazing! I do not see one grey hair."

"What do you see?" I asked, knowing Bernal would be truthful.

"A queen," he replied. "You are a woman now, Beatriz, and lovely."

"My lord told me once that he wished he could see me a woman grown," I said, and felt, for no apparent reason, a cold stab of fear. I grasped Bernal's hand.

"Don Pedro is on his way home, isn't he?"

His eyes avoided my own. Don Bernal cannot lie. "If you were my lady, I would be riding home."

His remark pleasured me, and I told Don Bernal he must be my right hand and help me with all the details of the splendid fete I planned.

I ordered every corner of my castle scrubbed and whitewashed. The hearths must be cleaned, and logs of cedar, oak, and tamarind prepared. Fresh pine needles were spread on my floor, and I made certain we had sufficient beeswax tapers, charcoal, and pine-knots for torches.

Guatemala's harvest was brought to me: avocados, frijoles, plantain, vanilla and chili beans, peppers and prickly pears. The Indians sensed my excitement, and though their stores were slender, they brought me baskets of papayas, oranges, cherries, quinces, custard apples, and the fruit of the passion flower.

I planned a feast: the meat of the armadillo and the iguana, chickens, wild turkeys and doves, red crabs and shrimps packed in ice. I wanted wild honey, corn cakes, spiced beef, and wine enough for everyone in Santiago.

The weather that June was ill-humored. Thunder shook the earth. *El Volcan Fuego* belched fire, and there was lightning so brilliant it showed the color of a man's eyes.

Paco told me there was a new crack on the high slopes of Agua, and more than a seepage of water. "We must construct new dams, Beatriz," my brother said.

"Don Pedro will be home soon," I assured Paco. And I gave Bishop Marroquin the same answer when he told me his hospital roof was leaking. He said there was much sickness and he feared an epidemic.

"We will make an epidemic of merriment," I said. "There is too much talk of sickness and dying, good Father!"

Léonor and I planned our gowns for the masquerade. I gave the affairs of the town to Paco. He told me he would need a secretary, and against my better judgment—I did not like the man—I chose Don Robledo. Loose-lipped, squint-eyed, he resembled a ferret. He was always whispering behind a sheaf of papers. I sensed his obstinate dislike of me.

It was this gentleman who came to me saying he had received word that Don Castellanos, the Royal Treasurer, was on his way to Santiago. The great lord would arrive in early August, Robledo said.

"Then Don Castellanos will be our guest of honor," I replied, "My fete is planned for the 29th of August."

"A *fiesta* is an extravagance at this time, Doña," Robledo

warned.

"But it is Paco's Name Day. And Don Pedro is on his way home," I said, and my heart was so set on my desire I refused to admit the gleam of interest in the secretary's eyes.

"Are you certain Don Pedro returns?" he asked.

"Almost," I replied lightly. "Go now, and help my brother. You must write his letter for him. He has a clumsy hand and little patience."

I ordered new crimson draperies for my walls. Each castle servant was given a bolt of green cotton and a pair of leather sandals. Bowls, cups, and platters came each day from the busy kilns.

Every morning I awoke to the smell of brown sugar cakes and wheat bread baking.

Don Castellanos arrived, leading a caravan of mules, horses, and soldiers. His stoutness lent him majesty, I thought, but we were hard put to find a bed strong enough to support his gross obesity. He wanted Pedro's room, but that I refused—the fire was laid and the linens fresh for my lord alone. I said as much, and I ignored Don Castellanos' genuine surprise that I expected Don Pedro so soon. I added also, because the Don was overly attentive, that Pedro did not often use the royal chamber, he preferred to sleep in my apartments.

The royal treasurer brought me a gift from King Charles, a necklace of rubies. And, from deep in one of his leather pouches, Don Castellanos took a small box which was tightly sealed and knotted with twine. "From your uncle, Don Francisco, my lady." He hesitated, hoping perhaps to see me open the gift but I did not. I waited until I was alone.

Tio Francisco's gift was a yellow diamond, cleverly cut in the shape of a heart and suspended on a fine silver chain. It was beautiful, but it was the accompanying letter I was most interested in. Tio Francisco saluted me with affection; he inquired after my health; he said my parents grew frail and then, between the polite phrases, I caught the important message.

"Being informed of Don Pedro's lengthy absence from

your side, I send you Don Castellanos, a gentleman of merit and intelligence, nobly-born and well versed in the affairs of New Spain...."

So many words, all in praise of the royal treasurer. And the gentleman a widower too, my uncle wrote, and childless. Then at the very end:

"You have my heart, little Beatriz." (And it is cold as your diamond, I thought.) "I pray you, girl, do not believe you can govern that savage kingdom by yourself. Heed my advice. Do not reject the attentions of my lord Don Castellanos."

"Little Beatriz!" I threw the letter into the fire. So? It was all to be repeated over again? Another husband for me! But Tio Francisco was premature, believing Pedro dead, myself a widow. I shuddered. Once, I had believed my uncle wise.

He is arrogant, I thought. He seeks to move us all about like pawns, at his pleasure. No—my dear uncle, I am not your little Beatriz anymore. I would not marry the fat royal treasurer if he were the last man on earth. Which he is not! And my kingdom may be savage, dear Uncle, though I do not find it so, I have managed by myself for one long year.

"My lord lives!" I told the empty room. I caught sight of my reflection in my long silver mirror, a blurred reflection—it was like looking at myself through tears, or still water. My lord Pedro would find me thinner, a trifle pale perhaps, but red-headed and proud as he had left me: his Conquistador's Lady.

By all the Saints! I thought—Pedro will laugh when I tell him of Tio Francisco's scheming. He will laugh, yes, and then boot the royal treasurer from the castle.

I held Tio Francisco's diamond to my throat. A gift for a queen, I thought, and if my lord Pedro does not hurry home, I myself will boot the royal treasurer across the sea into my uncle's lap!

The diamond cut my mirror's sheen with a dart of fire. I decided to wear this jewel for my *fiesta*. It would replace the emerald I missed. Pedro had not returned me my jewels, and I wondered where they were locked away.

And then I remembered that fireworks were still to be fashioned. My lord must breast the mountaintop, and rein in his horse then, to see a golden rush of stars falling on Santiago.

August 29th. There was little time left, and I clapped my hands impatiently for my servant girls, and cursed the day's black clouds—and bit my tongue and whispered a prayer instead.

CHAPTER 38

I WORE WHITE SILK embroidered with gold and silver leaves. My slippers were silk, white with silver heels. My *manta* was Flemish lace, held to my hair with a jeweled wreath. When I lifted my overskirt, my petticoats showed their edging of silver. My hair was smooth, piled high in layers of curls. I know I heard Don Castellanos catch his breath when I took his arm. He appeared a vast purple mountain, and I noticed even his fingernails were oiled.

I gave the stout lord a wooden mask which was carved to resemble a wolf. "Don Lobo," I said, rapping his snout with my fan. My mask was chalk white, the face of the Queen of Hearts with cut glass eyes and a crimson heart of a mouth, sliced in two.

We feasted at the long table in the banqueting hall. The meats and stuffed poultry were served on what were once Moctezuma's gold platters. Italian crystal held water for our lips and fingers, and each guest had an Indian to do his bidding. Don Castellanos said he was delighted to dine with the ladies. The wine made him amorous; gross and wheezing, he made no secret of his intentions toward me.

Paco toasted Léonor, then I gave the signal and Indian music-makers entered the hall. They were garbed in green feathers and each of them wore the mask of a bird. First came the *tuns*, which are hollowed logs struck with sticks; the tone is heavy as a roll of thunder. We heard the *tambors*, drums covered with deerskin, and then the small *chinchines*, the calabash gourds filled with seeds. Flutes and conch shells lifted the sonorous music to the harmonics of bird calls. My guests sat spellbound in the forest music.

I summoned the guitars and banjos, and we watched the Dance of the Bear, the Jester's antics, and the whirling of the Bullfighters. The Bullfighter's combat brought me to my feet, and I applauded the appeal to a dancer dressed as the King of Guatemala to kill the bull figure. There were shouts from the company, *"Viva Alvarado! El Conquistador!"* when the bull dancer pretended to die.

"A delightful evening, Doña," Don Castellanos congratulated me.

"But it is not yet over," I protested. "Look up, sir." I pointed to the *piñata* floating like an orange moon above our heads. Don Castellanos had never seen this game, and I explained it to him. "The clay pot holds rich surprises." I said. "Each of us in turn is blindfolded. We try to break the pot with a long stick. My majordomo, Négri, has asked to go first."

Négri's antics made us laugh. A silk scarf about his eyes, he stood on tiptoe and struck blindly at the swinging pot. Léonor leaned across Paco and whispered, "Did you put the jewels in it, Doña, as we planned?"

"The stones were struck from our own mines," I said. "I gave the pot to my women and asked them to fill it full. I am assured it was done."

Paco stood. "I will be next." He failed to hit the pot, and sat down again amid much teasing. Léonor followed, and she succeeded in making a crack in the side of the vessel.

Each of my guests then, the ladies of my Court and their gentlemen—all tried to spill the treasure, but without success. The *piñata* spun drunkenly under the onslaught, and I laughed until my sides ached.

Don Castellanos said it was his turn. "I will pour jewels into your hands, my lady."

"I doubt you will succeed, sir," I returned cooly.

He flourished the ribboned stick and staggered about for so long, with so many curses, that he was at last hissed back to his place at the table. "Let me try again, sweet lady," he begged.

I shook my head. "Your aim is unfortunate, sir. If my lord Pedro was here, it would rain jewels."

A gust of wind then, and the door blown open. I held my breath, turned my head. Hoofbeats, yes! And the watchman—"Halt!"

Silence. The company sat still. We waited, watching the drizzle of rain beyond the wide-open door.

Rosita entered—feathered, painted as if for a masquerade. "Doña—" she cursied low and before I could protest, she had seated herself near the head of the table.

"She was not invited," I told Paco.

"Don't let her spoil our party," he replied. "I will speak to her myself, later."

Again, footsteps, and my heart jumped. At any moment now I was certain my lord would enter.

But—Belial this time. Filthy with mud, her feet bare, and cursing the guards who tried to stop her. I stepped forward. This I would not permit!

Again, Paco stayed me. It was he who escorted Belial to a stool in a far corner. The company whispered; I knew they were uneasy. All looked to me, and I smiled as I never had before. No—this *fiesta*, my lord's homecoming, would not be spoiled.

I clapped my hands. "Who next? Who will try to spill the treasure? Yes," I rattled on, "that clay pot holds real treasures, I promise.

"Who will try again? Perhaps a gentleman, that one there—" I pointed, "his arms look strong—yes, try!" I pleaded.

"No!" Belial's voice rasped. "It is you, my lady, who must strike now." She nodded at Rosita and the girl ran forward, grasped my arms and spun me about. The guests, believing it was all in fun, laughed at my clumsiness.

"A scarf, a shawl," Rosita begged, and someone flung her a strip of crimson. "Stand still," she told me, her hands on me, so cruel they bruised.

She bound my eyes tightly. She turned me around and around until the floor tilted under me, and I almost fell. Dimly, I heard Paco's voice. All of the company applauded me. Rosita set the heavy stick in my hands. I smelled her scent, and the stable odor of Belial, near her.

"My lady's turn," Rosita purred.

Belial hissed—"Now, Doña!"

Why was the wretch so intent on my playing this game? I wondered, the stick heavy in my hands. Belial is mad, I thought, she must be silenced.

I stood quietly a moment, wanting the direction of the *piñata*. Blindfolded, I felt all the masked faces, grotesquely grinning, mocking me. I raised the stick to strike, then paused—I heard horses, a man's shout, dogs barking.

"Who comes?" I asked, and would have removed my blindfold but Rosita caught my hands.

"Once more, my lady. Try again," she urged.

I swung hard, and my stick met the jar with such a jolt my shoulders ached. A shower of objects rained down and I tore the scarf from my eyes. "I have won!" I cried.

There was a shocked silence all about me. Masks askew, the mouths beneath gaped. Paco dropped his cup with a clatter; a lady swooned, and Léonor crossed herself. Belial yelped, and pointed at my feet. I looked down and saw that I stood in a welter of stones and bones. The grin of a split skull rocked at my feet.

Fists pounded my door. The horseman entered. I saw his boots, mud-stained, his gloved hands shaking from his long ride. Knocking the strewn bones aside, he knelt at my feet. He gave me a crumpled letter.

"Forgive me, Doña. I bring sad news to the Queen of Guatemala. Don Pedro is dead."

CHAPTER 39

NOT EVEN BELIAL could have foreseen such an ending. She had only wished to frighten me: with Rosita's help, she had filled the *piñata* with bones. Not the gypsy, not anyone in Santiago, had known my lord was dead.

I did not know. For two long months, since June, Don Pedro has been dead. I have the black letter by heart.

Ten thousand Indians had fortified themselves in the village of Nochilstlán, Guadalajara, Mexico. Governor Cristobal Onate requested my lord's aid in subduing the marauding forces which tormented both the Province of Chiapa, and the boundaries of the Royal Territory of Guatemala.

On the 24th of June, the Captain General Alvarado halted his force beneath the mountain heights of Nochistlán. The Indians hid themselves in deep trenches on the hillside.

My lord became impatient. He could have starved the Indians out, forced them to surrender. Instead, he rode his horse straight up the slope, calling on his men to follow. The Indians loosed a rain of boulders, forcing the Spanish to withdraw.

The savages descended in two long lines. Don Pedro and a small group were surrounded, and my lord ordered a further retreat. In this manner, he lured the Indians a good distance from their stronghold. Then Don Pedro pulled in his horse and ordered a charge, uphill again.

The terrain was rough, pitted with swamp holes. Horses and soldiers were kneedeep in mud.

Seeing the struggle hopeless, my lord placed himself in the rear and ordered his men to retreat, to seek a suitable battlefield. I am told it was my lord's sword that protected his men as they stumbled downhill. The Indians followed closely, and it was my brave lord who struck them down. (With the same gallantry, years ago, Pedro Alvarado had defended Cortez's withdrawal from the Aztec city.)

The Spanish Army retreated for ten miles, the Indians

fierce on their flanks. My lord gave his horse to a wounded soldier and continued the battle on foot. At last, firm ground was reached.

But a scribe named Montoya took fright. He set spurs to his horse, believing the Indians still pursued him.

"Be tranquil, Montoya," my lord said. "The Indians have left us." [1]

Montoya did not hear. He struck his horse and the animal reared and fell. Man and horse fell on my Captain General, crushing him.

My lord lay bruised in the mud, on the stones. He refused aid. Thinking of his men's safety, he gave orders that his armor be removed and put on another officer.

"It is not well that the Indians know my danger," my lord said.

The new captain, in my lord's heavy armor, led a charge toward the Indians. On the flat ground, the Indians fled. My lord was lifted to a crude stretcher, and he gave the order to retire to a nearby village.

Hearing his officers curse Montoya, my lord was heard to say, "What has happened cannot be helped, and it should happen to anyone who takes with him people like Montoya." [2]

One of the captains bent over Don Alvarado. "Where does your lordship feel the most pain?"

"In my soul," my lord murmured. [3]

The Last Sacrament was administered, and a brief will was drawn and transcribed. My lord left his whole fortune to me, his widow.

1, 2, 3: Pedro Alvarado—Conquistador

CHAPTER 40

SO WAS THE NEWS of my lord's death brought to me—months after it had happened.

At first I thought to die myself. Indeed, I hunted death. Only Négri prevented me; he was the one I allowed to enter my rooms. He brought me food and drink, all or most of which I ignored or struck from his hands. He said nothing; he came and went like a ghost.

A ghost? Dear God! my sleep was haunted. There was Ana, her caresses cold. And Luisa—her sound was that of dead leaves blown. Francesca carried my lost babe at her skeleton breast; her tears puddled his empty eyes. Only the shaman brought relief; his form stood tall, endlessly repeating, "There are no goodbyes, there is no death."

My lord never visited me. I prayed his spirit come and take my own. Does he wander, lost, believing Beatriz does not mourn him? Or does the promise of gold still lure him? I have been told a host of Conquistadors rides the mountaintops in the moonlight, seeking the Seven Cities of Cibola. He loved me, and I hold to that knowledge. But it is not enough! Stolen, my love! Who will dare tell me God is not cruel?

Bishop Marroquin. His hands are dry as paper and his words are that thin. He counsels me, his voice plaintive as a mourning wind: "Accept, Beatriz, bend to God's will."

I will not bow my head. I cannot accept. I have shouted at the bishop, my old friend—yes, sent him stumbling, with bowed head, from my chamber.

I hate myself for my behavior. I curse each day and night. My holy statues are turned to the wall; I will not look upon their bland faces. God is merciless. He has taken from me again, and still again. I cannot believe otherwise.

I asked Négri what the place was called where Pedro met his death: Muchitiltic, he said, the Indian word for black.

I ordered the tapestries removed from my walls, the rugs and draperies folded away. I told Négri I wanted every room from the kitchens to my third floor chapel stained black with a mixture of oil and water. I commanded that my roofs and patios, the cobbled courtyards and the garden path be stripped of growing things and darkened, black as my mourning.

When I had no tears left, and no strength for raging, Bishop Marroquin visited me. He told me my behavior was unbecoming to a noble woman—a Christian woman, he said. He scolded that my rantings were being taken literally as blasphemings against God and the Church.

"The weather is unkind," the bishop warned me. "*Fuego* rumbles and spits fire. The people are saying, Beatriz, that you will bring God's anger down upon us all."

"God does not care—that much!" I replied, snapping my fingers in the good man's face. Then remorseful, I fell on my knees to him. "Comfort me," I begged.

"Nine days—you will lose your senses, Beatriz, if you remain so, locked in your room." He raised me to my feet.

"Once you wanted to be queen," he reminded me. "You are losing your kingdom, my lady. Don Castellanos plots against you. His behavior has been so arrogant these days I have had to send him from the castle."

Here was news to turn my mind from sorrow. "Don Castellanos would be Governor, king of Guatemala? In my lord's place?" I heard my laughter hard, metallic.

"Don Pedro left me his kingdom. Guatemala was promised me—yes, it is in my marriage contract."

The Bishop nodded. "True," he said. "Paco is interim-governor and he tries to keep the peace. But—" Bishop Marroquin sighed, "without Don Pedro—God rest his soul!—the gentlemen revert to their old greeds. Ambitions battle now, Doña."

"I am queen!" I cried. "They must elect me governor. The crown will agree."

Before the bishop's astonished eyes, I threw a log on my fire and knelt, my skirts above my knees, to blow upon the ashes. I pushed the black velvets from my windows. I lit all the tapers I could find.

"I must make order," I said. And the dust flew. I flung open my windows and gulped the fresh air. Rain stung my face.

"Send for my waiting-women," I said. "I will go down immediately."

I bathed and dressed with care. I insisted on black, without adornment. My silver mirror showed me a wraith, pale but resolute. "Go ahead of me," I told Négri. "Tell the gentlemen of the Council that the Queen of Guatemala and Honduras commands their presence in the Council Chamber."

Paco and Léonor waited for me at the foot of the stairs. I saw they had respected my wishes: both were clothed in deepest black. Léonor held me close a moment, then, supporting me on either side, they led me outside to the wide balcony that overlooked the town. I saw that fire had ravaged parts of Santiago and garbage littered the streets.

I turned angrily on Paco. "How could you let this happen?" I demanded. "Is there no law, no order here?"

Immediately I relented; his face was stark, a mask of tragedy. "Many knights have departed," he said. "Those who remain are drunk, day and night. Those dogs we import from Spain to hunt the Indians—the beasts are destroying sheep and swine, Beatriz. Cattle are loose in the planted fields. The air is foul with fevers—"

There were tears in my brother's eyes. "I swear we have buried more Spaniards these past days than ever died in the wars of New Spain. Curse the day Don Pedro rode from Santiago!" Paco swore.

Quickly Léonor placed her fingers on his lips. "Enough blaspheming," she murmured. She turned to me. "Beatriz—*mamacita*, it is only you can take control. First, you must rid us of that spider, Don Castellanos. It is rumored you will marry him. Oh, Doña, say it is not true!"

I held tightly to Paco's hand, to Léonor's hand. "If I could, I would order Castellanos killed!" I exclaimed. "Oh God!" I moaned, "this unhappy August!"

Paco managed a smile. "In September, Beatriz, you will be the first elected lady-governor in all the Americas." His face turned grave again. "It was my lord Pedro said that—that you must be lady-governor—one day in Council when you were absent. The gentlemen present laughed at our lord's words but he remained serious. He swore it would come true."

I replied solemnly, "It will be so, my brother."

Later that same morning, in Council, I decreed the last solemn Mass for my lord's soul would be celebrated September 6. It was on that day, I ordered, the *Cabildo* must begin its sessions. I must be formally elected governor, I declared.

The gentlemen proceeded according to my orders. Bishop Marroquin celebrated the Mass and, before all the Court and the townspeople, I took Communion from the bishop's hands, thus signifying repentance, my obedience to God's will. I felt nothing, just a faint gratitude that my body had at last turned to something unfeeling as stone.

I retired to my rooms after Mass. I waited for the voting to be done; Négri came and went as usual. "They will not forget you are a de la Cueva," he assured me.

Yes, I knew it was my noble birth, my powerful relatives—their strength across the sea, the King's affection too—that would secure me my titles. Fiercely I wished one man at least would forget my name, forget that I was woman and widow. Would anyone at Council now recall my intelligence, my bravery, my endeavors on behalf of Santiago?

It was not long—just two days. On September 8, Paco came to fetch me. I was ready for him. In my black dress, my hair braided stark and plain, I entered the Council chamber. It was dim, the candles hooded, and black cloth covering my lord's great chair. The gentlemen appeared uneasy. They stood as I entered.

"Yes?" I asked, "Is it done?"

The vote, I was told, was unanimous. The Council president, a skinny alderman whose clothes fit him so badly he resembled a scarecrow, asked me to repeat the oath. I promised to serve his Majesty "as if I were Pedro Alvarado who was then in glory." I knew my voice was strong, my bearing royal as befit my name and titles. But I felt no elation.

The official document was presented me. I took the quill in my right hand and bent to sign my name. Suddenly, my courage deserted me. The parchment beneath my hand blurred; I saw my future like a long dry desert ahead of me. Feeling I could not take another step, I leaned on the table. All sat silent. I knew they looked at me without compassion. They waited, still as vultures, and I felt small in their eyes, helpless as they deemed me to be.

What matter if I am queen, my heart cried. I am alone. I am young, twenty-two—and all I know of soldiering is as Don Pedro's wife. Can I command veterans twice my age? Who here will follow me? Who will advise? I looked from one gentleman to another and saw only those who sought to depose me.

The quill fell from my hand. Once, I remembered, I had wanted just this future. I had cursed my marriage, and Santiago. I had longed to be a queen—yes, to reign alone.

Guilt froze me. I heard the rain, it flailed like the claws of an army of rats against my castle walls. Thunder crashed. I felt gripped by doom. The candles flickered and a thousand memories pinpointed the dark. All that I had foretold, in anger and despair, had come to pass.

My hands spread emptily on the table. I searched each face, seeking a rescuer. It was Paco who smiled kindly at me, and his lips formed the words: "Sign, Beatriz."

Shakily, I raised the quill. I signed my name: Doña Beatriz de la Cueva de Alvarado.

I looked at my signature and saw myself—a small girl at her uncle's knee, victorious because, for the first time, she had signed her own name neat and clear.

My name, and now my lord's name after—signifying I belonged to him. Of Alvarado, yes—Conquistador's Lady. He had called me brave, his own.

But how to mark me now? I wondered. My future lay blankly before me and I had no care for it. I wanted nothing more, no one.

Then I knew the mark I must make. With a firm hand I crossed out Doña Beatriz, she who once belonged to Alvarado. I wrote, in large slanting letters:

'La Sin Ventura.' She without a future. [1]

1: Signature extant, Guatemalan Archives, Guatemala City.

CHAPTER 41

THERE WAS FEASTING that night, to celebrate my victory. I did not attend the festivities. For the majority of citizens, mourning for their dead Captain General was over; all that remained now was to divide the spoils among the living. I resolved no man should profit from my lord's death. I decreed Paco lieutenant governor and, fully aware of the plots and avarice about me, I reserved for myself all matters pertaining to the allotment of lands and Indian slaves.

My first visitor that next morning was Don Castellanos. He came through the rain, his stoutness such that three umbrellas could not protect him from the downpour. Paco had lent Castellanos a palace on the outskirts of the city, and now he professed to have walked so far I had to offer him haven from the elements.

He had not heard the news of my election the day previously, and he said he had come to commiserate with me. And to offer himself for the governor's post. I replied, trying to hide my smile, that the Council had duly elected me governor of Santiago. I said also that I had heard of his imminent departure and that I wished him well.

He was stunned. And then indignant. No lady could be governor, not anywhere, he protested—it was unheard of, impossible! Sorrow had turned my head, he suggested; I needed a man like himself to take care of me. "Your uncle," Castellanos said, "your good uncle, being concerned for your welfare, Beatriz, he has blessed our union."

I bit back my anger. "My good uncle," I replied, "has not seen me for years. He thinks of me as a mere child. My lord, I would remind you—I am a woman grown. And capable. Besides, I will not marry again."

This gentleman's effrontery, his fawning, the pirouetting of that gross body—I could not hide my disgust. I bid him depart, immediately. "You will leave Santiago tomorrow," I said, turning my back on my stout suitor.

He sent me a note that afternoon. He stated he would

not recognize me as governor. Santiago is a shambles, he wrote, the king must be informed of recent happenings. In his position as king's treasurer, Don Castellanos insisted he was interim-governor, guardian of the Crown's welfare. On his orders, his letter continued, Doña Beatriz, her brother Francisco, and Alvarado's illegitimate *mestiza* daughter, Léonor, were all confined to the castle. Usurpers, Don Castellanos named us, rebels and traitors.

I summoned Paco, and read him the letter. We ordered the arrest of the king's treasurer and his companions. Paco called for his secretary, Robledos, and dictated the order for the arrest. It was dated September 10, and noted "Immediate." Paco and I waited together in my chambers for Don Castellanos to be brought before us.

We were disappointed. Robledos proved false; I had always mistrusted this man. My soldiers entered through the front door of Castellanos's palace, but he escaped through the back entrance. Robledos had warned him just in time. My loathsome suitor had vanished. "I pray he drowns in a river!" I said fervently.

"All of us may drown, Beatriz," Paco said. "My lord Castellanos will have to find a mountaintop. Santiago's streets are flooded. Adobe houses and wooden shelters are melting away in this rain." He stared out my window at the storm.

I joined him. Curtains of rain hid any view. "That is an enemy I cannot control," I said, trying to keep my voice steady because the lightning struck terror to my soul.

"Those who can have left the city," Paco told me. I sensed a grave concern in his voice. "I have sent the servants to seek high ground," he said. "Negri has gone with Pedro's brothers to fetch wagons. We must abandon the castle, Beatriz."

"No," I said, "never, Paco! My lord left the care of it to me."

He grasped my hands. He pleaded with me. "Many have drowned in the streets, Beatriz. The *arroyo* in which this castle is built is filling with water. Tonight all can be swept away!"

I looked at Paco. His concern for me touched my heart.

"Do you know," I said, my hands warm in his, "I love you very much."

I turned to the window again. "All will be swept away? You forget, Paco. My all was taken from me months ago."

"Beatriz!" Léonor called me from the doorway. I saw she was dressed in riding clothes and wrapped in a warm cape. "There is little time left," she warned. "Bishop Marroquin has ridden off to help the Indians—he swears he will return tonight, but—" she shook her head, "I doubt it.

"Beatriz, prepare yourself. Our horses are waiting, saddled. Look, here is Anica—bundled like a lamb." I smiled to see the child, only her small nose showing from her furs. She stretched her arms to me. "Mama!" she cried, and I took her from Léonor.

Anica in my arms, I returned to the window. "All shutters must be bolted," I said. The rain rattled like spears on shields. "Those who have no horses?" I asked. "And those imprisoned?" I was thinking of Belial and Rosita, jailed since my ill-fated *fiesta*.

Paco told me the jail was flooded and all prisoners had drowned. I thought of those two whose lives had tangled with my own. "Poor wretches," I whispered.

Thunder shook the castle. Léonor cried out. "*Mamacita*, you must not stay here. It is dangerous!"

I heard the rasp of stones falling. Faint, above the storm, I heard the shaman's prophecy: "My lady, beware the dark waters!"

I must prove it all untrue. Only I could lift the curse off my days. But memory stabbed again—I had written it myself: *"She without a future."*

No, I would not run for safety, that I knew. Always I had faced forward. God, I prayed, do what You will with me.

Do what You will with me. My prayer was spoke in earnest. Peace flowed through me, soft as the name of love. I saw the shaman's face. *"There is no death."* His was ancient teaching, and one I had disbelieved. Now I raised my head and listened to those words.

219

CHAPTER 42

"YOU MUST LEAVE NOW, both of you," I told Paco and Léonor. "Leave Anica with me. I will take her up to the chapel on the third floor."

Paco knew I had made up my mind. "Négri is certain to return," he said, "and perhaps Bishop Marroquin. I will take Léonor to the nearest Spanish settlement and request aid."

He held me strongly in his arms then. "There is no one I love more than you, my sister."

"There is one," I replied, trying to hold to lightness. "It is Léonor. You must get her to safety at once, Paco. Someday you and she will rule Guatemala. It was Pedro's dream that you two marry. And it is fitting."

I embraced my brother and Léonor with my eyes. "With your union, Spanish and Indian are joined. There will be peace, and the territory will prosper."

Léonor begged me one last time to leave with her. "There are no servants here," she said. "Beatriz, water seeps in through wide cracks—the walls crumble." Her voice faltered, and I saw tears in her eyes. "Eleven ladies await you in the hall. Their husbands have gone for help, leaving these women in your care. You must order all to safety."

Eleven ladies? Eleven bedraggled barnyard hens! What would I do with them? Their terror would ignite my own. "Take them with you," I begged Léonor.

She shook her head. "They will not leave without their husbands. And there are no horses."

I swore under my breath. "By Heaven! Always I am trailed by ladies!"

Paco grinned. Then he embraced me. "God keep you, my sister. Your spirits are high, and your *Señorita* is saddled. I will see you again." He held me closely and I felt Leonor's arms encircle the two of us.

"I love you, Beatriz," Paco said again. His lips near my ear, he whispered, "When I was a runt, I wished for a brother. Here in Guatemala I am proud to call you sister."

"Thank you," I replied softly. We stood quietly, my brother and his lady, and I. Peace wrapped us light as a long ago summer. "I will see you again," I promised.

For a moment, as the door closed behind them, I was seized by panic. I would go with Paco and Léonor: "Wait!" I cried, but a clap of thunder stole my voice, shutters slammed wide and wind swallowed candle flames. Anica sobbed. She was a deadweight in my arms....

I will hold courage foremost in my mind. I must go upstairs now, a step at a time. Négri will come soon. The noise is awesome. Why is it so bitterly cold?

I will take my ladies and Anica to my tower room. We will be safe there, above the storm. Once, I remember, when I was young and careless, I climbed an apple tree. That girl, she dreamed she would be queen.

I cannot climb beyond this storm. If only Anica would stop crying. And these wretched women—they huddle in a corner, their cries beseeching the very God, I think, who sends this storm. The women look to me for comfort. When have they not? And they are frightened always and that angers me, and thus I am impatient. My ladies will believe me unkind. When have they not?

Has the storm slackened its grip? Hush—please! We are arived in my tower. It is a tall ship riding the wind. *La Estrella*...the Star....

Ladies, let us pray here together, to my own Virgin. She has my mother's face. Or is it Ana's love shines through the gloom? Holy Mother—mother mine—whoever made this holocaust must stop it now.

Mother, listen—if the rain continues, the volcano will burst from the weight of its waters. My castle will fall in the flood. Dear sweet Mother, neglected one, remember your Beatriz now. Have mercy on me!

There—Anica is quiet at last. It is my love comforts her. Would that I had someone to hold me! Always I have wanted that.

Always I forget! Because I have had it all, the full cup of it. Life, the shaman called it. I name it love. Pedro—my heart's desire. If I wish, he can fill me now.

Yes. Many have loved me. Négri will come soon. And Bishop Marroquin will not forget me. Don Bernal, and Pedro's brothers—their faces light my dark like candles. I pray all have escaped this storm.

Such a thunder below stairs! My world shakes under my feet. I fear the water has got in at last. If my lord were here, he would barricade the doors. I shall pretend he is here, then I will have that same courage he did admire.

My Virgin trembles. How can these stones be moved? I remember a globe set spinning and Guatemala split in two. Tio Francisco, forgive me. I will not diminish my kingdom now, at the last. I am a Conquistador's Lady.

I hold tightly to my blessed Mother's feet. She will not let harm come to me, Her child.

Mother! Ana! I did not mean it to end so.

The earth quakes. My castle sways. I hear the hoofbeats of a thousand horses. The Conquistadors! Dear God, let my lord be riding at their head.

"My *Tonatiuh*, Child of the Sun, so he was called." I see tomorrow in his hands, bright as gold....

CHAPTER 43

BISHOP MARROQUIN came on the morrow. The castle had collapsed. More than ten feet of water and ice from *El Volcan Agua*, and debris, filled the corridors. Even the roof of the third floor, Beatriz's tower room, was washed away. In the shambles, only the altar stood untouched, and the Virgin. The bishop found Beatriz, her arms clasped tightly about the Virgin's feet, and Anica too, in her embrace.

The eleven ladies were washed away in the flood that had burst from Agua's side. And Négri, his body was never found.

That day, September 11, the survivors straggled home to scavenge the leavings. They blamed Doña Beatriz for the disaster. They called her witch and heretic. They demanded her body be thrown to the wild animals. Some said her corpse should be set on a raft and floated down-river to the sea.

It was Bishop Marroquin who defended Beatriz. He ordered her body interred in the cathedral she had helped to design. Its walls had withstood the catastrophe. Beatriz's tower bells, polished and hung just in time, she believed, to welcome her lord home, now tolled her death. It is written that those who heard the bells had little time or inclination to pray for the soul of their Conquistador's Lady whose only sin, if sin it was, was loving overmuch.

Santiago was abandoned. On October 22, 1541, a new site for another capital city was located. Francisco de la Cueva and Bishop Marroquin were elected joint Governors, and the city now known as Antigua was founded.

Léonor, who became Paco's wife, ordered her father's body brought from Mexico City and laid in the new cathedral, in Antigua. There, in 1580, Beatriz was interred beside her Captain General.

Years later, fate dealt still another blow. In 1773, an earthquake rocked the new Santiago, and the walls of the cathedral fell, burying the tombs of Don Pedro, Conquistador, and his lady-wife, Beatriz de la Cueva de Alvarado.

Again, in 1976, another earthquake partially destroyed Antigua, leaving its cathedral in ruins, its domed ceiling fallen and further concealing the whereabouts of Don Pedro's and Beatriz's graves.

❖ ❖ ❖

APPENDAGE

Don Bernal Diaz del Castillo, a Captain with Cortes and chronicler of the times, survived the flooding of the first capitol and resided later in the new capital, Antigua.

In recording the death of the Captain General and his lady, Bernal wrote, in part, "The loss of Alvarado was sorely felt in his family.

"As soon as the fatal intelligence arrived in Guatemala (Don Pedro's death), the Bishop Marroquin of excellent memory, and all the clergy, assisted in rendering him the funeral honors. His majordomo also, to show his sorrow, caused the walls of his house to be painted black, which color they remained ever after. Many cavaliers waited upon his lady Doña Beatriz de la Cueva and her family.

"In order to console her, for her distress was very great, they told her that she should give thanks to God since it was His Will to take her husband....As a good Christian she consented but observed that she wished to be free from this melancholy world and all its misfortunes.

"These circumstances I mention because the historian Gomara attributes the unfortunate event which shortly afterwards befell her to her having spoken blasphemously, in saying that God could do her no more injury than she had already suffered. She met with her death in the following manner. A deluge of water and mud broke from the Volcano which is at the distance of half a league from Guatemala (Castle), and bringing with it great quantities of large stones and trees, overwhelmed the house of Doña Beatriz who was at the time praying with her women. As to the words which Gomara ascribes to her, she never uttered them, nor was her oath a judgment of God in any respect."

BIBLIOGRAPHY

Barrett, Meca. *El Caballo Rojo*. Editorial Escolar "Piedra Santa" (1959).

Brigham, William T. *Guatemala, the Land of the Quetzal*. University of Florida Press (1965).

Chinchilla, Carlos Samayoa. "The Emerald Lizard." *Tales and Legends of Guatemala*. Joan Coyne Maclean, transl. The Falcon's Wing Press, Indian Hills, Colorado.

Defournfaux, Marcelin. *Daily Life in Spain (in the Golden Age)*. Newton Branch, transl. Praeger Publications, New York.

Diaz del Castillo, Bernal. *The True History of the Conquest of Mexico*. Maurice Keatinge, Esq., transl. Robert McBrice and Company, New York (1927).

Kelsey, Vera and Lily de Jongh Osborne. *Four Keys to Guatemala*. Funk and Wagnalls (rev. ed.).

Killy, John Eoghan. *Pedro De Alvarado, Conquistador*. Princeton University Press, New Jersey (1932).

Parry, J. H. *The Spanish Seaborne Empire* in *The History of Human Society*. Alfred A. Knopf, New York (1970).

Scholberg, Kenneth (ed. and transl.). *Spanish Life in the Middle Ages*. University of North Carolina Press, Chapel Hill (No. 57).